THE EARTH CONCURRENCE

COLONIAL EXPLORER CORPS BOOK 1

JULIA HUNI

IPH MEDIA

The Earth Concurrence © 2020 by Julia Huni

All rights reserved. No part of this book may be reproduced in any form or by any electronic or mechanical means including information storage and retrieval systems, without permission in writing from the author. The only exception is by a reviewer, who may quote short excerpts in a review.

Cover Design © J. L. Wilson Designs
https://jlwilsondesigns.com

Editing by Paula Lester, Polaris Editing
https://www.polarisediting.com

This book is a work of fiction. Names, characters, places, and incidents either are products of the author's imagination or are used fictitiously. Any resemblance to actual persons, living or dead, events, or locales is entirely coincidental.

Visit my website at juliahuni.com

Printed in the United States of America

First Printing: November 2020
ISBN: 9798564590457
IPH Media

BOOKS BY JULIA HUNI

Colonial Explorer Corps Series:
    The Earth Concurrence
    The Grissom Contention
    The Saha Declination

Recycled World Series:
    Recycled World
    Reduced World

Space Janitor Series:
    The Vacuum of Space
    The Dust of Kaku
    The Trouble with Tinsel
    Orbital Operations
    Glitter in the Stars
    Sweeping S'Ride
    Triana Moore, Space Janitor (the complete series)

Tales of a Former Space Janitor
    The Rings of Grissom

Krimson Empire (with Craig Martelle):
Krimson Run
Krimson Spark
Krimson Surge
Krimson Flare

If you enjoy this story, sign up for my newsletter, at juliahuni.com and you'll get free prequels and short stories, plus get notifications when the next book is ready.

*To the high school and college students of 2020:
May this year make you stronger.*

CHAPTER ONE

"Make a hole!" a voice called over the rumble of conversation. I stepped to the side of the corridor, glancing over my shoulder as I moved. A squad of men and women jogged in formation, their faces focused. As soon as the group passed, those of us pressed against the bulkheads relaxed and returned to our business.

"I wish they'd stay in the gym," a man in front of me muttered. His coverall identified him as a ship's engineer.

"They say it's too crowded now," a woman wearing lieutenant's bars replied with a hint of disbelief. "I think they just like to make the rest of us feel inferior. We haven't woken that many of them, yet."

"How many we got this turn?" the engineer asked.

"Fifty," the woman said. "Plus his excellency and the princess. We'll wake the other fifty when we park."

Anger kindled in the pit of my stomach. *His excellency and the princess?*

"His excellency?" the man asked. "You mean Kassis? Who calls him that?"

The woman glared at her companion.

"Sir," the man added.

The woman's glare faded. "Just something I heard at the club. Don't spread it around. I'll deny saying it."

"He seems okay to me," the man said. "And that nickname sounds kind of derisive. Sir."

"There are a few people who don't love Kassis," the lieutenant said. "And don't forget it." She gave the man a hard look, then caught me glaring from behind him. Her eyes widened a little. "Good morning, Ms. Kassis."

"Good morning, Lieutenant," I replied as I pushed past them. "Sergeant."

"Did she hear us?" the sergeant muttered as I sped away. "Sir?"

Terkvards. I glowered and swung into the grav-lift.

I stepped out on the recreation deck and headed for the gym. The passageway rumbled with a dozen different conversations. The ship's crew bustled around me, everyone moving with purpose. They hurried past, discussing scrubber status and drive vibrations and dilithium crystals.

Not really. Dilithium crystals aren't real. They're from an old vid series my dad liked to watch on *Ancient TēVē*. I thought it was pretty hokey—transporter rays, phasers, and warp drives. And the effects were terrible. But he liked the characters. He said it was a remake of an even older series that originated on ancient Earth. That's why he studied it, I guess.

My name is Serenity Kassis, and my father is Nathanier. Yes, *that* Nathanier Kassis. The guy who discovered the first sentient non-humans in the system. He liked to tell people it was a team effort, but he was the commander on that expedition, so he gets the credit. And, to be honest, he really was the one who spotted them first.

Exploring new worlds takes a toll, so Dad decided to retire on a high note. But when they offered him one more mission—this mission—he couldn't say no. I wondered why that lieutenant disliked him. I'd keep my ear to the deck and see what I could learn. I'd also access the crew's directory and find out who she was.

This ship, the *ECS Return in Glory*, was a long-distance vessel run by the Colonial Exploration Corps. The *Glory* was one of the largest explorer ships, capable of carrying colonists as well as EC teams. We didn't have any colonists aboard this time because the planet we were exploring wasn't open for colonization. Yet.

Usually, the EC sent smaller vessels, like the one my dad commanded on that famous trip to Darenti Four. But a mission of this importance required a larger team. So, the EC refitted the *Stalwart* and gave her a snazzy new name. She carried a hundred CEC Explorers plus a public relations team. The ship's crew, under the command of Captain Tisha Hydrao, ran the ship, and Dad led the exploration team.

The exploration team, including me, Dad, and the PR guys, had been asleep for the last twenty years while Captain Hydrao's crew flew us to our destination. The crew did shorter shifts in the deep sleeper, but Captain Hydrao stayed awake the whole time. An EC captain could spend half of their career on a single mission. Not the way I'd want to spend my life, but Captain Hydrao seemed to like it. Not that I spent a lot of time chatting up the captain.

The gym overflowed. Long deep sleep required regular exercise to recondition the muscles. I hated working out, but Dad would check my health stats, so I had to keep it up. I slapped my hand on the access plate to log in and wandered to the Refit class.

"Hey, Siti." A young explorer stood by the door. Her red curls stood out from her face in an uneven, frizzy blob. A generous serving of freckles covered her pale nose and cheeks, making her look younger than her twenty-two standard years. She yawned. "I'm still so tired."

"Hey, Marika," I replied. "Me, too. Porter told me the effects wear off after a few days."

"I've been awake for a week, and I'm still yawning all the time," she said, demonstrating again. "There must be something wrong with me. Maybe they didn't give me enough jazz juice."

I laughed. "The system is automated. I doubt they got your dose wrong," I said. "Besides, I'm not sure it works that way. Either you wake up or you don't."

We both shuddered. Deep sleep had been perfected over the centuries, but most civilians didn't know how safe it was. They remembered the horror stories from history class about the early deep sleep colony ships. It didn't help that the techs were required to warn us about the one guy out of four hundred who didn't wake up. Although, with a hundred of us on this ship, that meant one of us had a twenty-five percent chance of not making it. Or something like that. Math isn't my strong subject.

"Have you heard anyone using a nickname for my dad?" I asked Marika as we moved to our stations. "His Excellency?"

Marika sputtered a laugh and clamped her hand over her mouth. Her wide blue eyes peered over her fingers. "N-no."

I narrowed my green ones.

She rolled hers and sighed. "You have to admit it's kind of funny. I mean…" She trailed off.

According to some of the explorers who were with him, the Darentis tried to make Dad their king when they finally understood what he was and where he came from. The Corps had kept that under wraps, but rumors swirled.

"I've never heard anyone in the Corps call him that," she said, pulling her hand away from her mouth and holding it vertical, with the palm out, in the Corps salute. "Who was it?"

"Some lieutenant. Ship's crew, not Corps." The display at the front of the room flashed. I read it and groaned. "I don't want to do deadlifts."

AFTER THE WORKOUT, Marika and I agreed to meet for dinner, and I returned to my cabin for a shower. The explorers had dorms on a lower deck of the ship, but since I was the commander's daughter, they'd given me a cabin in officer country. The Corps didn't usually send family members on missions, but they'd made an exception to get Dad to take command. That's probably why they called me the princess. I hated it, but I wasn't going to give up a comfy cabin to change anyone's mind.

My unit had a private bathroom, complete with dual-mode shower. Water was rationed, of course, but two minutes of spray was better than a sonic bath any day. I cleaned up and pulled on a pair of colorful leggings and an even brighter shirt. Everyone else on this boat wore uniforms, and it got a little monotonous after a while. I figured it was my duty to brighten things up.

I arrived at the mess hall a little early and took a seat in the lounge, scrolling through the feed on my holo-ring while I waited. We didn't get news from back home, of course—it took too long to arrive at this distance. But I could read the latest gossip from the crew and Corps. And of course, there were always the daily news updates. They weren't very exciting: We're this much closer to orbit. The emergency drill stats need improving. The L3 scrubbers are down for refit.

I swiped the feed off and looked for a game I could join. Before I found one, I heard a rustling sound. I froze, listening.

There. It came from the back corner of the room. I moved forward quietly, peering under the couches and tables, stopping every few steps to listen again. As I approached, a tall potted plant rustled.

Every ship has rats. That's what they say. Most ships also have cats to take care of that problem, and the *Glory* was no exception. But cats didn't climb spindly potted plants. Moving slowly, I parted the leaves. Two bright green eyes blinked at me.

"Hello," I whispered. "What are you?" I moved a hand toward the creature.

It leaped out of the plant and flew at me. The tiny, furry body stretched out, revealing membranes between the arms and legs. The face seemed to grin as it landed on my outstretched arm and scrambled up to my shoulder.

I squeaked and froze in place. My pulse pounded in my ears. Any second, those pointy teeth would sink into my ear or face.

Nothing happened. I released my held breath. Slowly, I lifted my hand to shoulder level and held it away from my body. The little creature launched itself again, landing in my palm.

"Where did you come from?" I'd never seen a rat in real life—that's what the cats were for—but this didn't look like the pictures. In fact, it didn't look like any creature I knew of. For one thing, the fur was blue and white striped. For another, it seemed to like people. "You're friendly! And so cute. But so skinny!"

The little guy's ribs showed through his fur, which was patchy and matted. He shivered in my palm. When I lowered my hand, he scurried up my arm to my shoulder again.

Definitely used to humans. I flicked my holo-ring and pulled up an item identification app. "Smile for the camera." I centered the creature's face and flicked the icon. The icon turned green, and "identifying" appeared above my palm.

The creature snuggled into the cover of my neck, shivering. "I'd give you part of my protein bar, but I want to make sure it's safe for you." And that it wouldn't turn into a destructive, evil monster like in that *Ancient TēVē* vid. Of course, it wasn't after midnight—at least not on the ship's clock. But this creature could be operating on a different time zone.

My ring pinged. The creature was a sair-glider from Kepler Three. They'd been domesticated and were popular on Armstrong where they helped keep the insect population down. Sair-gliders lived forty to fifty standard years, so someone must have smuggled him aboard when we launched.

If he'd been smuggled aboard, someone was probably desperately searching for him. But the app said gliders had an incredible sense of smell and could locate their owner in vast areas. If that was true, why wasn't he trying to find his owner? Maybe he didn't want to be found? He didn't appear to be well cared for.

The good news was sair-gliders could eat anything humans did except chocolate and coffee. Which meant more for me! I pulled a packaged protein bar out of my pocket and ripped it open. The little guy went still, as if the sound had triggered some memory.

I broke off a bit and held it toward my shoulder, twisting my head around so I could see. His little hands reached out as I brought the piece nearer. He grabbed it but didn't pull it away. Either these things were naturally polite, or this one had been trained. I let him have the chunk, and he shoved it into his cheek.

"What ch-ya doin'?" Marika asked.

I spun around, and the little animal leaped back to its potted plant. "I, uh, did you see that?"

"See what?" she asked. "Doesn't matter, I'm hungry. You can show me later." Without waiting for a reply, she hurried away.

I glanced at the animal. "Do you want to stay there or hide in my pocket?" I asked, holding out my hand.

The eyes blinked, and the creature leaped onto my arm. I grabbed his squirmy body before he could move and pushed him into my deep shirt pocket. "Stay there," I whispered. I broke off another chunk of bar. As I slid it into my pocket, I took a peek. The little guy had curled up into a ball. His green eyes blinked, and his jaw chewed furiously. I held out the second piece, which he grabbed and cradled to his chest. He seemed content to stay, so I sealed the top of the pocket, leaving a gap for air.

As I followed Marika into the mess hall, every monster video I'd ever seen flashed through my mind. Aliens poking out of people's chests. Mysterious creatures going berserk after getting wet. Little monsters becoming big monsters. I chuckled under my breath. This was obviously someone's pet. I'd give it a snack and see if I could find its owner.

In the mess hall, I grabbed a tray and loaded it. Food on the ship was heathy and surprisingly tasty. This mission rated top-grade food synthesizers, so the kitchen produced large quantities of a wide selection. I slid a glass of pink liquid onto the tray and headed toward the table Marika and I considered ours.

Two other uniformed women sat with Marika. The blonde I knew from Refit class. She was a new Corps recruit. The other woman was the lieutenant from the corridor.

"Hi, Anivea." I slid into the empty seat and nodded to the blonde. She smiled weakly. Then I looked at the officer. "I'm Siti."

"This is Petra Wronglen," Marika said, her eyes wide. "She's—"

"Lieutenant Wronglen," the woman cut in. "I'm Captain Hydrao's aide."

"Nice to meet you," I said, watching her closely. The striped creature wiggled in my pocket. I clamped a hand over him, and he settled.

We ate in silence for a few minutes.

"I thought Lieutenant Stein was the captain's aide," I said after a while, wondering why this woman had joined us. She clearly outranked my friends and was several years older. Besides, ship's crew and Corps rarely mixed. Every table but ours had a monochromatic theme. Gray uniforms for the crew, black for Corps.

Wronglen lifted her chin. "Stein was moved to navigation. Now that we're nearing our destination, they needed additional help. They brought me out of deep sleep to take the position."

"What did you do before you went down, ma'am?" Anivea asked.

Wronglen's nostrils flared, as if her previous assignment were distasteful. "Maintenance. But they already have an OIC this shift." She turned to me. "An OIC is—"

"Officer in charge," I said. "I'm familiar with the term. What does the captain's aide do?"

"I'm responsible for organizing all of the revivals," she said proudly. "I woke you and your father."

"Ah. A sentient alarm clock." I rolled my eyes at Marika.

Wronglen's lips thinned. Anivea gasped. Marika stifled a giggle.

No one spoke for a while. Finally, I sighed. "So, did you want something, Lieutenant? I mean, this doesn't seem like your usual. There aren't many officers in here." I gestured to the room at large.

She leaned forward, then glanced at Anivea and Marika on either side. "Would you give us a moment?" It was not a question.

The girls leaped to their feet, grabbing their trays. "We'll just…" Anivea said.

"See you after dinner," Marika mumbled.

I glared at her. "Don't leave. She only wants a minute. Right?" I looked at the officer and raised my eyebrow.

"It's okay," Marika said hurriedly. "I have some studying to do. I'll see you later." They hurried away.

I sat back in my chair, folding my arms over my chest. The creature in my pocket started to wiggle again. I clapped my hand over him once more, trying not to look awkward. "What was so secret you had to send my friends away?"

Wronglen leaned forward again. "If you know what's good for you, you won't mention that conversation in the passageway."

"Conversation?" I asked, trying to be cool. "You mean where you insulted my father and me to a junior crewmember?" I'd been around the Corps long enough to know she shouldn't be doing that.

"I—yes." Wronglen looked uncomfortable and changed tactics. "I'd like to apologize. I don't know your father and had no business using that nickname in conversation with a subordinate." Her robotic tone didn't sound very apologetic.

"So, you think it would be okay if you'd been talking to another officer?" I wasn't going to let it go easily.

She flushed. "No. I shouldn't disparage the hero of Darenti." Her lips pressed together as if she wanted to take it back.

"Thanks," I said. "I forgive you."

The lieutenant's nostrils flared again, but she clamped down on whatever she was feeling. "I'll leave you to your meal in peace, then." She lifted her tray and hurried away.

Weird. Why would she seek me out to threaten me then apologize? That felt over the top—as if she were trying to distract me from something else. I finished my meal alone, pretending I didn't mind. The gently vibrating creature in my pocket soothed me a little, and I smiled faintly.

"Attention, crew and Corps." A deep, feminine voice echoed through every holo-ring in the room. I flicked mine and swept the announcement up.

Captain Hydrao smiled at me from the hologram hovering over my palm. I glanced around the room—she appeared multiple times at every table. I giggled at the mirrored effect.

"As you know, we'll be arriving at our destination soon." Hydrao nodded at a man standing next to her. "Commander Kassis and I would like to thank you for your hard work in getting us here. We know the ship is a bit crowded right now, with the explorers being revived, but we want a full team available as soon as we land. In the meantime, we thought you'd all like to witness this historic occasion."

My father stepped closer, smiling at the camera. "We've launched a probe. In just a few moments, video from its long-range cameras will reach us, and we'll be able to see our destination."

The holo changed to a dark star field. The left side of the field disappeared in a glow of light from the system's star. The software kicked in and dampened the brightness.

"If you watch the right side of the video, you'll soon see the planet. We'll be there in a few weeks."

A faint pinprick of light grew larger, resolving into a tiny blue-green sphere. As the probe zoomed toward it, the planet grew, revealing the familiar landmasses we'd all learned about in school.

"There it is," my father said. "Earth."

CHAPTER TWO

My holo-ring vibrated the incoming message signal. Unless it was from Marika, I usually let it go to message, but this time, the sequence indicated a call from my father. I checked to make sure Liam—the sair-glider—was hidden in his nest in a drawer. When he wasn't flying around my cabin, he rode in my pocket. Several times, he'd tried to climb up my arm when we were out in the public areas of the ship, so I took to spending more time in my room. Dad was probably getting suspicious. I flicked the accept button

"Can you meet me for lunch?" Dad asked.

"I guess," I replied, a little sulkily. Lunch was one of the few times I could see my friends—they had jobs. Aside from my required Refit classes, I had nothing to do, and I was bored. Liam helped, but a friend to hang out with would have been even better.

"Great," Dad said. "See you in the officers' mess on the bell."

"Aye aye, sir!" I said, just as I had since I was a little girl.

He smiled, winked, and broke the connection.

I sent a message to Marika, telling her I'd have to miss lunch, and played with Liam for a while. A little more research had indicated sair-gliders were considered planet-neutral. They carried no diseases or parasites, so they were safe to take to other planets. How odd that the perfect space-faring companion had evolved on Kepler Three—or anywhere, for that matter. Rumors indicated CEC explorers frequently brought them along on missions. But I hadn't seen any others on the *Glory*.

I made it to the officers' mess two minutes early. My father expected punctuality. He strode up to the door and wrapped me in a hug just as the bell rang. We went in and sat as his usual table. Four places were set.

"Is someone else coming?" I asked.

"They'll be here in a few minutes," Dad said. "I wanted to talk to you first."

"About what?" I asked.

"Your job."

"I don't have a job," I reminded him.

A waiter arrived and took our drink orders. Officers' messes located on planets had human waiters, but on the ship, a bot did the job. They could have programmed the tables as touch screens, but that didn't give the same ambiance, I guess. But it meant more possibilities for mechanical failure. The military is all about tradition, and the Explorer Corps is no different.

We ordered drinks. "Are we taking those to the surface?" I asked, nodding at the boxy little bot. It had rounded corners and two big orbs on the front to give it a humanoid appearance. It slid across the deck using maglev tech. A box in its "chest" carried food and beverages kept at the appropriate temperature.

"Don't be silly," Dad said. "Not enough infrastructure for them to operate properly. We'll have a camp mess. You know what those are, right?"

"Just like the enlisted mess, but with humans serving?" I said.

"Usually self-serve, but yeah." He cleared his throat. "I want to give you a job."

"Doing what?" I asked. A job sounded like a lot of work. And a lot less time to play with Liam.

"There are several possibilities on the ship," he said. "You need something to keep you busy until we hit the dirt."

"Then what?" I asked. "How about I work with Marika? She has an interesting job."

"Marika LaGrange?" he said. "She's a first-term explorer."

"Yeah, and she's going to do cool stuff on the planet," I said. "She'll—"

"I know what she'll do on the planet," he said. "She'll help set up the camp, monitor security, shift loads. It's grunt work."

"That's why I've been working on my muscles," I joked, flexing my biceps. "But it's not that hard. They have grav-lifters for moving stuff and automated security cordons. And we know what to expect on Earth. It's not like Hurley-Behnken, where you ran into that flesh-eating fungus."

He nodded. "That's true. But we don't know *exactly* what to expect here. In five hundred years, there could have been massive changes in the air, water, and flora. We'll be carting a lot of lab equipment, and we've brought many more scientists than we use on a typical mission. I might be able to set you up as a lab assistant."

"You think I'm too good to be a grunt?" I demanded.

The little robot trundled up to the table. Servos whined softly, and mechanical arms removed our drinks from the box, placing them carefully on the table. "Would you like to order?" an androgynous voice asked.

"We'll wait for the others," Dad said. The little robot scuttled away. Dad glanced around the room, then looked back at me. "I don't think you're too good to be a first-termer. But you haven't gone through the training they have, so you aren't prepared for that position. Lab assistant is a little less strenuous."

"I—" I started, but he cut me off.

"The explorers work directly for me," he said. "I don't want anyone thinking I'm playing favorites, and they will, no matter what happens. It's better that you're assigned to one of the science teams."

"They work for you, too," I snapped.

"They're assigned to support my mission, but they don't work directly for me in a technical sense." He sipped his drink. "They report to Dr. Niles Gatens. He's university staff on loan to us. It's either that or join the ship's crew." He nodded toward the door where Captain Hydrao had just entered. The annoying Lt. Wronglen followed on her heels.

"No," I said. "I'm not working for Wronglen. And I'm not joining the crew. They have to stay up here."

"They'll come down for visits," Dad said. "It's safer. Have you met Wronglen?"

I didn't get a chance to answer as the two women stopped at our table.

"Thank you for joining us, Captain," Dad said, rising from his seat. I followed his lead and got a brief smile in reward. "You've met my daughter, Serenity?"

"Nice to see you again, Siti," Hydrao said. "This is my aide, Lt. Wronglen."

I nodded. "We've met."

Wronglen ignored me. Hydrao sat, and Dad and I followed. Wronglen took the fourth chair next to me. *How delightful.*

"You young women have a lot in common," Hydrao said, smiling politely at me. "Your father tells me you graduated from the Mount Wellesley Institute. Petra attended there, too."

"Salutatorian, class of twenty-three," Wronglen said with a condescending smile. "I'm sure I was long gone by the time you started."

"Yes, you're much older than me," I said sweetly. "I graduated from the honors program in thirty-one. Valedictorian."

Wronglen's eyes narrowed.

I smiled. *You started it. Witch.*

"So, Siti," Hydrao said. "Are you interested in taking an assignment on the bridge? Petra would be an excellent mentor if you're considering applying to the Space Academy."

I hid a smile at Wronglen's sour face. "I've thought about the academy," I said, "but I haven't decided yet. This is kind of a gap year for me." I laughed. "Or a gap twenty years. Time to figure out what I want to do with my life. I'd really like to be part of the landing team. I could probably get into any university in the galaxy with that on my resume. Dad and I were just talking about a lab assistant placement." Hopefully, I wouldn't have to work too hard. I wanted to see the sights.

Hydrao tipped her head to the side, considering. Her eyes flicked to Wronglen, who quickly blanked her expression. "Interesting proposition," she said. "A Mount Welleslian valedictorian should certainly have the skills to provide support in one of the labs. You might check with Dr.

Gatens, Nate," she said to my father. "He asked me just yesterday if I could spare anyone."

Dad nodded. "Thanks, Tisha, I'll do that. Now, let's order. I'm starving!"

A FEW HOURS LATER, Marika met me at the mess hall for dinner. She'd obviously stopped for a shower before coming up from the dorm—her hair was still wet. "You got a real shower?" I asked.

"Every four days," she said with a grin. "Sonic showers are okay, but real water is worth the wait. I can't wait to get dirtside where we can have them every day."

"If the water passes the testing," I said.

"Look at you being all reasonable and tech-y." She grabbed the tray I held out. "Did you have to look that up?" She nodded at my holo-ring.

"I am now an environmental lab technician, I will have you know." I lifted my chin and looked down my nose.

"How did that happen?" she asked.

We loaded up our trays. "You won't believe this." I told her about the lunch with Wronglen and Hydrao.

"That was close," Marika said. "Can you imagine working with her?"

"With whom?" Wronglen asked from behind Marika.

Marika's pale face flushed pink. I tried to ignore the heat in my own. "What are you doing here?" The best defense is an offense, right? Or something like that.

"I'm here for dinner." Wronglen's nostrils flared. "What's it to you?"

"You're an officer," I said. "I thought you didn't fraternize with the troops."

"I'm allowed to eat here if I want," she huffed. "You clearly don't understand how the service works. It's a good thing I talked the captain out of her insane plan to have you work on the bridge."

I laughed. "That is *so* not what happened. Come on, Marika, let's leave the delusional L.T. to her meal." I picked up my tray and headed across the mess to our usual table.

THE NEXT MORNING, I reported to the environmental lab promptly at eight. I waved my holo-ring at the access panel, and the door slid open. A woman in a lab coat leaned against a table, scrolling through screens and drinking from a tall, silver cup.

She looked up as I walked in. "You must be Serenity Kassis."

"Yes, ma'am," I said. "Call me Siti. Are you Dr. Gatens?"

She laughed. "No. You won't see him until later. He likes to give us plenty of time to set things up before he arrives." She rolled her eyes and flicked off her holo. "I'm Li Abdul-James. You want some coffee?"

"No, thanks," I said, lifting my own silver cup. Mine had the ship's logo on the side and my name engraved beneath. And it contained chai latte, not coffee.

"Drink up. We can't take 'em inside the lab," she said. She chugged her coffee and set the cup aside.

She showed me around the lab, pointing out experiments that would be run and data that would be recorded. "Obviously, since we're looking at the chemistry of the environment, the actual experiments have to wait until we land. But we'll spend the next few days setting up the equipment, making sure we have the proper materials, then packing it all into these transport cubes." She gestured at a stack of sleek crates in the corner.

"Why did you unpack everything if we're just going to pack it back up?" I asked.

"Most of these instruments were not assembled a few weeks ago," Li said. "New, fresh-out-of-the-box equipment. Well, fresh twenty years ago. But we don't want to do the assembly on the dirt—too easy to lose things in transit. We set up all the equipment here, run some diagnostics and test procedures to make sure it's all running correctly. Then we box it for transport."

We spent the morning doing just that. About two hours after we started, Dr. Gatens swirled into the lab. He was a short, skinny man, with thick white hair, piercing gray eyes, and a huge lab coat that flapped away from his stick-like body when he moved.

"Welcome to the lab, Sara," he said.

"It's Siti," I replied. "Thanks for hiring me."

Gatens waved a hand, as if my name were unimportant. Or maybe my whole existence was unimportant. "Li will direct your activities. Do as she says, and all will be well." He swung away from me, focusing on Li. "What's the status?"

Li gave him a twenty-second overview of what we'd done that morning. He cut her off before she got half-way through. "Excellent! I'll see you tomorrow." And he swept out of the room.

I stared after him, my mouth open.

Li laughed. "He's quite dramatic, isn't he?"

"That's a good word." I pulled on my earlobe. "Will he be back?"

"Every day at eleven," Li said.

"He just sweeps in, gets a report, and disappears?" I asked. "What does he do all day?"

"Not a clue," Li said with a sigh. "When I signed on to this mission, I was told I'd be working with the best. I'm starting to wonder: the best what?"

I laughed. "Maybe he switches on when we hit the dirt," I suggested as I loaded the test slide into another microscope. "You know, like an actor hitting the stage."

Li smirked. "He has the persona down pat."

THE NEXT THREE days followed the same pattern. I worked in the lab all morning, took an hour lunch to visit with Marika and play with Liam, then went back to the lab. On the third afternoon, we stacked the last crate. I looked at my broken nails, wondering if there was anyplace to get them done on the ship.

"Now we'll shrink-wrap these and move them to the shuttle," Li said.

"Shrink-wrap?" I asked. "Why not a gravitational clamp?"

"Never use technology if there's a lower-tech way that's just as effective," Li said. "It's kind of a mantra for the Exploration Corps. Tech has a way of crapping out just when you need it." She pulled a basket off a shelf. "Throw one of these over each pallet. Then activate it." She unfurled a length of thin, dark blue material and tossed it over the closest pallet of equipment. The CEC logo glowed in large golden letters on each side. Walking around the stack, she adjusted the cloth until it stretched evenly over the entire pile. Then she pressed the yellow activation button on one of the corners. The fabric tightened around the crates, holding them in place.

"That's lower-tech?" I asked.

"Maybe not, but it doesn't require power to maintain once it's been activated," she said. "This will hold the equipment in place until we land. Now we can use the grav-lifters to move it to the shuttle bay."

We had just wrestled the second pallet through the narrow lab door when my holo-ring pinged. The captain's voice issued from the ship's speakers as well as through my audio implant. "We will enter Earth orbit in five minutes."

Li abandoned the wrapped pallets in the outer office and lunged for the door. "Let's get up to the observation deck!" she cried, leading the way.

Every holo-ring and view screen on the ship appeared to be focused on the planet below. We'd been approaching for days, the blue-green orb filling a larger portion of the screen as we drew near. But everyone wanted to witness the moment we arrived.

A queue had started to form at the float-tubes. "This way," Li whispered, leading me away from the lines. "There's a maintenance hatch here." We rounded a corner, and she tapped on an access panel next to a meter-high hatch.

"Why do you have access to maintenance?" I asked.

"My partner works in ship's maintenance," she said. "He gave me access in case…" The door popped open. She pulled it away from the wall and motioned for me to climb in.

Ducking my head, I stepped over the high threshold and onto a platform. Some tools hung on the wall of the small, circular room. A hole in the floor revealed a ladder to the deck below. On the opposite side, another ladder led through a hole above.

"In case of what?" I asked as she shut the hatch behind us.

"I dunno," she admitted. "In case we needed to bypass the float-tubes, I guess." She started climbing the ladder. "It's only two decks."

We climbed to the deck above, then crossed the tiny room to the next ladder. "They're built this way to prevent anyone from falling all the way down," she said. "Plus, there are automated blast doors that close in case of atmo breach.

"Automated blast doors?" I echoed faintly. As I climbed through the next deck, I noted the thickness of the decking, and the heavy plate waiting to snap across the hole. "This thing would cut me in half if it shut while I was here," I noted as I scrambled through as quickly as possible.

"I think they have sensors," she replied. "But let's face it—if there's an atmo breach, they'd rather cut a couple of us in half than lose the whole ship."

I glared at the hole while she opened the hatch.

"Observation deck is to the right."

We got some funny looks when we climbed out of the hatch, but no one stopped us. A steady stream of Corps personnel streamed through the corridor, with a few ship's officers peppered in. I didn't see any of the enlisted crew.

We crammed into the wide lounge, probably exceeding the maximum occupancy by about half. No one seemed to care about that, though. Thick transparent plates covered the ceiling, allowing us a brilliant view of the planet below. We worked our way into a corner, hoping to avoid the worst of the jostling as more people attempted to enter the lounge.

"Parking orbit in thirty seconds," a male voice said. "Twenty-five."

No one spoke. Every head cranked toward the ceiling, staring at the beautiful blue-green curve.

"Ten seconds," the voice said.

Everyone else joined in. "Nine. Eight. Seven…"

The chant grew louder. "Four. Three. Two. One. Mark!"

Deafening cheers erupted all over the room. People hugged and kissed. The guy next to me grabbed my shoulder, then recoiled—probably when he realized who he'd manhandled. He took a half-step back, nearly crushing the man behind him. He held out a shaky hand.

I laughed and threw my arms around him, squeezing fast and letting go.

Li grabbed my arm, jumping up and down. "We're here! We're here!"

The captain's voice echoed through the room, cutting off the cheers. "Congratulations one and all. We have reached Earth!"

"I'd like the thank Captain Hydrao and the crew of the *Return in Glory* for bringing us safely to our destination," my father said. "On behalf of not just the Colonial Exploration Corps, but the entire human population of the galaxy, thank you for bringing us home."

CHAPTER THREE

I PERCHED on the jump seat, my restraints pulled tight as I tried to lean forward. The back of the co-pilot's chair blocked the bottom of the view screen, so I leaned out into the aisle.

Thunk!

"Ow!" Dad and I exclaimed together. He'd leaned in from his side at the same time.

I glanced at him, laughing as I rubbed the top of my head. "Why aren't you flying?"

"I try to share the wealth," he said. "Plus, D'metros and Evy are more current than I am. I don't get enough hours. This should be a routine landing, but when you get complacent, then you make mistakes."

On the screen, the clouds cleared, and we could see the planet below us. Green stretched across the landscape, washing up to brown ridges and mountains. I gasped. "It's amazing!"

"It is," Dad agreed. "Every new planet takes your breath away. Seeing the birthplace of mankind is even more incredible."

"We're headed for that empty plateau," Paulus D'metros said, pointing at the viewscreen. "There's room for all three shuttles to land, and we can set up camp against that cliff."

I peered at the screen, not seeing anything he described. I saw only rolling green, and a winding darker green. To the left, a blue expanse of water. "Where's the plateau?"

Sarabelle Evy glanced over her shoulder but didn't say anything. She returned the data flowing across her screen. "All green," she said. "Looks good."

D'metros grunted. "Excellent." He slid his fingers along the viewscreen, then flicked them over his shoulder. "You can open that in your holo and zoom in, Ms. Kassis. I've marked the landing site."

"Thanks," I replied. "Call me Siti." I flicked open the file, and a smaller version of the viewscreen opened in my palm. I compared the two as we drew nearer the landing site—my copy changed with the master on the viewscreen. Although the shuttle appeared to have large windows, the view outside was an illusion. Even transparent aluminum was too vulnerable for repeated reentry, and these shuttles made the trip many times. They used dozens of cameras and redundant computer equipment to create the illusion of windows.

On my palm, an arrow blinked, designating the landing site. A tiny brownish area lay above a river, almost like a step between the valley and the cliff beside it. "That's big enough to land on?"

"We're still pretty far away," Dad said. "Plenty of room." He flicked his ring, and an overlay appeared in my view, showing a schematic for the campsite.

"Huh," I said, flipping the holo around to view it from all sides. The cliff above the landing site looked like a rough wall. The top of it stretched in a rocky ridge along the foot of the mountains. "Why here?"

"We picked the plateau because it's easily defensible," Dad said. "Scans from the ship indicated there were no predators on the plateau, but that's the first thing we'll check when we land."

"But why here?" I repeated. "Why this area? Why not near one of the big cities? There wasn't a city near here, was there?"

"No. We'll use this as a base camp," Dad said. "Once we've got it set up, we'll send smaller teams to each of the continents to do a survey."

"Yeah, I've read the briefing," I said, zooming out the view on the holo. "But why did we choose this part of the world for the base camp?"

"We were told to," Dad said.

"By your boss?" I persisted.

"No," Dad said. "When humanity left Earth five hundred years ago, there were a number of instructions left with the colonists. One of them was if we ever returned, this was the location we were to land. There was more information, but after this long, much of it was corrupted. We only know this is the place. Maybe this was the last place people lived?"

"Huh," I said. Mysterious instructions from the past. Cool.

"What is that?" Dad demanded.

"What?" I asked, shifting the holo.

"That." His hand speared through the holo and pointed at my chest.

Liam's blue and white striped head poked out of the cargo pocket on the front of my landing coverall. Crap.

"Uh, that's Liam," I whispered. "He's a sair-glider."

Dad's eyes narrowed. "I know what it is. Where did you get it?"

"I found him," I said. "Or more accurately, he found me. In the crew lounge near the mess hall."

"You found an unauthorized animal on the ship, and you decided to keep it?" he asked.

I shivered at the cold in his voice. I hung my head. "He was almost starved to death. I nursed him back to health. And I checked the research. Sair-gliders are safe."

"They're safe to take when you visit your grandmother on Tereshkova," Dad roared. "That doesn't mean you should introduce them to virgin planets on a survey!"

D'metros and Evy exchanged a look.

"What?" Dad growled.

"Falina has one," Evy said. "She's taken her on every mission we've done."

"Yeah, it saved her life on Tremos Seven, remember?" D'metros put in.

"Bit that serpent's head right off," Evy agreed.

Dad's lips pinched together. "You two are not helping. Falina's glider was authorized. And well-trained. This one isn't."

"But he's still safe to bring to Earth, right?" I asked in my best 'daddy's little girl' voice.

He shook his head, but I saw the corner of his lips twitch. "You had no way of knowing that."

"Actually, the stuff I read talked about Tremos Seven," I said. "It didn't identify Falina, but…"

"Too late now," Dad admitted. "But I want you to leave it in the shuttle when we land. Once we get the camp laid out, you can bring it to the living mod. But it stays in camp."

"Yes, sir!" I raised my hand in the CEC salute.

"Cute," Dad grumbled.

"We're approaching the landing site," Evy said.

The shuttle swooped lower, individual trees now visible on the viewscreen. We skimmed over the vast stretch of green. My stomach dropped when the land fell away to a river, and then we hovered over the rocky plateau. The shuttle eased down and settled in place.

"Nicely done, Evy," Dad said.

"The computer did most of it," Evy said. "But I put on the final flourish." She swiped an icon. "This is the pilot. We have arrived. Feel free to get out of your seats and retrieve your equipment. The commander will meet the environmental team in the airlock. PR folks, you can send your remotes to the lock, but please stay in the seating area."

While the pilots ran through their shut-down procedures, Dad and I unfastened our restraints. As I waited for Dad to stand, stretch, and move out of the aisle, I moved Liam to my bag and stowed it under the seat. He cheeped at me, but I'd fed him right before the drop, so he curled up and went back to sleep.

Dr. Gatens met us at the airlock, with Li hovering behind him. Gatens wore his usual baggy lab coat, but Li had donned the same sturdy landing suit the rest of us wore. They both swiped furiously through data screens on their holo-rings. A pair of newscasters pushed in behind.

Dad glared over Li's shoulder. "You were told to wait in the passenger area."

"But we—"

Dad held up a hand, and they stopped talking. "This is a CEC mission. When you were embedded with this unit, you agreed to the rules. If you can't follow instructions, you will be returned to the *Glory*, and your remotes will be confiscated."

Both reporters backed away. Before they reached the end of the corridor, two tiny holo-cam drones swooped over our heads and hovered by the airlock hatch. They turned to focus their main cams on Dad.

Evy and D'Metros joined us. Evy unlocked a compartment by the airlock and passed out weapons to Dad and D'Metros. She tried to give them to Gatens and Li, but they both refused. She didn't offer me one.

"Give Siti a stunner," Dad said. "She knows how to use it."

"Yes, sir." Evy handed me a compact hand weapon before relocking the compartment.

Dr. Gatens, practically dancing in excitement, lifted his hand, a holo of data swirling over his palm. "The readings look excellent!" he said. "Just as the probes indicated. Perfect oxygen-nitrogen mix. Argon and carbon dioxide are well within parameters. No toxins. Temperature is currently eighteen degrees—much lower than the last reported temperature for this location and season."

"As we expected," Dad replied. "Let's open her up."

Evy squeezed past me with an apologetic grin and flicked the control panel by the airlock. She straightened her spine and nodded formally at the drones. "The commander has given the go-ahead. Opening the airlock now."

Our arrival on Earth was an historic event. Every second of the arrival would be recorded and later analyzed and discussed. Every decision would be hashed over after the fact by viewers throughout settled space.

I bit my lip. Probably should have thought about that before bringing Liam on this trip. No wonder Dad had been pissed with me.

Evy placed her hand on the access panel and leaned forward to peer into the retina scan. She typed in a passcode, and the hatch popped. She swung it wide and marched into the airlock. The drones zipped over her head and hovered beside her.

"Everyone in," D'metros said, making pushing motions. Dad and I followed Evy. Once we were all inside, D'metros closed the hatch behind us.

"Last chance," Dad said with a grin. "Anyone want to chicken out?"

"Hell no!" Evy and D'metros cried in unison. It sounded like a ritual thing.

"Of course not," Gatens mumbled, although a sheen of sweat covered his face. Li grinned from behind the short scientist.

Dad addressed the drone. "This is an historic moment. Mankind returns to Earth. All our readings show a veritable paradise restored, and it only took five hundred years. Evy, open the hatch."

The airlock cycled and the outer hatch popped. Cool air rushed in, scented with resin and earthy notes. Sunlight streamed down, making my eyes water. I dashed away the tears and stared through the hatch.

Rough stone stretched away to a sheer drop. The sun glinted off water in the distance. Beyond the second shuttle, tiny coniferous trees swayed in the breeze. Soft whooshing, like the oceans back home, came and went. After a moment, I realized the sound was caused by the wind in those trees.

The drones streaked out the door, making us all duck. They hovered and spun to focus on the hatch. Evy and Dad stepped out onto the narrow platform formed by the side of the shuttle and paused. Dad cleared his throat. "To quote a famous early explorer: One small step for man. One giant leap for mankind." He jumped to the stone.

We cheered.

"This is the commander," Dad said. "All clear."

A voice piped in through our audio implants. "Shuttle two to commander. Clear."

And another. "Shuttle three, we're clear, too."

Dad turned and gestured to us. "Come on out."

I climbed onto the step and jumped to the stony ground.

"Stay close," Dad told me. "We don't know enough about possible predators."

"Aye, sir," I replied before wandering toward the edge of the cliff. I could practically hear Dad rolling his eyes and gritting his teeth. I ignored him—he could still see me. Besides, what was going to get me? A giant bird?

As I neared the edge of the stone, I realized the trees weren't tiny—only the tops were visible. They were many meters tall, with their roots dug into the ground far below. Beyond the trees, a ribbon of water wound away, and in the distance, the sun glinted on a wide lake.

The clanging of the shuttle's hatch rang across the stone. I spun around. D'metros had disappeared—probably cycling the lock to let more people out. Dad stood with Evy and the two scientists, looking at data Gatens projected on the side of the ship. I wandered over, figuring I should probably be doing my job.

"That's great," Dad interrupted Gatens' enthusiastic speech. "Keep an eye on the readings and let me know if you see anything extraordinary. At least we don't have to worry about parasites or toxins. We've been here before."

"Actually, both are possible," Li said. "We don't know how the contaminants we left behind might have impacted the evolution of plants and animals here. But we're probably safe. The scans should alert us if there's any problems."

"That's what I said," Dad muttered. Li didn't give any indication she heard it.

I hid a grin and followed Dad and Evy around the end of the shuttle. Six other explorers joined us in the space between our shuttle and the next one.

"Offload shuttle three and return to the ship," Major Tam Origani said. "Then move the other two over there. This plateau is surprisingly level. There's running water at the back, near the campsite."

"That's why they chose that site," Dad said. "Check out the entire plateau. We don't want to find out the hard way that we've encroached on a wild animal's den. When we're clear, you can start unloading the equipment."

As he spoke, more people trickled around the shuttles, joining us in the center. Origani took command, directing the armor-clad explorers to clear the space. They moved away in pairs, eyes watchful, heads swiveling.

Dad put a hand on my shoulder. "You see how they stay in pairs? Until we've determined otherwise, this is a hostile planet. We think we know everything there is to know about it, but that makes it even more dangerous. As Li mentioned, things change in five hundred years. Evolution doesn't usually work that fast, but all it takes is one unusual mutation. You stay within the camp at all times. If I give you clearance to leave, you'll go with at least one partner."

I heaved the expected sigh but nodded. "Aye, sir."

He grinned. "Once they clear this plateau, you're free until Li needs your help. But stay close." He marched away to receive reports from the teams returning to the center.

I leaned against the side of the shuttle, careful to not touch the exhaust ports marked "hot." The sun poured down, and I turned my face upward, eyes closed. The optical shield built into my suit would prevent me from sunburn, and the warmth felt good on my skin. I wished I could strip off the heavy jacket, but until we'd established a base, that was against protocol. Being the daughter of Nate Kassis, I could appreciate the importance of protocol, even though I chafed at the thought.

"Enjoying a life of leisure, I see," a scathing female voice said. Wronglen.

"Just taking a short break before getting to work," I said. "What are you doing here? I thought the captain had to stay aboard until Dad gave the all-clear."

"She does," Wronglen said. "That's why she sent me. To report back."

"She didn't trust Dad's reports?" I asked, feeling offended on his behalf.

"Captain Hydrao prefers to get her information firsthand." Wronglen sniffed.

"Secondhand," I said.

"I beg your pardon?" the woman snapped.

"Secondhand," I repeated. "She'd have to come down here herself to get it firsthand."

"Whatever," Wronglen grumbled, striding away.

I grinned and closed my eyes again.

"All clear!" Evy's voice rang through my audio implant. My eyes snapped open. Time to explore.

I hurried around the prime shuttle. The hatch opened as I went by, and another handful of explorers jumped out. I scanned them quickly, but Marika wasn't with them. She'd be assigned to a detail anyway, so she couldn't cut out and explore with me. They streamed toward the central area. I headed the opposite direction.

The stone plateau was probably a half-kilometer long, in the shape of a shallow wedge. The two straight sides were bounded by the cliff stretching another ten or fifteen meters above our heads. On the long arc, the stone fell away in a sheer cliff to the tree roots below. The camp would be set against the cliff walls behind me, with the outer edge being used for shuttles.

Once the shuttles had been unloaded, two of them would return to the ship to pick up the remaining equipment and personnel. The rest of the team had been awakened shortly before we left—by the time the camp was set up, they'd be ready to join us.

I strolled along the cliff until I found a place where the trees below ended. I sat on the stone, my legs dangling over the edge. About forty meters below, a narrow sandy beach hugged the bottom of the cliff, with a wide river flowing beside it. Trees grew close to the water on both sides, but here, the river had washed them away or they hadn't had enough soil to get a foothold.

Behind me, one of the shuttles blasted its hover engines. I glanced back to see the first one had unloaded several large crates and now hovered above the stone. It slowly drifted away from the people and equipment. When it reached the edge of the plateau, it dropped over the side. Engines fired, and it swooped away.

Another shuttle lifted and slid toward the rear of the plateau. Dr. Gatens' equipment was in that shuttle, so I reluctantly got to my feet and joined the others.

The crates from the first shuttle were even bigger than I'd realized. Three meters on each side, they held the basics for a planetary base camp. Half a dozen explorers guided the grav-lifters on the crate, nudging it into place about a meter from the cliff face. Another crew moved the second crate.

"Over here," Li called through the audio implant. I turned. She stood near the back of the now stationary second shuttle. The rear door of the craft hinged upward, allowing direct access to the cargo bay. A ramp extended from beneath the opening.

I circled around the craft and reached the ramp as it touched down on the stone. Li and I climbed up the steep slope and slid along the narrow gap between the smaller crates secured there.

"The other labs will have to get their stuff out first," Li said. "But I wanted to do a quick review. Our lab will be in the Mod B. We'll take these stacks of crates and that one." She pointed to our equipment. "The rest, we'll store behind the camp until we need it."

"Behind the camp?" I asked as I squinted at the markings on the crate behind ours. "Is that food?"

"Could be," Li said. "Explorers gotta eat. We've got an experimental chef on this trip. Usually they'd just send meal pacs, but with all the publicity this trip is getting, they decided we should have a cook." She grinned. "Therri is a culinary historian and master forager."

"A what?" I asked.

"He knows a ton about the foods people used to eat on Earth," she translated. "Plus, he's good at finding edible plants and animals. That's his Corps specialty. Initial exploratory missions usually eat meal pacs, but the later colony reviews have to find edible sources of food—if a colony can eat the native stuff, they don't need to bring in costly synthesizers. Therri figures out which foods colonists can eat."

"Native foods?" I pulled on my earlobe. "I'm not sure I like the sound of that. I'll take a good synthesizer any day."

"Gotta have power for an AutoKich'n," she said. "We don't like to be dependent on technology that can break, remember?" She patted the stacks of shrink-wrapped crates. "And colonists plain can't afford it most of the time."

"AutoKich'ns aren't that expensive," I said doubtfully.

"They are at scale," Li said. "Heavy to ship. Once a colony has manufacturing set up, they can build 'em local. But most colonies want independence from that kind of technology. So that's what we look for."

The crates in front of us lifted and shifted away. Light streamed in as the tall stacks moved down the ramp and into the camp.

"Our turn," Li said. "Follow me. We're in Mod B."

We activated our grav-lifts and slid our wrapped crates down the ramp. Li pushed her pallet across the stone to the newly unfolded module. Each enormous cube provided living and working space for twenty-five or more explorers. We guided our loads through the door and into the single large, open room. A pair of explorers followed behind, bringing our remaining stacks.

"Put these in that corner." She pointed across the room then turned to the last guy. "Those go behind the building for storage." He gave a thumbs-up and disappeared. She turned to me. "Now that we've got everything inside, we build the lab."

"Build?" I asked, gulping. "I've never built anything. Except a sandwich."

"This is almost as easy," Li said. She pulled up a schematic on her holo-ring and flung it onto a projection pad laying on top of her pallet. "This gives us directions. See? Fit tab A into slot B."

It was almost that easy. The schematics told us where to erect walls. We peeled thin layers of flexible plastek from the internal walls of the mod. Once free, we dragged them into place, with Li's schematic lighting up red if we got it wrong. When we'd put them in place, she activated the section through her holo-interface, and the plastek stiffened. In effect, we built the lab around our stacks of crates.

"It's solid enough to hold light shelves," she said, knocking on one. "Or someone leaning against it. It wouldn't stop a rover or a large predator, but we set up external security to keep them out. Now we can unpack."

We spent the rest of the morning unpacking. After a few hours, Li declared a lunch break. "If the kitchen is set up, we'll get a good meal, but if not, they'll be handing out meal pacs. Let's go see which it is." She closed and locked the lab behind us.

"Why bother locking?" I asked. "You know everyone on the team."

"It's policy," she said, leading me down a hallway that hadn't existed before. We passed open doors, revealing other scientists building and unpacking their own labs. "I trust the Corps, but I don't know the ship's crew as well. Not that I distrust them, but I don't trust them either, if you know what I mean. And the journalists will be down soon. They're an unknown quantity. Plus, the lock will keep out curious animals. They shouldn't get through the external security shield, but there's always a chance. They learned that the hard way on Darenti Four."

I raised my eyebrows, but she didn't expand. I could always look it up later—if I cared. We entered a small lobby. Ahead, an open door and two windows allowed sunlight to stream onto the plas-tile floor.

"First lunch lottery!" a deep voice sang out behind us.

Li grinned over her shoulder. "I'm betting on meal pacs."

A tall man with broad shoulders and a slight paunch grinned back. "This is Earth. We knew what to expect. I predict we'll have the full meal deal."

"They're following all the regular protocols," Li said, pausing to let the man exit the building ahead of us.

He stepped through and waited for us to come up beside him. "I know. Doesn't change my bet." He turned to me and held out a fist. "I'm Rico Abdul Jones."

I bumped my knuckles against his. "Siti Kassis."

"I know." He winked. "Everyone knows the commander's daughter."

I curtseyed and fluttered my eyelashes. "Of course you do."

The last shuttle stood on the stone plateau ahead of us, but it had been moved parallel to the front of the modules. We turned right and walked to the end of the cube. The second cube had been opened up, creating a dark, narrow alley from the front of the buildings to the stone cliff behind.

We continued to the third building—the common mod, as it was known. This one was smaller, with an open frame of beams stretching over the space in front. Chairs and tables lay scattered in the striped shade. Beyond them, double doors stood open, and a delicious scent wafted out.

"Huzzah!" Rico said, pumping his fist. "Pay up."

Li woke her holo-ring and opened a pay screen. She flicked a few icons, and a ch-ching sound came from Rico's ring.

Li rolled her eyes. "I can't believe you turned that noise on."

"Lots of credits to make on landing," Rico said with another wink. "Gotta let folks know how much I appreciate their business."

"Does it make a crying baby sound if you lose?" Li asked as we trooped through the door.

"If I ever lose, I'll let you know," Rico said.

Along a side wall, a buffet was laid out. Three serving stations held a variety of warm and cold food. At the end of the table, a water cask stood guard over a tray of glasses and pitchers of colorful liquids. Beyond that, a small table held a stack of meal pacs.

"The food on the first day is kind of hit-or-miss," Li told me as we lined up and grabbed plates. "If you aren't quick enough—"

"Or if the chef is too adventurous," Rico put in.

Li chuckled. "Or that, you can grab a meal pac. But always try the real stuff first. It's usually much better."

I glanced dubiously at the first station. This table held a large thermal pot that steamed gently and a stack of flexi-bowls. Li ladled out a thick brown liquid with chunks. It smelled okay, so I grabbed one of the flattened bowls, popped it open, and scooped in some food. Following Li's example, I sprinkled on some green stuff and some yellow stuff.

"This one is shredded cheese," Li said. "They bring wheels of if down from the ship. The green stuff might be herbs from the ship or something local that tested safe."

"Who does the testing?" I asked as we carried our food out to the tables on the patio.

"The chef works with the botanists." Li glanced at the sun, then took a seat with her back to the view.

I sat across from her, where I could watch the tops of the trees sway in the wind. A team had installed meter-tall bollards at regular intervals along the edge of the cliff. These would form a force shield when activated. It would keep out local wildlife and prevent any careless explorers from falling to their death. Gates could be opened in the shield at any bollard to allow explorer teams access to the outside world.

"The camp shield filters the air and keeps out wildlife," Li said. "But the temporary one doesn't filter light. It's going to shine right into your eyes if you sit over there. Rookie mistake."

"I got my shades," I said, activating my suit's optical shades. "But the sun would feel good on my back." I started to rise so I could move around the table, but Rico took the other chair.

"Too slow, your majesty." He smirked.

My eyes narrowed. "Don't call me that."

"Whatever you say, Ms. Kassis." Rico bowed and held out his hands. "Please don't have my head on a pike."

"Shut up, Rico," Li said, slapping his bulging arm.

My face heated, but I tried to grin back. I'd have to get used to this kind of treatment. These people worked for my father. For some reason, they expected me to be a pampered princess. That reflected more on their relationship with him than on me. Or so I told myself.

"I prefer 'your imperial highness,'" I said.

Rico burst out laughing. "You got it, your imperialness."

As we ate, more of the team trickled in. Most of them returned to the patio with trays of real food. Wronglen chose a meal pac, of course. Marika waved at me when she arrived, but she sat with her teammates. I tried not to feel neglected.

Li and Rico talked about missions they'd worked in the past and how they felt this one would stack up against those. Rico thought Earth would be the easiest ever because we already knew what to expect. Li disagreed, citing the opportunity for mutations. I let their conversation rumble around me as I gazed out at the view.

A bird swooped low over the camp, squawking when its talons hit the force shield. Blue sparks trailed in its wake as it fought to pull up.

"Eagle!" someone yelled. "That's a bald eagle! I can't believe they survived!"

The bird flapped its wings, battling away from the camp. Then it soared out over the river and dropped below the cliff top.

"So cool," Li said. "I wonder what kind of mutations it needed to survive. According to the records, the air was toxic when we left." She rose and took her tray into the building.

Rico grinned. "Li's first puzzle. She'll mutter about that eagle for days."

"But she's not a zoologist," I protested.

"Doesn't matter," Rico said. "It crosses her area of expertise—atmosphere, weather—her whole focus is how those things affect life on the planet. Have fun!" He rose and followed her inside.

I grabbed my own tray and returned to the cafeteria. Following Rico's example, I scraped my dishes into a tub then placed them in another tub. We filled our water bottles at the cask and returned to the lab.

All afternoon, Li muttered about the eagle. After a few aborted attempts to get her to talk about anything else, I gave up and focused on my work. We put collapsing counters together, then moved crates of supplies under the counters. Scientific gear was set up on top, but Li did that.

Dr. Gatens breezed in a few hours later. He glanced at the half-unpacked lab and frowned. "I thought you'd be further along by now."

"It takes a full day to set up," Li said shortly. "Check the schedule." She turned her back and continued working.

"You, Sana!" Gatens said.

"It's Siti," I said.

"Whatever. Let me know when the lab is ready." He turned, his lab coat swirling around his body, and left.

"It would go faster if you helped," I muttered.

"No, it wouldn't," Li said. "Trust me, we're better off without him."

"What's he going to do?" I asked. "He can't start working until we get this set up. What's he going to spend his time on?"

Li shrugged. "Gazing at his navel? Annoying the commander? Practicing dance? Who knows? As long as he isn't doing it here, I don't care."

"Doesn't it bother you that you do all the work, and he gets all the credit?" I asked.

"He doesn't get *all* the credit," Li said. "My name is on every report we sent back to HQ. They know who did the real work. Besides, he doesn't work for CEC. He's on loan from the University of Grissom. He's a tenured professor, which means he doesn't have to work much at all. They only sent him because he's a history buff, and he begged to be detailed to this mission. And he has influential friends in the right place."

"So, he gets a free vacation because someone higher up likes him?" I demanded.

"It's the way of the world," Li said. "Someday, when I'm too old to do this anymore, I hope I can find such a sweet job. Just gotta work on schmoozing the right people."

"You'll never leave CEC," my father said. "But if you do, I'll put in a good word for you."

Li and I snapped upright. "Hello, Commander," Li said. She glanced at me, her face clearly saying, "How much did he hear?"

I shrugged. "Hi, Daddy! How's the mission going?"

He gave me his "I know you're up to something" look. "It's going fine. Textbook camp set-up. Security is live. Extra shuttles are unloaded and returned to the ship. Kitchen is up and running. We'll even have hot showers tonight."

"Hallelujah!" Li said. "Last up, first down. You know you're done when the showers are running."

"That sounds like a really bad song." I opened another crate. "Did you need something, Dad?"

"Just checking in," he said. "I assume she's working hard, Li?"

"She's been really helpful," Li said. "We're ahead of schedule. In fact," she looked around the room. "We'll be done early. First ones to the showers."

"Is that one of the things Rico bets on?" I asked.

Dad laughed. "Rico bets on everything. Don't take any of his action. He always wins." He gave me a one-armed hug. "I'll see you at dinner." At the doorway, he turned back. "Now that the field is set, you can let Liam out. But keep an eye on him."

"Thank you, Daddy!" I ran to the door and hugged him again.

"Who's Liam?" Li asked. "And why do you keep him locked up?"

CHAPTER FOUR

We weren't the first to the showers but close. Clean and dressed in our more comfortable camp uniforms, we returned to the dorm. This was a larger space in front of the communal showers, with reinforced columns set at regular intervals. Li showed me where to get a hammock and how to hook it into the sturdy metal loops.

"I always take a top bag," she said, clipping her hammock just above shoulder height. "Harder to get into, but less likely to get tripped over at night. Plus, no one can drop things on your head."

I picked a spot next to hers and clipped in my hammock. "How do you get up there?"

She showed me how to grab the hammock from underneath and flip up in. "If there's another one below to climb on, it's even easier," she said.

I tried to follow Li's example. "This is not as easy as it looks. Does everyone sleep here?" A vision of Dr. Gatens flying into an upper bunk using his lab coat as wings flitted through my head.

"No, the top folks have quarters behind the kitchen," she said. "That mod has four separate rooms and two semi-private bath modules. Your dad, Gatens, Origani—they'll sleep over there. The pilots sleep in the shuttle—there are bunks behind the cockpit."

"I saw those—they look more comfy than these." I plucked the fabric of my hammock.

"Good reason to become a pilot, I guess," Li said with a grin. She put her hands on both sides of her hammock and flipped over to drop to the floor. "Lockers are over here." She grabbed her duffle bag and strode to the wall.

I followed her example. My flip was a little sloppy, but I didn't end up on my butt. I struck a pose, then grabbed my duffel and picked out a locker near hers. We stowed our gear. Liam scampered out of my bag and up my arm.

"Is that a sair-glider?" Li asked.

"Yeah," I replied. "He, uh, found me on the *Glory*. I don't suppose you know anyone who lost one?" I held my breath, hoping the answer was no.

She shook her head. "No. Does the commander know?"

I nodded. "He said as long as I keep him inside the force shield, I can have him."

"Lots of explorers have them," Li said. "You'll see them flitting around the camp." She showed me how to register my thumbprint on the locker.

"No holo-ring unlocking?" I asked.

"You can set it up, but most of us don't bother." Li shut her locker and went back to her hammock. She grabbed her wet towel and headed for the door. "It doesn't save much, and we try to use holo-rings as little as possible when we're dirtside. We have a net set up here, but out there, there's no access."

I followed her out of the room. We dumped our damp towels into the recycler. "Don't we have coverage from the ship?"

"Sure, but it's slow and spotty. Besides, they'll be leaving to launch the jump beacons soon. Best not to rely on something that might stop working."

"That's kind of a mantra with you, isn't it?"

She tapped the patch on her shoulder. "That's what this says."

"What language is that?" I asked, craning my neck to peer at my own shoulder. Liam leaned out of my hair to look, too.

"I think it's ancient Latin," she said with a shrug. "Or Klingon."

"Siti!" Marika squealed as I emerged from the cube. "Where have you been?"

I glanced at Li, but she had turned away to talk to someone else. "Working. Showering. Setting up my bunk."

"We call it a bag," she said, dragging me toward the patio in front of the chow hall. "Not a bunk. Come on. Everyone is over here." We joined a group of first-termers seated around a table. Someone had brought cards, and a young man dealt out a hand. "You remember Ralph."

I nodded. I'd met most of these lower-ranking explorers onboard during PT or meals but hadn't connected with them the way I had with Marika. We played cards for a while, and the others admired Liam. Within moments of him leaving my arm, four other gliders joined him in aerial acrobatics across the patio. We watched and played until the kitchen crew announced dinner.

"Do we all take a turn in the kitchen?" I asked Ralph as we stood in line. In the military vids on *Ancient TēVē*, working in the kitchen was always required—sometimes as punishment. That seemed like a good way to get sub-standard food.

"Hell no." Ralph laughed. "You would not be able to eat anything I prepare. I burn water. These guys are pros. On smaller missions, you might have to take a turn handing out meal pacs."

We ate outside, then sat in the gathering darkness. The tables started to glow, providing just enough illumination to see each other and our food. Stars spread out overhead. Tired from his rampage with the other gliders and full of whatever the kitchen crew had fed us, Liam slept in my pocket.

It was early summer in this part of the world. That meant we'd worked almost ten hours today after landing—that had to be some kind of record for me. One of the older explorers brought out a small stringed instrument and started strumming. Dr. Gatens lit up a pipe. Dad and Maj. Origani hunched over a holo-map, talking in low voices. My eyes drooped as I played with the remains of my meal.

"Fire!" The shout shook me out of my stupor.

"Where?" Dad asked, rising from his chair.

"On the beach," the first voice answered. A man stood silhouetted by the meter-high glow of the force shield warning strip. It was set to yellow to keep anyone from stumbling into it—or over the edge if they got through. "It looks...contained."

"Show me." Dad hurried across the plateau, stopping beside the barrier. "Origani, get a team—we'll check it out." He turned and rushed around the side of the chow hall cube.

Around me, holo-rings flashed as Origani assembled a team. Then my own audio activated. "The rest of you," Origani said, "after the team assembles, we'll call for defensive weapons and form a perimeter. Lt. Evy has command."

Everyone jumped to their feet, and half a dozen people hurried to the mods. "As soon as they get geared up, they'll start calling us," Marika whispered to me. "You probably won't get tagged."

"I kind of figured that," I said. "Why do they need a team? And a perimeter? Isn't there a guard?"

"There's always a guard set around the camp," Ralph said. "The force shield keeps most wildlife out. Heck, just the glow keeps nocturnal animals away. But we have full perimeter camera coverage and real-time observers. We all take a turn on rotation. It's a five-person team. They report back any unusual activity, and then a recon team assembles if needed. If it's potentially dangerous—large animals, fire, whatever—we add to the perimeter guard."

The recon team hurried across the space in front of the patio and gathered near the man who'd raised the alarm. Immediately, rings flashed, and another ten people leapt up and headed to the armory.

"Just stay there," Marika said as she jumped to her feet.

Dad strode around the side of the kitchen cube again, dressed in his soft-armored gear. I jumped up and ran to his side.

"Siti, sit down."

"But Dad—" I broke off when he slowed to glare at me. "Aye, sir." I wandered back to my table, standing there uncertainly as more people around me hurried to the armory.

"Origani," Dad called." Make a hole!"

"Aye, sir." Origani flicked his holo-ring. A meter-wide gap appeared in the yellow glow. "I'm leaving the pest screen set. Are you coming, sir?"

"Wouldn't miss it," Dad said. The yellow light glinted off his teeth as he grinned.

Origani gave him a hard stare, then nodded. "Ready, team?"

"Ready, sir!" The team snapped to attention as they responded. They activated their grav-lifters and marched through the gap in the force shield. As one, they descended beyond the lip of the cliff, as if riding a float-tube in a ship or space station.

I looked around, but no one paid me any attention. Trying to look inconspicuous, I meandered toward the spot where they'd disappeared.

"Halt!" Flynn called.

"Oh, it's you," I said. "You startled me."

"Please return to the common area," Flynn said. "We need to keep the perimeter clear of civilians."

"I just want to see what they're doing," I protested.

"You can watch on the unit channel," he said. "Didn't anyone show you that?"

"What? No!" I flicked my holo-ring. "Where do I find that?"

"Look under mission broadcasts," he said, his tone clearly marking me as an idiot. "And go back to the common area before you fall off the edge."

I glared at him and kicked my foot at the force shield. "I may be a civilian, but I know I can't fall off the edge." Before he could retort, I beat a retreat to the tables.

Li waved me over. Most of the table lights had been switched off, but a holo-projection hung above hers. Three other scientists sat with her. I pulled up a chair and joined them.

The holo appeared to be projected from a single explorer's helmet. The name "Kassis" glowed in the lower left corner. The team had reached the beach and spread out in a ring around Dad. Their names, glowing softly in the display, showed where they stood.

Li reached forward and twisted the holo to the right a few degrees. "There's the fire."

"That looks like an oil lamp," I whispered.

CHAPTER FIVE

DAD and the others returned to the camp. He immediately took his team to the VIP conference room in the back of the kitchen mod. Evy opened an all-hands channel. "Curfew in ten minutes. If you aren't on guard, go to bed. It will be your turn soon enough."

"Curfew?" I said in outrage as people obediently moved toward the mods. "There are people here! People, on Earth! How are we supposed to sleep after a bombshell like that?"

"You don't have to sleep," Li said, getting to her feet. "You just have to go back to your bag and be quiet. G'night all."

"I'm going to find out what's going on," I muttered to myself as the others filtered away to their billets. I waited until most of the others had left, fiddling with my holo-ring. Then I rose and hurried around the side of the common mod.

The back half of this module was dedicated to VIP quarters. An external door led to a hallway. I hadn't been inside this mod before, but I'd seen virtual mockups as a kid. Four private cabins on the right side, with plenty of sound-proofing to protect the sleepers from kitchen noises. The VIP rooms shared a bath between each pair. On the left, a small lounge and a large meeting room against the external wall.

I slid through the unlocked door and down the empty hallway to the conference room door. Apparently, the designers hadn't worried about people listening at keyholes because I could hear the conversation fairly clearly. Not that there was a keyhole. I settled down on the floor next to the door and listened.

"...they're from—they can't be from here!" Maj Origani said. "The Exodus emptied this planet. If there are people here, Gagarin dropped them. They broke the treaty. We need to alert Headquarters."

"We'll send a message as soon as Hydrao gets the jump gates open," Dad said in a calm voice. "In the meantime, we can gather more information. Our translators flagged their dialect as unknown, not Gagarin."

"They're actors," Origani said. "Putting on whatever bizarre dialect Gagarin Planetary Security invented."

"If they're from Gagarin," Dad said, "their base must be well-hidden. None of the *Glory's* scans picked up signals of any kind. No communications, no common household electronics—nothing."

"They're probably living like natives would have," a female voice said.

Wronglen! What was she doing in that meeting? The idea that she could be in there, participating, while I was stuck eavesdropping made me grind my teeth.

"...even GPS agents aren't that dedicated to their cause," Evy said. "Live at a subsistence level on an undeveloped planet? They'd at least bring a mod."

"Do they have mods?" Wronglen asked.

"Obviously not our mods," Evy said, her voice clipped. "But they must have something similar. They steal our technology all the time."

"They have their own support tech," Dad said. "We ran into them on Behnken—I mean Zhigang, as they're calling it now. Didn't we, Tam?"

"They beat us by hours," Origani replied with a growl. "We had to cede the whole system to them."

"We're not doing that here," Dad said. "Earth belongs to all of us. Wronglen, contact Hydrao. Ask her to run a scan of the planet and find their base. They've obviously hidden it, so it will take a more in-depth scan than we did. Look for any indications they've gone native."

"They've already left orbit," Wronglen said doubtfully. "She won't be in a position to scan the planet."

"I'm sure you launched observation satellites," Dad said, an impatient edge making his voice rough. "Use them. Origani, organize tomorrow's party."

"Already on it, sir," Origani said. "I've got a security team and equipment ready to go. They'll drop just before dawn."

"No, don't send them down early," Dad said. "We don't want to upset these people. Drop drones down to watch, of course, but don't send the team until, say, half an hour before the designated time. Get some drones looking for their camp now. The real camp, not the tents in the trees."

"Aye, sir."

"And make sure we take some food with us," Dad said. "Put Ahuja on it. Tell him this is a major summit and to plan accordingly."

"They said they'd provide the food," Origani protested.

"Are you going to eat what they're serving?" Dad asked.

"Uh…"

"That's what I thought." Dad cleared his throat and chairs scraped the floor.

I jumped to my feet and ran for the door. Against protocol, I'd left it ajar, hoping to make an escape before they caught me. I hit the door mid-stride.

Blam! It was locked.

"Ow!" I twisted the handle with one hand, rubbing my nose with the other.

"Serenity," Dad said from behind me.

I turned slowly. He stood in the doorway, glaring at me. Humiliation washed over me like lukewarm bath water. I shivered.

"Would you wait for me in my quarters?" He pointed at the first door on the right.

I straightened my spine. No one had dared to crowd around him, watching, but I was sure they were all listening. "Aye, sir," I said. I executed my best pivot and marched into his room.

The VIP quarters weren't much better than the dorm. He had a bunk instead of a hammock and a desk in the corner. His locker was larger than mine, and he had two instead of one. A closed door would lead to the shared bath. But that was it. No fancy carpet or plush bedding or any of the trappings I'd seen in the virtual tours as a kid. I guess those were to impress the civilians.

I pulled the chair a few inches away from the desk and sat. I knew from past experience he'd leave me waiting, but I'd taken up meditation while at Wellesley for this express purpose. I straightened my back, closed my eyes, and took a deep breath. Besides, I had a lot to think about. Apparently, the team had not only found people, but talked to them. Set up a meeting—

The door rattled, and my eyes flew open in surprise. Was he on to me?

"I was going to call you in," Dad said as he pulled the second chair away from the desk. He sat, running a hand through his hair. "I had a job for you, but now I'm not sure that's a good idea. Didn't I teach you not to eavesdrop?"

I opened my mouth, but nothing came out. I'd been prepared to meet his anger with self-righteous indignation, but his sorrowful tone threw me. I hung my head. "I'm sorry, Dad. I just wanted to know…"

"As does everyone in the camp," Dad said, his tone stern now. "You don't see them lurking outside my conference room door. I'm going to have to lock the module if you can't honor my privacy."

I took a deep breath. "I know. But there are people on Earth! That's not some little political secret. That's huge!"

"If you were listening—" he raised an eyebrow at me "—you know where they're really from. That's a pretty big political secret."

"Did you expect them to be here?" I asked in shock. Now that I thought about it, he'd been awfully calm when the report came in. No surprise at all. "You knew!"

"I didn't *know*," Dad protested. "When we left Grissom, we had intel that indicated Gagarin had sent a mission to Earth ahead of us. When we got here and didn't detect any signals, we thought we'd beaten them. Now we know we didn't."

"What did you want me to do?" I asked.

"I can't have someone I don't trust on my team," Dad said. "If you're going to be an effective part of this mission, you need to follow the rules like everyone else."

"I will, Daddy," I said. I thought about doing the salute, but that would be too cutesy. "Really, I will."

He turned away, tapping his fingers against his chin. "I can get one of the explorers to do it. Someone who's been trained to follow orders."

"I will follow orders; I promise," I said, putting a hand on his arm. "Please, Dad, I want to help. What do you want me to do?"

He looked me up and down. "I want you to come along tomorrow. From what I could see, those agents were young. Having someone closer to their age could help facilitate the conversation."

My eyes widened. "You want me to flirt with Gagarian spies?"

He chuckled. "Not when you put it like that! I want you to be friendly. If they're as young as they look, they might be susceptible to a pretty face. But if you don't follow my directions to the letter—" his eyes narrowed "—I will send you back up here so fast your head will spin. And I'll get Wronglen to do it instead."

"I'll do exactly what you say!" I said. "Besides, Wronglen is too old. Evy looks younger."

"We have a deal," Dad said, ignoring my comment. "You follow orders, immediately and without question." He held my eyes for a long time.

I nodded gravely.

"Good." He stood and held out his arms for a hug. "Get some sleep."

I wrapped my arms around him and leaned my head against his shoulder. "You too, Daddy."

"You'll call me 'commander' tomorrow," he said, releasing me. "I don't want them to know you're my daughter. And if you don't behave, I'll take Marika instead of you."

"Maybe she should come, too," I suggested as he gestured at the door.

"I think one teenaged girl is all I can handle at a time," Dad said.

"She's twenty-two," I argued. "And she's much prettier than me."

"Are you trying to get out of this?" he asked.

"No! I wanna go!" I spun around, putting my hands up. "I just thought two would be better than one."

"I'll think about it," he said. "She could keep an eye on you." My face fell and he grinned. "Go to bed. I'll see you at breakfast at oh-seven-hundred."

"Aye, aye, sir!" I hurried back to my dorm.

CHAPTER SIX

"Hold still," Marika hissed at me. "We have to get this fastened, or you'll fall to your death." She fussed with the grav-belt around my waist.

"Just get a larger size," I said. "I don't mind wearing a medium."

"You aren't that big," she muttered. "I don't know why this one doesn't fit!"

"Because it was built for twigs like you," I said. "We aren't all small enough to blow away."

She heaved a sigh and slid the belt back into the drawer. "All the girls on the team are smalls."

"Marika, I'm fifteen centimeters taller than you and proportionately larger all the way around," I said. "That's why they make different sizes. There's no shame in being a medium."

"It's just you don't look that huge."

"I am not huge!" I grabbed the belt out of her hands and snapped it around my waist. "I'm a normal size for my height. Stop making it weird. Come on, we're late. Dad's going to be pissed."

"Please don't tell him it's my fault," Marika whispered.

"I won't," I said, but my heart sank. I'd just promised last night that I would take everything seriously, and here I was holding up the delegation. "Hurry."

As we raced out of the supply depot, something tweaked my ear. Crap! Liam! I'd forgotten about him. He'd climbed onto my shoulder this morning when I left the dorm early to have breakfast with Dad. I didn't have time to take him back, but I wasn't supposed to take him outside the force barrier.

"You'll stay in my pocket, right?" I whispered to Liam. I scooped him off my shoulder and pushed him into my pocket.

"Come on!" Marika called over her shoulder.

We pelted across the stone plateau and skidded to a halt beside Dad. "I'm sorry we're late," I told Dad. "It was my fault. I should have gotten my gear together last night."

Marika snapped to attention.

His lips twisted. "No, it's my fault. I told you to go to bed last night, not get your gear. I guess if I ask you to follow orders, I should expect you to actually do it."

I smiled. He was in a good mood today—I'd noticed it at breakfast. "Were you waiting for us?"

"Yes and no," he said, beckoning for us to follow him. "The plan was to send the team down first to secure the area. I just made them wait a little longer. The other side might see it as a power grab, but that's okay. We want them to think we have the upper hand."

"Don't we?" I asked.

"That depends." He nodded at Anivea to open the barrier. "Set your belt to neutral and follow me." He walked through the barrier, tapped his belt control, and pushed off the edge of the cliff. The belt caught him, and he drifted away from the stone.

I took a deep breath. I'd used grav-belts before, of course, but never in the wild. This was no different than any training facility, right? I stepped out of the force shield, a mild shiver of electricity tingling over me. Then I tapped the engage button and pushed up and away with my toes.

I drifted up a few centimeters from the cliff. The feeling of flying swept over me, exhilarating and terrifying. I'd never pushed off anything this high before. Marika joined us, and Dad connected his comm through our holo-rings. "Down at quarter speed on my mark. Three, two, one, mark."

I hit the drop control, and we slid downward like fruit through gelatin, sinking toward the beach at a sedate speed.

On the beach below, a thin brown mat covered a stretch of sand parallel to the river. A long table stood on it with a rank of chairs on either side. A ring of explorers stood in a loose oval around it. As we drew closer, another group stepped out of the shadows of the trees. The Gagarin contingent. A bald man led the group with an older man on one side and a little girl on the other. They walked to the far end of the table and sat. More people followed: three young men and a tall woman. Two others stayed in the shadows.

"Our drones didn't locate any more of them, but they've got to have backup hidden. Maybe they have some kind of unknown stealth technology," Dad said. He looked at each of us. "Don't tell them anything about our tech. Be friendly, but don't give anything away. And watch out for the journalists."

He nodded toward a pair dressed in blue jackets with the G'lacTech-News logo on their chests. The man and woman stood by the cliff, away from the meeting participants. Both of them swiped continuously at the bubble of holo-screens surrounding their upper bodies. "They aren't allowed to talk to anyone, but they've got drones recording everything." As he spoke, a cloud of tiny drones swarmed out of a bright blue pouch on the man's belt, disappearing across the sunlit beach.

We landed on the sand between the water and the rank of explorers. None of them turned to look at us—they could see us in their heads-up displays. Dad strode up the beach between two guards, and Marika and I followed.

"Thank you for meeting with us," Dad said as he approached the table. "I am Commander Nate Kassis. This is Major Origani, my second in command, and Lieutenant Petra Wronglen, the captain's aide." Origani and Wronglen stepped out of the ring surrounding us and moved toward the table. .

My jaw clenched. When I discovered Wronglen was on the team, I'd wanted to argue with Dad. But I didn't have a reason to get rid of her, and Captain Hydrao would insist on including her if she knew what was going on.

Dad took the seat at the end of the table, putting his back to the Gagarin camp. It must make his shoulders squirm to know those two enemy guards were behind him, but his own people stood between him and them. As we'd been briefed at breakfast, Marika and I stood behind Dad. The guards behind us turned to face the external threat.

"I am Zane Torres," the bald man said. "This is Levi, Tiah, Everest, Eric, Peter, and Seraphina. We represent several different communities here on Earth."

"So you say," Dad replied. "When did your communities settle this planet? The Inter-Colony Treaty of 2430 made Earth a protected planet."

"We didn't 'settle this planet'," Zane said. "We never left. Every one of us was born on Earth, and our ancestors before us all the way back to the dawn of creation. Or when apes descended trees. However you want to say it."

"Earth was evacuated in the late twenty-first century," Dad said. "There was no one left."

"The evacuation continued through the early twenty-second century," Zane corrected. "And there were many left behind. Many who didn't survive the desertion." His eyes grew hard, as if he'd lost personal friends in the event. Way to nurse a grudge.

The conversation went back and forth. Dad tried every trick in the book to get them to admit to their origin. Zane kept insisting they had never been off planet. I gave up listening after a while and took some time to check out the rest of their team.

The little girl, Tiah, sat on Zane's right, with her back to the cliff. She wasn't as young as she'd looked from above—maybe my age, perhaps older. She was short, with brown hair, thick eyebrows, and a slightly hooked nose. She didn't say anything but watched Dad with an unnerving laser intensity.

The old man, Levi, glared across the table at Tiah. His animosity seemed to be aimed more at her than at us. After a few minutes, he settled back in his chair and closed his eyes. I'd seen elders use this trick back on Grissom, pretending to be asleep when they were listening to every word.

The red-head, Eric, grinned when he caught my eye. I smiled then looked away coyly, watching him from under my lashes. He had wide shoulders and pale skin. None of them appeared to have solar screens—he was going to burn badly. Maybe that was why he sat with his back to the river and the morning sun.

Blond, blue-eyed Everest sat next to Eric. He was even bigger. The two of them exchanged glances and body language that made me think they might be a couple. Or maybe just good friends.

Peter sat next to Tiah. He had dark hair—almost black—and almond-shaped eyes. His head swung back and forth, watching Zane and Dad like a grav-ball match. He was almost as tall as the other two boys but less bulky. I got a more serious vibe from him, too. Another, younger boy, possibly his brother, sat next to Peter. He hadn't been introduced. In fact, I hadn't even noticed him until now. Odd.

I glanced at Marika and activated my comm link. "Who's the boy?" I whispered.

She started, darting a glance in my direction. "Which boy?"

"By Peter. Dark hair, dark eyes. Wasn't introduced."

"Which one is Peter?" she asked.

"Seriously? The one next to him. They look a lot alike."

"Oh, yeah, you're right. Huh."

I closed my eyes and shook my head, then deactivated the comm. She was useless as an observer. But she was an explorer, not a diplomat.

Seraphina sat halfway down the table with empty seats on either side. Was she trying to be friendly with us? Or did she not get along with the rest of her delegation? She looked like a warrior woman, with a strong body and serious face. A thick brown braid fell down her back.

I glanced over my shoulder, but the two in the trees weren't visible from here. Besides, my job was to watch the table, not the woods.

My eyes ranged around the table and snagged on Eric. He was watching me again, and when he saw me looking, he smiled broadly. I smiled back. I looked up and rubbed my nose with a finger then raised my eyebrows. He nodded, his lips quirked on one side, and rubbed the back of his neck. When Zane stopped talking, Eric leaned over and said something to him.

"My friend reminds me the sun is hot," Zane said with a laugh. "At least for those with fairer skin. We'd like to take a break to bring some water and refreshments."

"We brought some food," Dad said, raising a hand. High above, right on cue, two people stepped away from the lip of the cliff, a box suspended between them. As they descended, I recognized two of the kitchen team. "Chef Therri Ahuja has lent his expertise and prepared some mid-morning snacks."

"You didn't have to do that," Zane protested. "We promised to bring food." He gestured to Eric and Everest. The two pushed back their chairs and hurried toward us.

Dad stood so quickly his chair tipped over. Marika and two of the explorers nearest us reached for weapons. Eric and Everest froze. Zane, Seraphina, and Peter leapt to their feet.

"Stand down," Dad snapped at his team. Marika moved back a pace, her hand dropping. The other two explorers held their hands out from their sides to show they hadn't drawn their weapons. Dad stepped away from his chair and half bowed to the two boys. "Sorry about that. My people are very protective. Please, proceed."

Eric glared at the rank of guards, but Everest simply nodded and stepped past Marika. She watched them as they walked away, not turning back until they'd passed the outer circle of guards. Then she jumped forward and righted Dad's chair.

Dad's voice came through my audio implant. "Stand down. Unless there is a direct threat to a team member, I don't want to see anyone moving toward their weapons. Is that understood?"

"Yes, sir," the team muttered, the sound coming through loud and clear.

I glanced at the Gagarian team. Zane leaned over to speak to Levi. Tiah whispered something to Peter. The young boy made eye contact with me for a fleeting second, then looked away. After a moment, he stood and touched Peter's arm. Peter turned and looked at me. I smiled. He didn't smile back.

Zane came around the end of the table, walking slowly toward us. He kept his hands out to the sides where we could see them. As he passed

Seraphina, she stood and followed him. They stopped when they reached Dad.

"This is getting us nowhere," Zane said. "Perhaps we can take a few minutes for a break and more informal discussion. A chance to get to know each other better."

My father nodded. "Excellent idea."

Dad must have signaled the chef, because Ahuja and his assistant pushed their crate forward, lowering it to the table. He popped the front open, and the assistant started pulling trays and dishes from inside. "We have samples of some foods from our systems. If we'd known you'd be here, we would have brought more refined delicacies."

"Thank you for your gifts, but they were unnecessary," Zane said. "We brought food to share with our guests." He stressed the last word, as if to remind Dad they were claiming the role of hosts.

I caught Marika's eye and jerked my head slightly. Now was our chance to chat up the interlopers. Marika and I circled around Seraphina and made our way to the other end of the table.

I stopped by the younger boy. "Hi, I'm Siti," I said, holding out a fist to him. To my surprise, he bumped it with his own but didn't say anything.

"That's Jake," Peter said. "He doesn't talk much."

"You two brothers?" I asked.

He nodded. "Is that guy your dad?"

"How did you know?" I asked in surprise.

"You look like him," Peter said. Then he flushed and backpedaled. "Not that you look like a guy! But you look kind of like him. Same eyes, same smile."

"Yeah, I've been told that before," I said. So much for keeping our relationship under wraps. "This is my friend Marika."

Peter and Marika exchanged nods. "What's up with the two hunks?" she asked. "Are they a couple or what?"

My head snapped around, and I glared. "Marika!"

"Hey, I don't want to waste time flirting if they're not interested in girls."

Peter gawked at us. "I, uh. I dunno. Everest is gay, but I didn't think Eric…" He trailed off as if reevaluating years of interactions. "Maybe."

Jake smiled a little, his eyes downcast.

"What about your friends in the woods?" Marika asked. "What's their deal?"

"Joss and Zina?" Peter asked.

Marika's shoulders dropped. "Oh, are they a couple?"

Peter laughed. "No, they're twins. Joss definitely likes girls. And he's single."

Marika grinned. "Maybe I'll go chat up Joss," she said, heading purposefully across the beach, her hips swinging a little more than normal.

Peter glanced at the explorers standing around the edge of the carpet. "Seems like there are plenty of guys with your team. Why's she so keen on meeting someone new?"

I shrugged, trying to spin a good answer. "Dating in the CEC is tricky. You can't hook up with anyone in your chain of command or anyone in your sub-unit. And most of these guys are kind of, uh—"

"Brawny?" Peter asked.

I laughed. "Yeah, but she doesn't object to that. Actually, now that I think about it, I'm not sure why she hasn't hooked up with any of them. Maybe because we haven't really had time."

"Why not?" he asked.

"We haven't been awake very long," I said.

Pete's eyebrows drew down. "Awake? Did you come here in suspended animation? How long did it take?" His questions came out rapid-fire.

"We call it deep sleep, but yeah," I said. "Twenty years. It's weird to think all my friends back home are old now." Not that I had a lot of close friends. We'd moved around too much for that. CEC dependents tended to make friends fast and move on to new ones easily.

"How long did it take *you* to get here?" I asked.

Peter's lip twisted up. "Five hundred years."

CHAPTER SEVEN

I LAUGHED. "You guys won't give it up, will you?"

"Give what up?" he asked.

"This local boy thing," I said. "We are Earthlings."

"You won't give up, either," he said. "This Gagarin thing." He rolled his eyes, then glanced at the table. "You hungry? Eric's oatmeal is better than Joss's but I could use a refuel right now."

"After you," I said, sweeping a hand.

We picked up plates and looked at the offerings. Ahuja's foods were laid out in shiny plastek dishes; each variety of food in a different shaped container. He'd brought standard breakfast pastries, sliced meats, and breads. My eyes narrowed. Someone was holding out—some of this stuff was clearly Autokich'n food. Nothing cooked on this planet had ever looked like that.

Rough, heavy pottery held other items I didn't recognize.

"What are those?" I asked, pointing at some strips of dry brown...something.

"Jerky," he said. "Dried meat." He put one on his plate and offered the tongs.

"What kind of meat?" I asked.

"Beef," he said. "Domesticated herbivore."

"I know what beef is," I said, picking up a piece and turning it over. "I've never seen it jerkied, though."

"It's a good way to preserve the meat," he said. "The outsiders—we—" He stopped. "Our electrical power is spotty," he continued after a long pause. "We dry the meat, so it stays good even if the power goes out."

"Makes sense," I said. "A kind of primitive version of meal pacs. Meal pacs are shelf-stable meals. Easy to transport."

He opened his mouth, but nothing came out. After a second, he said, "Exactly. What's all that?" He pointed to Ahuja's trays.

"Hm, let me see," I said. I rattled off some names.

"Uh, okay. Are any of them sweet?"

I indicated the pastries. "Those are nice with coffee. Good mid-morning snack."

"Perfect." He grabbed a couple of the squares I indicated. "Hey, how do you know what coffee is? In fact, why are you so understandable?"

"What do you mean?" I asked, my nose wrinkling.

"I mean, it's been five hundred years since you left here," he said. "Both our languages should have shifted—and not the same way."

"Oh, we have translators." I pulled my jacket collar away from my neck, revealing a small button.

"Real time translators?" he marveled. "How does it work? Why can't I hear you saying things in your dialect?"

It was my turn to open my mouth then clamp my lips shut. "I don't know," I said slowly. "I don't understand how they work."

"And you probably weren't supposed to mention them to me," he said with a chuckle.

My face flamed. "Don't tell anyone, okay?"

"Your secret is safe—" he broke off. Consternation crossed his face. I could tell he'd just realized he couldn't keep secrets for me—I was with the other side.

"It's okay," I said. "I know you have to tell them. Dad's used to me screwing up."

He changed the subject. "Tell me about your home."

"I'm not sure I'm allowed to do that," I said softly. "I mean, I can tell you I'm from Grissom."

"Your dad already told us that," he said. We finished eating in silence. "The food was good."

"Yours was too," I said, although I hadn't eaten any, of course. I'd put a couple items from our side of the table into my pocket for Liam, and I'd crumbled the cookie bar, so it looked like I'd at least tasted it.

"You afraid we'll poison you?" He laughed.

My face heated red again.

His eyes widened. "I, uh, will you excuse me?" He hurried down the table toward the older members of his party.

Dad and Zane sat together at the end of the table, their plates full of untouched food. Peter stopped a few steps away, loitering until Zane noticed him. The older man excused himself and drew Peter aside.

"Let's get back to it." Dad's voice came through the audio channel. We closed in on the table, returning to our places.

Eric returned with a floppy hat covering his red hair and neck.

"Nice," Peter said. "Very stylish."

"Mara's sunscreen might work for you, but I have sensitive skin," he said.

"Sensitive?" he asked. "You mean pasty."

"Gentlemen," Zane said, glaring at them.

When everyone had returned to their seats, Zane rose. "Suppose you tell us what you want," he said, staring down the shining surface at Dad. "We want to live in peace on our planet. What do you want?"

"We want to preserve Earth," Dad said promptly. "It should be an historic monument. An interstellar reserve where all of humanity can come to learn about—and from—our past. We don't want to fight with anyone over it. But we will."

"You'll fight with us over it?" Zane asked. "This is our home. If you bring the fight to us, you'll regret it. People fight to the death over their homes. If you want to learn about Earth history, that's the top of the list."

"We won't allow Gagarin to control the planet." Dad rose, and the uniformed line behind me took a step forward.

"For the last time, we aren't from Gagarin!" Zane said. "Although, with the way you're behaving, we might prefer them to you."

"Sir!" Wronglen yelped. The woman hadn't said a word the entire time, her glittering eyes moving from speaker to speaker like a gambler watching his favorite sport. Now, she leapt to her feet and pulled her weapon. "You will not speak to the commander like that!"

"Wronglen, stand down!" Dad yelled.

Zane threw up his hands. "We're done here. When you can behave more civilly, come find us." He pushed over his chair and walked away. The rest of his team scrambled out of their seats and followed him. Pushing between the ranks of explorers, they stormed off the beach.

CHAPTER EIGHT

"Maybe they're telling the truth," I suggested as we stepped onto the cliff and shut off our grav-lifters.

"About what?" Dad snapped.

"About being from here," I said. "Maybe they aren't from Gagarin."

"Don't be ridiculous!" He stomped across the stone toward his quarters, unbuckling his grav-belt. "No one was left behind. They were brought here from somewhere, and the only place that could be is Gagarin."

"What about Liwei?" Maj Origani suggested. "Or one of the fringe worlds."

"The fringe worlds? Impossible," Dad said. He stomped into the conference room and threw his belt on the table. "None of them have the tech or the resources to mount a twenty-year flight anywhere. If they did, why would they come here? But Liwei is a possibility. Or maybe a joint Gagarin-Liwei initiative. Put a message in the queue asking about current Liweian politics and tech."

"Yes, sir," Origani said.

"The jump gates won't be operational for another few days," Wronglen cautioned.

"Can you get the information faster, Lieutenant?" Dad asked. "If you can, I'd like to know how."

Wronglen paled. "No, of course I can't," she stuttered. "I—I just wanted to remind you…"

"I know the queue isn't operational, Lieutenant," he said. "But getting the message into the queue means it will get to headquarters as soon as possible. Which reminds me, don't ever threaten our adversaries on my behalf. You are not authorized to speak for me. Is that clear?"

"Sir, they were threatening you!"

"Lt Wronglen, how long have you known me?" Dad asked, suddenly pleasant.

"I—uh—a few days, sir," she replied.

"And do you know how long Maj Origani and I have worked together?" he continued.

"No, sir."

Dad swung around to face Origani. "Tam, how long have we worked together?"

"About twenty-three years temporal," he said. "Eighty-five if you count all the cold sleep."

"Twenty-three years, Lieutenant," Dad said, swinging back to Wronglen. "With all the long-range travel, we've known each other since well before you were born. If my honor needs to be defended, Tam will see to it. I don't need your assistance."

"Yes, sir," she muttered, her eyes on the floor.

"And if you disrupt my summit again, I will call Captain Hydrao and insist she send a shuttle for you immediately. Do I make myself clear?"

"Yes, sir," she said, a little louder.

"Excellent." He sat in the chair at the head of the table and gestured toward the other seats. "Take a seat. What's the status on the jump gates?"

She ignored the chair, standing at attention. "Captain Hydrao said they'll be in position to launch the out-bound beacons in twenty-eight hours. Messages will go as soon as they're set. Then another fifty-seven hours to get in position to launch the in-bound gates."

"Roger," Dad said. "Tam, have the rest of the team join us when they arrive."

"Aye, sir," Origani said. "They're on their way."

"And have Ahuja bring the leftovers in," Dad said. "It's lunch time, and I'm starving."

Origani smiled. "Already done. Lt. Wronglen, please have a seat."

They sat, Wronglen sitting as far from my father as she could. I suppressed a smile at her discomfort. If she wasn't so obnoxious, I would have felt sorry for her—I'd been the target of Dad's anger more often than most.

Marika pulled me toward the chairs against the wall. "We grunts don't sit at the table," she said.

"Why not?" I asked.

"Because it's not our place," she whispered, glancing past me at my dad. "The officers sit there. If they want information from us, they'll ask us."

"How do you know so much about this kind of stuff?" I asked. "I thought you were a first-term explorer."

"I am," she said. "But this is the end of my first term. I had to contract for a second one to get on this mission. I've been in a few meetings like this. Believe me, you want to stay out of the way if you can."

That made sense. She was twenty-two—older than most of the first-termers on this mission. I always forgot because she looked and acted like one of my contemporaries.

The kitchen staff pushed in the grav-lift with the thermal cube. Ahuja's assistant spread the trays down the center of the meeting table and stacked plates and utensils at each end. Ralph showed up a few minutes later with a case of Hydra-Sweet and several carafes of water. As he heaved the case onto a side table, the rest of the summit team poured into the room. While they jockeyed for seats, Ralph stopped by Marika.

"How'd you get invited to the party?" he asked.

"Siti brought me in," she said. "The commander wanted us to talk up the younger members of the party. You know, spy stuff." She grinned and wiggled her eyebrows as she said it.

"Damn, you get all the luck," Ralph said. "I got stuck on guard duty. Nothing to do but stare out at the trees."

"Don't worry," Marika said. "I heard the regular mission will resume tomorrow. You'll be out there whacking bushes and fending off wildlife in no time."

Ralph flexed his biceps at us and left, whistling as he walked away.

"Fending off wildlife?" I parroted.

"What else is he good for?" she asked. "First-termers do the grunt work. Once you reach the upper echelons of your first term, like me…" She poked a thumb at her chest and looked down her nose at me. "That's when you get the choice assignments."

"Ah, of course, the upper echelons of your first term. Lofty heights." I smirked.

"Well, if you're smart, you befriend the commander's daughter," she said with a laugh.

I laughed, then stopped. "Is that why we're friends? Because you thought it would help your career?"

"Don't be ridiculous," she said, in a cajoling tone. "That was a joke. Besides, the commander rarely has a daughter to bring along."

"True," I replied. Most CEC officers didn't have family. When you were gone for twenty years at a time, relationships got tricky. Which was why Dad and I were on our own.

"If everyone has gotten some lunch," Dad said, "let's begin. First impressions. Major?"

Origani stood, and a holo-screen unfolded over the table. The picture was pixelated and the text unreadable. A couple of people scrambled to move the veggie tray out of the way. The screen resolved.

Origani paced around the room, whipping his hand toward the table as he threw each new point onto the screen. "Number one, we didn't find any support base. Either their base is extraordinarily well-camouflaged, or it's much farther away that we expected."

"Since we essentially chose the meeting space, the latter is quite likely," Dad put in.

"Yes, sir. However, we didn't give them a lot of time to find us. They were just here. Like they knew where we'd land," Origani said.

Dad raised an eyebrow. "Maybe they had the same return instructions we did."

Origani nodded and flicked his hand again, the movement audible. "Number two, we have set an automated drone to track them, as well as embedding tracking chips into their gear while they were distracted by the meeting. I can't believe they left their campsite unguarded. Most likely, this was done on purpose, to convince us of their ridiculous cover story."

Snap. That one sounded like it hurt. "Number three, they didn't hesitate to eat the food we brought. This indicates either a very unsophisticated level of diplomacy or a willingness to expend more junior members of the team. I noticed neither Torres, Levi, nor Seraphina ate our food."

"It could mean they have technology to test food remotely," Ahuja suggested from his place along the wall.

Every head in the room snapped around to stare at him. "Does such technology exist? Remote, non-destructive testing?" Dad asked.

"I've heard rumors it's being developed," Ahuja said.

"They didn't ask him a question—why does he get to talk?" I whispered to Marika.

"He's a subject matter expert," Marika said. "Food is his field of study. You'll notice he didn't volunteer anything about the other items. Plus, he's way senior to us."

"I had no idea CEC was this political," I muttered.

"We open new planets to colonization," Marika replied. "Of course we're political."

"Number four!" Origani cracked his hand again. This time, he winced. "They aren't worried about stretching this out. They have no ships in the system as far as we can discern; they are here for the long haul. I predict they will continue to claim they are natives until we prove otherwise. My gut tells me they landed several years ago and have been watching for us. Perhaps waiting for us to launch gate beacons, since they don't have that tech."

"Several years?" Dad gestured to Evy. After she pulled up some files, he continued. "According to our intel, they couldn't have launched this mission more than a decade before we did, and that's a stretch."

I covered a yawn with one hand and slid the other into my pocket to finger Liam's silky fur. I'd fed him some crumbs from the buffet on the beach; he should be getting antsy about now.

Except my pocket was empty. I jammed my hand in deeper, but there was no silky fur, no damp nose. Liam was gone!

CHAPTER NINE

"What's the matter with you, Siti?" Marika asked. We sat at our usual table on the patio. We'd spent the afternoon in meetings, rehashing everything that had been discussed on the beach. As far as I knew, no one had drawn any conclusions. Marika said that was typical for politics.

"Nothing," I said, my hand thrust deep into my empty pocket. The other sair-gliders were out enjoying the early evening sunlight, and I kept hoping to spot Liam. If he'd escaped outside the force shield, I'd likely never see him again. He'd be dinner for one of those wild animals the surveillance equipment had spotted while we'd been on the beach.

"What's going on over there?" I asked, pointing across the plateau. The force screen had flashed brighter at the edge, where a path down the cliff led to the Gagarian camp site. I squinted. "It looks like they've opened a gate."

"Rico said some of the Gagarians had climbed up the hill." Marika leaned back in her chair, enjoying the warmth. "Your dad went out to meet them."

"Without us?" I asked, affronted.

"Girl, we're nobody," Marika said without twitching a muscle. "If they don't think we'll be useful, they won't tell us anything."

"We'll see about that!" I jumped up.

"Siti!" Marika grabbed my arm. "You can't do that! He's the commander!"

I stopped. Dad had told me I had to act professional. And if I was going to get into the "family business," I needed to learn how to do it right. My shoulders slumped. That was the problem, though. I didn't know if I wanted to join the CEC. I sighed. "I guess you're right. But I can still loiter over there and see what I can learn, right?"

"Sure," Marika said. "But be careful. Say, where's Liam?"

I waved vaguely and tried to smile confidently. "He's flitting around. He'll come back when he's tired." I turned before she could ask again and strolled across the camp. When I glanced over my shoulder, Marika stood where I'd left her, staring up at the brightly colored gliders leaping from perch to perch.

I blinked the tears from my eyes and tried to focus on my mission: eavesdropping on Dad. I wandered up to the explorer on duty at the shield gate. "What's going on?"

A short woman with first-term stripes on her arm glanced at me. Her nametag read Laughlin. Though I'd met her last night, I couldn't remember her first name. I smiled pleasantly. She looked me up and down with a sneer. "Your majesty," she muttered.

Clearly not a fan. My worries about getting her into trouble vanished. I grinned hard enough to make my face hurt. "I prefer 'your imperial highness.'" I used yesterday's joke again.

Her lips quirked. "Funny. What do you want, Ms. Kassis?"

"Just needed to talk to my dad," I said casually, peering along the path. The plateau narrowed to a two-meter wide ledge. About ten meters away, the sheer slope of the cliff softened, becoming a steep hillside. Trees grew there, hiding the zigzag path I'd seen in the aerial shots Origani had shown in the meetings this afternoon. "Any idea how long he'll be out there?"

She blinked, as if surprised I knew he'd gone out. "He didn't say."

I nodded. "I figured. I have a message for him, from Captain Hydrao."

"Why don't you just leave it in his queue?" Her tone said, "you idiot."

I leaned closer and lowered my voice. "It's confidential. Eyes only, no record. You know."

Her face went blank, then she nodded wisely. "Of course. I don't think he'll be long."

Was that a real thing? Suppressing a grin that my bluff worked, I returned the nod and leaned against the cliff at the head of the path. The stone had soaked up warmth all day and now radiated heat that felt nice in the cooling evening. I closed my eyes, as if relaxing, and stretched my ears.

Nothing. If the path was as close as I remembered from the maps, I should be able to hear something. Unless the force shield blocked sound. I listened harder. Nothing but sounds from inside.

Maybe I could sneak out and listen. And maybe Liam would find me, if I was out there where he could smell me! I pushed away from the warm rock. "The thing is, it's time sensitive." I flicked my holo-ring to check the time. "Can you let me through? I'll just run over and tell him and be back in a flash. He'll be grateful."

Laughlin bit her lip. "It's against regs," she said hesitantly. "But if it's that important…"

"It is," I said, my hand pressed into my empty pocket. "Life and death."

"You shouldn't go out there without armor and a tracker," she said, eyeing my in-camp uniform. "And probably a weapon. There are wild animals. And Gagarians."

A chill crept down my spine, but I ignored it. "I'll be fine. I'm just going to the top of the path to talk to the commander, then I'll be right back." I pointed at the place where the ledge disappeared into the trees. "Believe me, I wouldn't go if it weren't urgent."

"Yes, ma'am," Laughlin said. "I'll open the gate." She flicked the control panel at the top of the bollard and pressed her hand against it. The meter-wide gate opened.

"Mind the edge," an automated voice said. "No shield beyond this point."

"You heard the woman," Laughlin said. "Don't fall off. I don't think the commander would be pleased."

"Thanks," I replied, ignoring her sour smile. It looked as if she would be more than pleased. What had I ever done to her?

I hurried along the stone ledge, staying close to the cliff. I wasn't afraid of heights, but I knew natural stone could be uneven and possibly dangerous. Although this ledge was smooth as glass. Maybe our guys lasered it. It was our primary equipment-free egress, so that made sense. The exploration plan called for the teams to be sent out via this path.

I reached the trees and slowed. When I glanced over my shoulder, Laughlin was watching. I waved and strode purposefully into the trees.

Once I was confident I was out of sight, I stopped to listen. Musical sounds echoed through the wood—probably birds. Something rustled in the undergrowth to my left—it sounded small. At least, I hoped it was small. The trees hid the low sun, and deep gloom covered the path. I moved forward a few more steps, listening for voices.

There. I continued along the path until it split. One going up, one going down. The Gagarians had a camp at the bottom of the cliff, so I chose that path. I should catch up to Dad and his team in a few minutes.

The air chilled as I hiked. I paused at a hairpin turn, but the voices drew me onward. My eyes adjusted to the darkness, but the narrow trail wound between rocks and tree roots. If I twisted my ankle, Dad would find me here, and I'd be sent back to the ship. I crept round another turn.

I stopped to rest and check the time. My holo-ring didn't respond to my flicking fingers. I tapped it again, twisting the device around. Nothing. Then I mentally smacked my forehead. Of course. The network ended at the force shield. Exploration teams would take a booster that connected to the network via the satellites Hydrao had placed in orbit. And once the *Glory* returned, she could boost the signal. But for now, anyone outside the camp without a booster was out of luck.

Surely, Dad wouldn't have come this far without a booster? I should be able to tap into his if I was close enough. I tapped the ring, but it didn't even turn on.

Crap. I should have shut it down to charge it last night. As long as I was inside the camp, it charged wirelessly. But when you had as many apps running as I did, the constant use would drain the power as quickly as it charged. This didn't matter if you were inside a network, but if you went outside, like we had this morning…

As soon as I got back to camp, I'd disable all my useless social media aps. I hadn't bothered before we left. And when I'd woken, I'd had twenty years' worth of posts to catch up on. Or at least as many as the ship had collected before we'd gotten too far away. Now those apps were just burning power.

I shouldn't be out here in the dark. Liam had had plenty of time to smell me and fly back. He was probably gone for good. I blinked back a tear. Fine. Time to head back to camp. I wasn't sure how I'd missed Dad on this single track, but I had to have done so. He wouldn't have gone this far unless he went all the way to the Gagarian camp.

I snapped my fingers. He must have gone down to meet with them in private! That was exactly the kind of thing the hero of Darenti Four would do. Should I follow him down and eavesdrop? Or return to camp and try to get it out of him later?

I stood there on the rough path, debating. The wave-like growl of the wind in the treetops soothed me in a primal way. Despite the darkness and unfamiliar rustling sounds, the resinous smell of the trees and their rushing sound greeted me like a friend I didn't realize I'd lost. I closed my eyes and drank it in.

A twig snapped. My eyes flew open, my heart pounding in my ears. I stared into the gloom, but trees and more trees blocked the last rays of sunlight.

"What are you doing out here alone?" a male voice asked behind me.

I spun around. A man with wavy dark hair, dark skin, and dark eyes stood on the path below me. He blended into the surroundings like he belonged there. I squinted, trying to see him better. "Who are you?"

"I'm Joss." He grinned, his teeth glowing faintly in the darkness.

"Oh, the tree boy," I said with a laugh.

"The what?"

"Did my dad come down here?" I asked.

"He talked to my dad and went back into your bubble. Haven't seen him since. What are you doing out here?"

"He just came out a few minutes ago," I said. Then I realized it was probably longer than a few minutes. In the time since I'd left the camp, the sun had set, leaving the woods in darkness. How long had I been walking down this path?

"If he came out, it wasn't to talk to us," Joss said.

"Wait," I said. "Who's your dad?"

"Zane Torres," he replied proudly. "Tall, bald guy? I'm sure you've met him."

I laughed. "Yeah, I met him. I, uh, I don't suppose you've seen my pet?"

"You brought a dog with you?" Joss asked.

"He's more like a—do you have sair-gliders on this planet?"

"Is that some kind of bird?" he asked.

"He's little and furry." I held up my hands to indicate Liam's size.

"Haven't seen him," Joss said. "It's getting chilly out here. You wanna come down to our camp and get something warm to drink? It's right over there."

"If my dad didn't come down here, I'm in deep trouble," I said. "I need to get back up—"

I broke off as a yell split through the trees.

"Down to camp, now!" Joss said. "Move!"

CHAPTER TEN

We raced into the Gagarian camp. They'd worked hard on their "local survivor" appearance. Several light-colored tents stood in a circle around a low fire, and a pair of wheeled rovers sat in a cleared space just off the path.

Joss dropped to a crouch, listening. A tent flap rustled, and Joss spun to confront it. Peter climbed out of his tent with Liam on his shoulder. "Check out the ninja squirrel!"

"Liam!" I cried, and he leaped to me. I caught him on my arm and cradled the tiny body to my cheek. "You found him!"

"How'd you get into camp?" Peter demanded.

"I brought her down," Joss said as he prowled the perimeter of the camp. "Everything okay?"

"Yeah, it's fine," Peter said.

"I heard yelling." Joss finished his circumference and turned to face Peter.

In the firelight, Pete's face darkened with a blush. "That was me. I was startled by the ninja squirrel."

"Apparently, our visitors brought pets." Joss nodded at me. "I gotta get back up the hill. Holler when you want to go home." He winked at me and disappeared up the trail.

Zane climbed out of his tent, standing with a soft groan. "You're awfully loud tonight, Peter. What's going on?"

Around the camp, other tent flaps opened and sleepy heads appeared. Eric still wore his clothes, but Zina's tank top and shorts were obviously sleep gear. She glanced around, spotted me, and ducked back inside. Eric stood, cradling a large, dangerous-looking weapon with a box strapped to the side of it. Cold washed through my veins as I realized I stood alone in the enemy camp.

"That squirrel thing was hiding in Joss's sleeping bag," Peter said. "It's her pet."

"Thank you for finding Liam," I said, trying to sound causal. "He must have climbed out of my pocket during the meetings."

"You brought an alien animal to Earth?" Zane asked, incredulous. "Have you people lost your minds? Introducing a new species to a planet is dangerous!"

"How would you know?" I asked, my voice sharp. "I thought you people never left Earth?"

"I haven't," Zane said. "But I know how cautious they were when they colonized the first worlds. They spent decades studying the ecology before introducing Earth flora and fauna."

My shoulders hunched. He sounded just like Dad. "Sair-gliders are eco-neutral. When properly trained, they're a low-tech addition to the security arsenal. Most CEC ships have a flock aboard." I'd done my research after Dad reamed me out.

"Then why haven't we seen them?" Zane asked.

I flushed.

"They aren't supposed to leave your camp, are they?" Zina emerged from her tent again, with a large sweatshirt draped over her pajamas.

"I was late, and he was in my pocket…" I muttered. Eyes downcast, I stroked Liam's soft fur. If Dad found out— "I need to go. They don't know I'm gone."

"I'm afraid they do." Dad stepped into the clearing. Behind him, Joss walked with his hands up, three uniformed guards with dark helmets following behind with weapons drawn.

Zane stepped between me and Dad. "What are you doing with my son?"

"He tried to stop me," Dad said.

"He'd be a pretty crappy guard if he didn't." Eric moved in behind Peter, raising his strange weapon.

"Siti, come here," Dad said to me.

Zane put out his arm, blocking me. "Not until you return Joss—and his weapon—to us."

Dad jerked his head at one of the guards. "He's not a threat to us." But he stepped aside to give Joss plenty of room.

Joss yanked his rifle out of the guard's hand and stomped past Dad. He stopped when he reached Zane, pivoting to stand between the two men. "I told you I'd escort you to the camp. You didn't need to take my weapon. Especially if you don't consider me a threat."

"My daughter was missing," my father said.

"So, you took a hostage?" Zane crossed his arms over his chest. "She came here of her own free will. Just showed up. Like you. We aren't in the habit of kidnapping people."

"Siti!" Dad repeated.

Crap, he was mad. I trudged past Zane. Before I reached Dad, Liam scrambled down my back and scampered away. I kept my eyes facing forward, hoping no one had noticed.

One of the helmeted guards reached for my arm, but I yanked it away. I lifted my chin and turned regally. "Thank you for your hospitality," I said, with a slight bow.

Zane nodded back. "*You* are welcome anytime." His eyes traveled back to Dad. "Bring her if you want to talk again." He spun on his heel and stalked back to his tent.

Dad barked a harsh word at his guard, and the three stepped off the path, dragging me with them. Dad swept by, giving me a hard glare. Then he disappeared into the woods.

"Sorry," I called softly over my shoulder before we followed.

CHAPTER ELEVEN

THE NEXT MORNING, I sat at the conference table, eating a bowl of beige gloop. When Ralph delivered it, he told me it was oatmeal, but I wasn't sure I believed him. It had no texture at all and very little flavor. Obviously, Dad's idea of prison food. But I was hungry, and I wasn't sure I'd get a chance at anything later.

When we'd returned to camp, he had confined me to the conference room. Marika had showed up a few minutes later with a hammock and a blanket. She hadn't said anything—clearly under orders. With a sad look over her shoulder, she'd left.

The conference room had a small bathroom attached. I finished the oatmeal and washed my hands and face. Then I sat on the floor and practiced my meditation. A few minutes later, the door opened.

I took a deep breath and raised my head. "Good morning, Sir," I said as Maj Origani walked in. I'd expected my dad, but maybe this was a power play. I'd known Tam Origani my whole life. Usually, he was the fun "uncle." Sometimes, he dropped the hammer.

"Siti," he said and dropped into a chair by the table. "Will you join me?"

I rose and sat across from him. "Did Dad send you to punish me, Uncle Tam?"

Origani's face tightened. "He has enough to deal with on this trip. He doesn't need a troublemaker."

"Is this trip different?" I asked, hoping to derail any lecture.

He blinked at me. "How could it not be? We're on Earth. Earth! Even without the media presence and the Gagarians, this would be fraught with political problems. Did someone put you up to this?"

"What kind of political problems?" I asked. "Isn't everyone excited to be back here?"

"Nothing is ever that simple," he said. "There are people who think Earth should be left to recover, undamaged by humans. Others think we need to get here before the Gagarians." He barked a harsh laugh. "Clearly, that didn't work."

"I didn't mean to cause trouble," I said. I hung my head. "I just—Liam is missing. I went looking for him."

"The fact that you're here at all is a problem," Origani said. "No one else brought family. I tried to convince Nate to leave you at home."

"What? I'd be like forty by the time he returned!"

"That's why he said no," Origani replied. "He didn't want to miss any more time with you. And since we were coming to a 'safe' location, Headquarters let you come. But the media are watching. If anyone catches you misbehaving, it goes on your father's record in a most public way. Those vultures are loading video into the message queue at an astounding rate. As soon as the jump gates are operational, everything we've done here will be splashed all over the galaxy. You need to keep your head down."

"I—I didn't realize—why didn't he just tell me?"

"Maybe he thought you'd try to use it against him?" Origani suggested.

"I wouldn't do that!" I jumped to my feet, affronted.

Origani gave me a level look.

I dropped back into the chair. "Come on, that was years ago. I'm much more mature now. And I promise, I will be more careful from now on. I'll stay in camp."

"No, you won't," Origani said. "You'll go where you're told. And today, we want you to go with the Gagarians."

"No, we don't," Dad said as he stepped into the room.

"Sir, we agreed—" Origani started.

Dad held up a hand. "Yes, Tam, we agreed. But it doesn't mean it's something we 'want'."

"Pedantic," Origani muttered.

Dad grinned faintly. His face hardened as he turned to me. "I am not happy with your behavior last night." I started to argue, but he held up his hand again. "However, I'm going to make use of it. The Gagarians seem to like you. Maybe they appreciate your rebellious streak. Or maybe they think they can use you against me. Either way, you've developed a connection that I don't have. I want to make use of that in the safest possible way."

"She'll be fine," Origani said. "She's not going by herself."

Dad nodded. "You and Marika will go with the team following our visitors to their base. They will expect us to follow them, so we'll be completely open about doing it. The hope is this will be a casual opportunity for you to expand your connection with them."

"My connection?" I asked. "I don't have any connection."

"You snuck out to meet them after hours," Dad said. "Young girls sneaking out to meet boys. It's as old as that ancient play—Romer and Juliann."

"It's older than that." Origani smirked.

"I didn't sneak out to meet boys!" I hollered. Dad and Origani glared. I lowered my volume. "I couldn't find Liam. I thought he might have gotten out."

"Gliders can't get through the force shield," Origani said. "If he was out there, someone let him out. That's highly illegal."

I bit my lip. I could admit to taking him out, and then I'd be confined to base for life. I'd probably never see Liam again. Or I could go along with this idea and hopefully get him back from Peter. I dropped my head. "I hope he comes home."

"He's here somewhere. He'll find you." Dad patted my shoulder. "Now, will you do this for me? I'm not sure entrusting you with a mission of this magnitude is a good idea. You haven't exactly proven trustworthy. But you're clever, and that's what we need right now. I need to know what those Gagarians are planning. We're counting on you and Marika to find out."

I sat up. "You can trust me, Dad. Really. I'll find out for you."

"Excellent." He turned to Origani. "Get her holo-ring fitted for surveillance and tell Wronglen she'll be along in a few minutes."

"Wronglen?" I cried. "What's she—why does she need to know?"

"She's going, too," Dad said. "I had no choice. The formal operating procedures for this mission require a member of the ship's crew to be present on all major activities. You'll have a media team as well."

"Is this normal for CEC missions?" I asked.

Dad laughed, a hard bark of sound. "Hardly. We never have media and rarely have interference from the ship. But this is Earth. A lot is riding on this. Tam says I can trust you. Can I?"

"I hope so," I whispered.

"That's not the most reassuring answer," Dad said.

"No, you're right," I replied. "I have acted badly several times, and I keep promising to do better. This time, I really will. You won't regret sending me." I held my hand up in the CEC salute, really meaning it this time.

Dad looked sadly at me, his eyes roving over my face. "I hope not."

A SUPPLY TRAIN waited at the cliff-edge above the beach. The three rectangular, anti-grav platforms held a full load of camping gear, food, water, and newly printed clothing packs as well as a network booster and a small force shield generator. Evy and Wronglen stood by the pallets, checking off items on their holos. While we waited for the rest of the team, I watched the sunrise. The sky turned pink and gold, then a brilliant edge of the sun appeared over the horizon. Our force shield darkened on that side of the plateau, blocking the brightest light to spare our eyes. I sighed, as it also dimmed the brilliant colors.

Marika appeared beside me, her eyes sparkling. "I can't believe they're letting you come," she whispered.

"Why not?" I muttered back.

"Rico said you snuck out last night. Tell me he was wrong!" She rubbed her hands together. "If he was, he owes me three green ration packs and a beverage of my choice when we get back to Grissom."

I was saved from answering when Evy cleared her throat. "Listen up, folks. I want to be ready to leave in ten minutes. Check the manifests. If there's anything missing, let me know yesterday!"

Marika pulled up a list on her holo-ring, so I hurried to do the same. "What am I looking for?" I whispered.

She showed me where to look for the mission briefing and support paperwork. An icon flashed red. "Click on that—the manifest. Make sure everything you need for—" she stopped mid-sentence to check her holo "—for a week is there. There should be a full complement of equipment for you—in your case, mostly food, clothing, etc. You don't need to check the common gear—that's Rico's job."

"I have a toilet paper ration?" I asked in amazement. "Paper? Ew."

"No personal sanitizers where we're going," Marika said with a laugh. "This is the wilds."

I clicked the "reviewed" icon on the manifest, and the document turned green. "What else?"

Marika shook her head. "You've got your grav-lifter on." She looked me over. "Did they issue you a weapon?"

"I have a stunner," I said, patting my holster. "And a solar charger for it." I tapped the small panel embedded in the shoulder of my jacket. Wiring ran through the jacket, and a plug dangled from the hem near the weapon.

"Plug it in," Marika said. "Best to keep them charging all the time. On primitive planets, there's no guarantee the sun will stay out."

"There aren't any clouds," I protested, but I reached for the plug. I slapped it against the side of the weapon, and it clicked into place.

"Not now, but I've seen storms pop up faster than you can imagine," Marika said.

"MOVE OUT!" Evy hollered.

I flinched at the bellow. Marika grinned. Evy and Wronglen marched through the open gate into the empty air over the beach. Rico and another explorer named Shabina followed them, with the supply chain tethered to them. The four people and the equipment dropped swiftly from sight.

Flynn and Chasin stepped out next, and Marika and I joined them. As we dropped below the lip of the cliff, the final two members of our team emerged above us—the media team on their air bikes.

We gathered on the beach, then moved into the trees. The Gagarians had struck camp. The only evidence of their existence was the ring of rocks they'd used to enclose a campfire and the pile of cold, soaked ashes within.

"These folks know how to camp," Evy said, nodding in approval. "Leave no trace."

"What do you expect from Gagarian agents?" Wronglen kicked one of the rocks out of the ring. "They're used to sneaking into places they don't belong and staying unnoticed. I'm surprised they lit a fire."

"They were trying to be noticed here," Evy said. "Remember the lamp on the beach?"

Wronglen muttered something under her breath.

"You have some personal experience with Gagarians?" Evy asked.

Wronglen ground her teeth. "I know those who have."

"Let's move out, folks," Evy said softly, her voice carrying through our audio implants. "We want to catch up with them as soon as possible. I don't want to have to send up a sub-orbital drone to track them. No point in advertising our tech if we don't have to."

"Set your grav-belts to a meter-high lift and tether," Rico said, fiddling with his controls. "We'll go for a fast pull. Stay within the train's force shield—don't want anyone decapitated along the way." He laughed loudly.

I flicked through menus to the grav-belt control and set my level. Tethering to a vehicle was new for me but easy enough to figure out. My feet floated off the ground, and as the supply train moved forward, we all swung in behind. Marika and I floated between the second and third cars.

"Decapitated?" I asked.

"Tree branches." Marika pointed up as the supply train towed us out of the camp and along the wooded path. Branches hung low over the narrow track, brushing the top of the force shield around the train. "You get dragged into one of those at speed, it ain't pretty."

I glanced behind. The media team in their bright blue G'lacTechNews jackets rode air bikes instead of using grav-belts. The guy wore his hair in a blond flat-top buzz cut. The woman had wavy brown locks streaming to her waist. They had specialized cameras sticking out at odd angles, making the bikes look like mechanical bugs. When their files got back to civilization, everyone in the galaxy would get to experience our trek in full-immersion virtual reality.

"We'll be on vid?" I asked.

Marika shrugged. "CEC usually does vid. Ours have face-blurring tech engaged. You don't join the CEC to get famous." She laughed. "These guys are news junket pros, though. I'm not sure what they'll post. They have to get signed releases if we're recognizable. Did you sign one?"

I shook my head. "Wasn't asked."

"She's fair game." The dark-haired woman connected through our audio channel. "Commander's daughter is considered a public figure."

I rotated my grav-belt, so I faced backwards. My holo-ring identified the woman as Aella Phoenix. His partner was Thor Talon.

"Are their names for real?" I asked Marika on a private channel.

"They're vid guys," Marika said dismissively. "Their names were probably issued by their company."

"I'm not a public figure," I said aloud. "Dad is, but family is off-limits."

"Sorry, sweety," Thor said. "When you joined the landing team, you became a public figure. Commander's daughter as explorer is ratings gold."

"Yeah, we need to get some conflict going between them," Aella said. "Father-daughter arguments would be platinum."

I rolled my eyes and swiveled around. Dad had known they'd be watching—he'd kept our disagreements private. I wished—again—that he'd kept me in the loop on this stuff!

Rico sat on the front cart of the train, guiding it above the rough terrain. In a few places he had to slow down to get between trees—we left some scars where the force shield peeled the bark away.

"The Gagarians drove a wheeled vehicle—that must have been tooth-rattling," I said.

"The wheels were for show," Marika said. "I'm sure they had grav-lifters, too. Gagarin has those."

"Actually, I was on the team that scouted their camp during the discussions," Flynn said. "Those vehicles were authentic."

"Authentic what?" Rico asked.

"I mean, they really are wheeled vehicles," Flynn said. "No other tech in them. They really want us to believe they're from here."

Everyone laughed. "That's not going to fly," Wronglen said sourly. "Everyone knows Earth was evacuated. I can't believe they tried to hide their tracks with that story."

"What if everyone was wrong?" Aella suggested.

"We have historical records," Wronglen said. "Proof of the Exodus. Passenger manifests."

"The numbers don't add up," Aella said. "The population of earth declined dramatically in the plagues of the middle twenty-first century—before they started evacuating. But there were still over a billion people here at the time of the Exodus. And the manifests show only seven million."

"Gawd, I can't believe they sent an *abandoner theorist* on this trip," Wronglen said. "Next thing we know, you'll be telling us Grissom is flat."

"The data doesn't lie," Aella said, her voice getting heated.

"Data doesn't lie," Wronglen agreed. "But it gets twisted. Or mis-read. Or outright embellished. Earth was evacuated completely. That was stated in all the historical texts."

"Except the scientists left behind," Thor put in mildly. "They're the reason we landed here, right? To see if we could recover their data."

"If we can find their base," Evy said. "That's why the Gagarians are here, too, I'm sure."

"The scientists were all past child-bearing age," Wronglen said, returning to the topic like a dog with a bone. "There were some old people who refused to board the ships, too. But nobody could have survived more than a few years."

"Enough arguing," Evy said. "Keep the primary channel free of chatter. You are giving me a headache. Flynn and Chasin, scout ahead. The rest of you, keep it down."

As the two advanced scouts zipped away, I looked around. The trail paralleled the river, winding closer then veering away in a seemingly random fashion. "This trail is packed hard," I said to Marika.

"So?"

"If those people are from Gagarin, why is there a vehicle trail here? Why would they be driving around?"

"Maybe it's a game trail," Marika said. "A lot of species follow migratory patterns that result in well-established trails."

"But it's the perfect width for their cart," I said. "That can't be a coincidence."

"Maybe they built the carts to fit the trail?" She shrugged. "Or they landed five or ten years ago."

"That's what Dad said. But their team is young," I said. "If they landed ten years ago, most of them—Joss, Zina, Eric—they would have been children. And Joss said Zane is his dad, and Zina is his twin sister."

Marika wrinkled her nose in thought. "Maybe the Gagarians send families on this kind of mission?"

"That's crazy," I said.

"Is it?" she asked. "We brought you."

CHAPTER TWELVE

THE SUPPLY TRAIN pulled into an open meadow. The Gagarians had parked their larger rover a few meters off the trail and spread cloths across parts of the grass. Eric and Peter were setting food out on the fabric. The smaller rover was nowhere to be seen.

"Come have lunch with us," Zane called.

Evy and Wronglen conferred, then Evy raised a hand. "Thank you," she called.

Flynn stopped the cargo train, and the platforms settled to the ground.

Zane strode toward us, the rest of his team in his wake. "We usually try to park a little farther from the trail," he said. "In case someone else needs to get by. But it's just us today, so no problem."

The two officers exchanged a look, and Evy stepped forward. "I'm Lt Sarabell Evy, of the Colonial Exploration Corps," Evy said. She waved at the rest of us. "This is my team. You've met some of them, I believe. Oh, and Lt. Wronglen."

Wronglen glowered. The rest exchanged greetings. Marika and I waved. Joss waved back.

Zane nodded but didn't say anything. For a moment, everyone stared at everyone else. Finally, Zane broke the silence. "If you wanted to visit New Lake, you could have just asked."

Wronglen flushed, but Evy just smiled. "You're right, we should have. Do you mind showing it to us?"

"Not at all," Zane replied. "But first, let's have lunch."

Evy's lips quirked. "Your companions aren't with you?"

"They've headed back to town to give folks a heads-up," Zane said. He turned and strode through his team to a meter-high metal box. "We've never had off-world visitors, and we want to look our best."

"I'm sure you do," Wronglen said sarcastically. "Need time to get your 'town' set up?" She made quotes with her fingers.

"Hardly," Zane said. He opened the box. "Everest made enough sandwiches to share. Help yourselves."

The rest of us stood back as Zane and Evy each took a wrapped packet out of the box. Peter took a step forward, but Zane gave him the stink-eye. He held up his hands and grinned.

"Please. We're happy to share," Zane said. "But only if you're really going to eat it. No need for show. I hate to see good food go to waste."

Wronglen's face went purple. Evy chuckled. "Sorry about that," she said. "We tend to be a little paranoid when accepting food from strangers."

"It's fine. Eat your own stuff if you like." He gestured to the rest of his group. "My team will be happy to demolish the rest."

Wronglen's lips pressed firmly together, and she reached into the box. Her hand hovered over two or three different packets, her eyes fixed on Zane. Finally, she selected one and moved away.

The rest of our crew stayed by the train. "Let's see if the officers survive before we eat that stuff," Rico whispered loudly.

With a shrug, Zane nodded at Eric. "Guess they aren't hungry." The rest of them each took a packet and spread out to enjoy the sun.

Joss grabbed two and sauntered over to us. "May I join you lovely ladies?" The sun glinted off his impossibly white teeth.

Marika fluttered her eyelashes and patted the pyramid of crates we sat on. "Come on up. Budge over, Siti, and let him sit down."

I scooted to the edge of my crate, and Joss sat between us. His broad shoulders bumped against mine, warm and solid.

"I'll share my meal pac with you," Marika said, ripping open her lunch packet. "The green ones are delicious, but don't bother with the others." She gave him a handful of ChewyNuggets.

"What are they?" He lifted one of the cubes, peering closely at the honey-gold coating.

She shrugged. "They're chewy, and kind of nutty and salty and sweet."

"Sounds like a girl I know". He tossed the handful into his mouth. "Mm!"

Marika laughed. I tried not to roll my eyes. He was corny, but when a guy has shoulders like that, he can get away with it.

"Pete! Pull up a box and join us!" Joss called out suddenly.

Peter stood on the grass nearby, his lunch in his hands. "Thanks, Joss," he said sourly as he settled on the grass. He unwrapped his lunch, spreading the cloth across his lap.

Joss waved at Marika's open meal pac. "Marika shared some rations with us. She said the green ones are good." He tossed the meal pac to his friend, then ripped open a green packet with his teeth.

Peter emptied the pac onto the cloth. It contained several smaller red and blue packets, but no green. He rolled his eyes. "Thanks. What are the red ones?"

"Some kind of stew," I said, my nose wrinkling. "It's nasty."

"It's okay warm," Marika put in. "But don't try it cold. The blue ones are fruit sauce. Not bad, but not as good as the nuggets." She waved an empty green packet.

"Thanks for sharing," Peter said. "I'll stick with this."

"I've got a few, if you want to trade." I slid off the crate and sat beside him, holding out an open packet. "Half a pack for half a sandwich?"

"Thanks." He gestured to his sandwich. "Help yourself."

I took half and sniffed. "Peabeege?" I asked in surprise.

"Peanut butter."

I peeled the sandwich apart. "This smells like peabeege, but what is this purple stuff?"

"Uh, the jam." He pointed to the brown side. "Peanut butter." His finger flicked to the purple. "Blackberry jam. What did you expect?"

"We have peabeege, but it's not in layers like this. It's just—" I sniffed again then flipped the top slice back onto the sandwich. "—one color.

Smells pretty much the same. The sweet part might be a different fruit." I licked some of the purple, which oozed out of the slices. "Yum!"

"Weird," he replied. "We get the peanuts from Thadome. They don't grow here. But the jam is from berry bushes. I probably picked some of this batch myself."

Joss cleared his throat and made crazy eyes. I looked from one boy to the other. What had Peter said that was out of line?

"Where's Thadome?" I asked.

His eyes slid away. "It's over that way," he said, waving vaguely in the direction we'd been traveling.

My eyes narrowed. "These peanuts grow wild?" They must have been here a long time if they'd already discovered sources for food. Marika said it might take weeks before Ahuja found suitable local food.

Joss laughed. "Not a chance. Peanuts are one hundred percent farm-grown. Especially around here."

"You've been here long enough to start a farm?" I took a bite. "This is really good."

"We keep telling you, we've been here our whole lives," Peter said. "We've had farms here for centuries."

"Right." I winked and took another bite.

I noticed Marika's sharp eyes watching our exchange. I felt a surge of pride. If she and I could ferret out their true intentions, it would cancel out my bad behavior last night. Dad would be proud.

"Hey, I have something that belongs to you," Peter said in a low voice.

From the corner of my eye, I saw Marika lean forward to listen. I suppressed a smile. "Liam?" I asked. A smile spread across my face as he pulled the little guy from his pocket. "You're such a naughty boy!"

Peter flushed.

"She meant Liam, not you," Marika said with a wicked grin.

AFTER LUNCH, we set out again. Joss had tried to convince me or Marika to let him try our grav-belts, but we declined. They wouldn't have fit anyway. Joss was in excellent shape, with broad shoulders and a narrow waist, but even my belt would be too small for him. Besides, giving our tech to a Gagarian was a bad idea.

As the boys reloaded their rover, the G'lactTechNews pair hurried over to Zane. I wandered closer to listen.

"Hey, I'm Thor Talon with G'lactTechNews." He tapped the logo on his chest then pointed at Aella. "This is Aella Phoenix. We'd like to take some vid of your team, right?"

"What will you do with this vid?" Zane asked.

"We'll queue it up to send to HQ," the woman said. "Capt Hydrao said the message beacons will be up in a couple of days. Then it will get back home almost instantaneously."

"Well, after the other messages go through." Thor laughed. "There's quite a backlog for the transmitter."

Aella laughed, too. "It's pretty fast. Anyway, this stuff will get back within the week, and anything we take after the backlog will get to HQ right away." She cast a dark look back at our team. "Unless the captain decides to censor."

Zane glanced at Evy. "You don't work for them?"

"Hardly." Thor tapped his patch again. "We're independent journalists. Embedded for the *Big Return*. But they control the beacons, so they control the data."

"And once it gets back to HQ—Headquarters?" At the man's nod, Zane continued, "Then what? Does HQ distribute it?"

"Oh, yeah, baby," Thor said. "All over the 'verse. That's our motto."

Zina chuckled. "Looks like you'll get your fifteen minutes, Dad."

Zane shot Zina an unreadable glare. "Go ahead," he told the news crew. "Not like we could stop them," he muttered as they lifted away.

Aella opened a pouch on her belt, and a cloud of micro-drones flew out. They spread out around the clearing, quickly disappearing.

"Are those drones?" Joss asked. "Cool."

"Let's get going," Zane said sourly. He started the rover and pulled onto the path.

"Gagarians don't want any press," Rico whispered loudly as the rover drove away.

"Shut up and drive, Rico," Evy snapped. "Better them than us."

CHAPTER THIRTEEN

The Gagarian rover was slow. I hadn't ridden in a wheeled vehicle in—well, I couldn't remember *ever* riding one. Anti-grav technology made the wheel obsolete, at least for passenger travel. And I could see why. They took forever to get up one side of a hill and down the other.

Meanwhile, Thor and Aella sent a steady stream of drones swirling around the group. Dad had insisted they keep their tech within half a klick of the convoy, and Evy monitored their locations with a flexible no-fly perimeter as we went.

The explorers took turns on "point." This meant someone scouted ahead of the main group. They also stayed within the boundary Evy set. They reported back at regular intervals, but each report was basically the same. More trail.

"Of course, we have a drone on the other vehicle," Marika said when she finished her stint as point.

"We do?" I asked.

"You didn't think your dad would let them just drive away, did you?"

"Huh. Never thought about it."

She patted my arm. "You'll learn when you go to the academy. Not that they spend a lot of time on counter-espionage. Explorers mainly visit untouched planets."

"That's gonna change," Evy said. She sat atop the crates on our pallet, having tired of Wronglen, I thought. "Now that we *know* the Gagarians are sending out teams, the academy will up their educational requirements on that subject."

Marika nodded. "Before, it was hearsay, but now we have proof."

Evy gave her a narrow-eyed look. "How do you know so much about the academy? You're a grunt."

Marika lifted her chin. "I did my pleeb year. But I got tired of the crap and decided to enlist instead." She grinned at me. "Started making credits a lot faster—my classmates just graduated last ye—well, a year before we climbed into our capsules on the *Glory*."

"And now they're more than half-way to retirement already," Evy said. "It's been twenty years for the paper-pushers back at HQ. The longer you stay, the faster they age. I've got classmates who are already sleeping late and eating dinner at four o'clock."

"Yeah, but they had to spend forty years pushing paper." Marika grinned. "We get to do this."

"So true." Evy smiled, then checked her holo-display. "Looks like the other rover is almost back at their base. Crap! What—I need to talk to the boss." She tapped her belt and lifted off, falling behind the convoy as she swiped through screens. "You seeing this?" she asked, but her voice grew fainter as we pulled away.

"I hate it when they do that." Marika balled her hands.

"Guess you shoulda stayed at the academy," I sniped. "Then you could be one of them. I'm sure we'll figure out what they're talking about when we get closer. Unless you have a drone hidden somewhere?"

"I wish," Markia said.

We crawled over a hill, but the view from the top was blocked by trees. Evy caught up and passed us, lying flat like a superhero. She streaked over the Gagarian rover and out of sight at top speed.

A few minutes later, we met Shabina where she sat on a large boulder beside the path. "Officers aren't supposed to take point," she muttered as she tethered to the rear car with Rico, Flynn, and Chasin.

"I'm going to see what I can find out," Marika said. She untethered and lifted above the train. She zipped forward and sat next to Wronglen on the first car. The two spoke for a few minutes, Wronglen getting louder and more agitated with each exchange.

"Flynn!" Wronglen hollered through our internal audio. "Front and center!"

Everyone winced and swiped at the volume control.

"Yes, ma'am." Flynn gave us all a wry look and flew to the front.

Marika lifted off and drifted back a couple of meters as Flynn passed her, but she stayed near the front car.

"You have the conn," Wronglen said, her voice still broadcasting. "I'm going to see—I need to speak with Lt. Evy." She handed Flynn a tablet and streaked away, her feet barely clearing the Gagarian rover's roof.

"Bet they're wondering what's up," Chasin remarked to no one in particular. "Coupla CEC officers speeding toward their base."

"You can bet they have defenses," Shabina said darkly.

Aella left her position behind the rover and waited until we caught up. She dropped down to face Marika and Flynn, her bike idling along as she spoke. "What's going on with Wronglen?"

We all leaned forward to catch the conversation.

Marika shrugged. "I guess she doesn't want to miss out on whatever fabulous scenery Evy sees first."

Aella grunted and flicked something in her holo. "Send a drone," she muttered, as if to herself.

Way ahead, Thor's bike rose above the rover, and he flashed a thumbs-up.

"You're supposed to keep the drones within the perimeter," Flynn protested.

"They will stay within a half klick of the convoy at all times," Aella said smugly. "Evy set the perimeter, and she's way up there. I'm just trying to stay compliant."

"She centered the perimeter on this." Flynn held up the tablet. "Not herself."

"Oops." Aella lifted and zipped away. She buzzed past the rover, and Thor pulled in beside her, streaking along the trail.

"Everyone's going to see it before us," I muttered. "Whatever 'it' is." I glanced at the others. "I'm going to see what the Gagarians say."

Before anyone could stop me, I untethered and increased my altitude.

I couldn't do the fancy horizontal flying like Marika, but I knew how to move independent of the tether. I doubled my forward speed and waved as I passed her and Flynn sitting on the front of the train.

In a few seconds, I reached the back of the rover. "Pull me in!" I cried, reaching out both hands.

Eric and Joss leaned forward and grabbed my hands. I flicked off my belt controls and dropped into their arms.

At least, that was my plan. Instead, I crashed into them. Both boys grunted. I rebounded, falling away from the moving vehicle. Eric and Joss pulled, and I ended up sprawled across their laps. Eric slid an arm around my shoulders, and Joss grabbed my hips.

With the impact, Tiah, Jake, Peter, and Zina jerked around to see what was happening. Zane glanced over his shoulder and hit the brakes, muttering something under his breath.

I slammed forward and my shoulder rammed into Eric's gut.

"Oof." His face scrunched in pain.

"Sorry," I said, putting a foot down and stomping on Joss's. "Sorry." We scrambled around, and finally, I sat between the two of them. My face flamed. Marika and Flynn burst into laughter. I tried to ignore them.

"You okay?" Eric asked.

"I'm fine," I said, my face heating even more. "I guess I need to practice."

"We're all good back here," Joss called out. "Proceed!" The rover started moving again.

I peeked over my shoulder. Tiah, Jake, and Peter gaped at me. Zina grinned from the front seat. Zane appeared to be muttering some more, but I couldn't hear what he said.

"What's up with all the zipping about?" Peter asked.

I shrugged. "Just wanted to see if you know what's going on?" I pointed vaguely forward with my thumb.

"We wanted to ask you," Peter replied.

"Evy got a look at something through her drone," I said. Since no one had said the drones were classified, I assumed they weren't. Now that I thought about it, that might not have been the best interpretation. Too late now. "She said something about your other rover reaching base, and then she wigged out. I think she talked to my dad."

"And then she zoomed ahead?" Joss grinned. "My bet is she spotted our village." He raised his voice. "Zina! Call Mom and tell her they might get visitors sooner than they expected."

Zane waved him off. "They already know."

"Know what?" Peter asked.

"We assumed they would have eyes on both rovers," Zane said.

When he didn't elaborate, I turned to Joss. "What did they see that's so, uh, inflammatory?"

"They saw our home—New Lake," Eric answered for him. "And they must be starting to realize our 'story' is true."

"Your story?" I repeated. "You mean you really are from Earth? Not Gagarin?"

"It's all true." Joss put one hand over his heart. "We were born and raised here. And our parents," he nodded at the front of the rover, "and grandparents before us. Back to the dawn of mankind."

"But—" I started, but Eric cut me off.

"Yes. People were left behind." His face darkened. "Lots of us."

"You say that like you were one of them." I laughed.

"I was."

CHAPTER FOURTEEN

The rover bumped over a rough patch in the trail. My teeth cracked together, and I almost bit my tongue.

"Eric," Peter snapped.

"You were here," I said, rolling my eyes as hard as I could. "Five centuries ago."

"We were here," Eric insisted.

"Eric!" Peter said again.

"Never mind." Zane stopped the rover and climbed out. I twisted around to watch. He circled the front and slid in next to Zina. "You drive."

They swapped seats so fast, Flynn—just a few meters behind us—didn't even notice. Zina hit the pedal and spun the wheels. A cloud of dust blew up, momentarily hiding us from the following supply train.

Zane turned around in his seat, leaning an arm on the back of the bench seat. "Maybe if you know the truth, you'll be able to help convince them. I suspect, even with the evidence before their eyes, they're still going to insist we're from Gagarin. Jake, swap seats with Siti, will you?"

Jake shot a quick grin over his shoulder at me and clambered past his brother. He grabbed the vertical bar that held the roof above the back seat and swung around the rover's rear fender, his feet flaring outward. The vehicle bounced a little as he landed on the rear step. Eric grabbed his belt to hold him on board.

"You can just climb over the back of the seat," Joss told me. "No need for fancy acrobatics."

I narrowed my eyes at him. "I have an anti-grav belt." I reached for the controls, but Jake still perched on the edge of the foot board, blocking easy egress. With a shrug, I scrambled around and climbed over the seat. Tiah and Peter slid to opposite ends of the bench to give me room. When everyone was situated, Zane nodded.

"I was born five hundred and eighteen years ago." He paused.

I laughed. "Right."

"It's true," Peter put in. "I was born five hundred and sixteen years ago."

I looked from the teenaged boy to the older man. "That makes even less sense."

"Pete, you're not really helping," Zane said, then turned back to me. "But it's true. Pete, Red—Eric, that is—Jake, and I were born before the Exodus ended. When I was seventeen, the Magellan departed early on its final voyage. It left behind roughly twenty percent of its manifested passengers—including Peter and Jake. Instead, they took the last dregs of the federal government and their families." His face twisted briefly, then cleared. "The Explorer—the ship I was supposed to take two years later—never arrived."

He took a deep breath, as if shaking off a bad memory. "I made my way across the country—long story—and arrived at the Dome. Peter and Red were already here. It was a research station intended to study the long-term effects of the Exodus on the planet. All of the scientists were older—they expected to live there, collecting data, until they died.

"I suspect that's why your shuttles landed here. Because your leaders knew there would be data to retrieve." He rubbed a hand over his bald head.

I nodded. "That's what I heard. Not that they tell me much. I'm just the commander's daughter."

We bumped along in silence for a few moments, then Zane went on. "After we'd been inside a while, it became clear the Dome was not a short-term research facility but, rather, a long-term solution." He glanced at the others.

"Mr. Roth, the guy who built the Dome—" Peter took up the story. "He built a suspended animation facility in the basement. Over the next year or two, over ten thousand people were placed in suspended animation with a wake-up date of five hundred years later."

The numbers sent cold rushing through my veins. "That's ridiculous," I sputtered. "Five hundred years? No one uses deep sleep for that long! It's untested—dangerous."

"It's been tested," Eric put in from behind me. "Tested on us."

My head swung around, and I glared at him. "Sure."

He nodded. "Yes."

"No way," I said.

"We're living proof," Peter said. "Jake and I were down there the longest. These losers stayed upstairs longer."

"Not my fault," Joss said. "I wasn't even born until a hundred years ago!"

I looked over my shoulder, eyeing Joss, then turned back to Zane. "Right. You have nothing to do with Gagarin."

"I'm not even sure where it is," Zane said. "I know—generally—where Sally Ride is because that's where I was supposed to end up."

"Me too," Peter said. Jake, kneeling between Eric and Joss on the seat behind me, nodded.

I stared at each of them, my eyes moving from face to face. It wasn't possible, but they sounded sincere. Then I turned to Tiah. "You haven't said anything. What about you?"

"I'm from the Dome." She shrugged. "I never went downstairs." She whispered the last word. With a slight shake of the head, she went on. "I was born sixteen years ago. In the Dome."

"This is crazy," I said. "I mean, it's a great story, but come on. Pull the other leg. No one survives deep sleep that long. The CEC uses deep sleep extensively—we send explorers on flights that take twenty or thirty years to complete. But no one does it more than three, maybe four times, tops. The trip here will be my dad's last one."

"That might be the recommended limit," Zane said. "But I can assure you it's not the true max."

I held up a hand. "None of this explains why Wronglen and Evy went racing away," I said. "What did they see?"

Zane shrugged. "I assume they saw New Lake—our village. It's exactly what we told them—a farming community. I'm pretty sure it looks nothing like a Gagarian base."

"It wouldn't, though, would it?" I asked. "I mean, you need it to match your story, right?"

Zane threw up his hands and turned his back. "Believe what you want," he said over his shoulder. "You'll see soon enough."

The trail we followed merged with another and widened. As we passed, I peered through the woods along the other trail, but couldn't see anything.

"I'm going back to my team," I said. "No need to stop. I got this."

"Are you sure?" Joss asked. "You wanna climb back over? I'll hold onto you." He smiled in a sultry way and winked.

"Thanks, but I'm good." I stood, crouching to keep from bumping my head on the roof, and climbed past Tiah. Perching on the edge of the foot rail, I held onto the pole like Jake had done. A couple of taps to my belt brought the grav-lifter online, and my feet lifted off the ground. I pushed away from the vehicle and waved as the rover continued on without me.

"That's why I didn't tell them," Zane said over his shoulder.

"Good call," Peter muttered as they pulled away.

I let the supply train catch up to me and dropped lightly onto the back of the first car beside Rico. Flynn and Marika still sat on the front, guiding the vehicle. Chasin and Shabina drifted behind, watching our six.

Marika handed the tablet over her shoulder to Rico. "Watch the drones, will you?" When he'd taken it, she tapped her belt and stepped off the hover cart to float back to me. "What did they tell you?" she asked.

I started to speak, then thought better. "I should probably report to my dad first," I said.

"Ooh, so something juicy?" Rico asked. "Come on, Siti, spill!"

"Not really juicy," I said. "Just the same stuff they've been saying. That they're from here."

Rico and Flynn both scoffed, but Marika just nodded. "I guess they're sticking to their story. As expected. What do you need to tell the commander?" She locked her deep brown eyes on me.

"Just trying to make up for last night," I said with an unconvincing shrug. "I've stepped in it enough times already. Want to stay on the side of good and right."

Rico laughed. "Good luck, kiddo." He ruffled my hair.

"Hey, hands off!" I lifted my chin and put on a snooty tone. "Do you know who I am?"

He laughed. "Sorry, your imperialness."

I smirked. "And don't you forget it!"

A tone sounded in my audio. "Emergency! We need medical and security, now!" Evy called.

CHAPTER FIFTEEN

Rico's eyes jerked to the tablet. "Crap!" A red circle flashed on the map about two clicks ahead of us.

Flynn grabbed it out of his hands. "Chasin, get your med bag. You and Marika are going ahead. Fast. Rico, stay with me, weapons hot. Shabina, stay on six!"

Before he'd finished issuing orders, Chasin appeared beside us, pulling a small white crate with a blue medical star. "Ready." He and Marika took off, streaking away at top speed, the crate bobbing along behind.

"I'm going with them." I flicked my grav-belt.

"He didn't tell you to go," Rico said. He handed a large gun to Flynn.

"He didn't tell me not to," I retorted, pulling my stunner out of its holster. I avoided Flynn's eyes.

"There are hostiles." Flynn waved the tablet at me.

I grabbed it, peering at the screen. "I don't see hostiles," I said. "I see the Gagarians' other rover and some damage. And there's Aella! If she's there, I can be there." I tossed the tablet at him and spun, flicking my belt controls. My feet lifted off the crates and my belt pulled me forward.

As I flew, Flynn hollered at me again, but I ignored him. My feet flew up behind me as I gained speed. Apparently, speed was the key to the superhero move. I flicked it up to max and swerved around Zane's rover.

"What's going on?" they called, but I was out of earshot before I could answer. Besides, I didn't really know.

I set my belt to lock onto Marika's signal. With the SmartFollow technology engaged, the belt backtracked her path and followed it rather than taking a direct course to her location. In thick woods like this, that was important. A direct flight likely would have plastered me against a tree trunk.

I sped along the path, about two meters above the ground, swooping below branches that hung across the road. I reached a corner and instinctively banked left. Then right. And right again. I burst out of the woods and shot out over a lake.

"Yikes!" I swung wildly as the SmartFollow corrected and pulled me onto a trail along the lake's edge. Heart beating double time, I pawed at the controls and slowed my forward speed a fraction. Luckily, I'd been out of sight of the team—and the Gagarians—before that wild correction.

With the lake on one side, the trail opened up a bit, and the trees fell back a few meters. Low bushes on my right marked the edge of the trail. Water lapped at the sand beyond the brush. Here and there, narrow gaps allowed access to the beaches, for those without a grav-belt. Probably animal trails, I thought.

The trail widened, and I heard voices. I increased speed, keeping my hand on the controls. As I neared a clearing, I dialed the speed down to minimum.

"Halt!" a voice cried out.

"It's me," I said, identifying Wronglen. "Serenity Kassis!"

She glared at me. "What are you doing here?"

"I came to help!"

Beyond the lieutenant, Evy and Chasin crouched over— "Are those bodies?" I yelped.

"The Gagarians were attacked and injured," Wronglen said. "They're alive. How are you going to help?"

"I have some first aid training," I said.

"So does everyone else on this team," Wronglen said. "Go back to the group. Tell them to get up here, fast."

"They're already moving at the Gagarians' top speed," I said, not sure it was true. Although, after watching us speed away, I was sure Zina was driving as fast as she could.

"Siti!" Evy called out. "Get over here and make yourself useful!"

I grinned at Wronglen. "Gotta go."

She glared but didn't try to stop me.

"Where's Marika?" I asked as I flew up.

"On guard duty," Evy snapped. "Get down here and hold this!"

Everest lay on the ground, eyes closed, face pale. Blood soaked the side of his shirt. Evy's hand pressed a pad against his ribs. "He's been shot by a projectile weapon. We need to stop the bleeding."

"Projectiles? Barbaric!" My stomach swooped as I landed, and I swallowed hard. I'd had first aid training, but I'd never had to use it. I knelt next to Evy, breathing deeply so I wouldn't pass out. So much blood! She grabbed my wrist and pulled my hand on top of hers.

"Press." She pulled her hand a way, and the blood on Everest's shirt seemed to darken. "Press harder. You need to stop the blood flow."

I pushed hard, my hand already warm and sticky. I put my other hand on top, holding the soaked pad against his side.

"Lieutenant!" Chasin called out.

We both looked up. Chasin held something up. When Evy nodded, he tossed it. She caught a device about the size of both hands together.

She lifted the edge of the cloth I held against the man's side and pressed the smooth, white device against his skin. "I'm going to count down from three. When I say mark, pull the cloth away," she said.

I stared at my hands, dazed.

"Siti, do you hear me?" she asked, snapping her fingers in front of my face.

"I—yes, I heard you." I took another deep breath. "I'm ready."

"Three, two, one, mark."

I yanked the cloth away. Blood pulsed out sluggishly. She slid the device over the gaping hole in his side. White foam flowed out from under it, coating his side as it oozed over the bloody skin. Within a few seconds, Everest's side was covered in a thick, hard cocoon.

She peeled the device away. "Field med ScanNSeal." She flicked the tiny screen and read it. "The projectile is lodged inside," she called out to Chasin. "I need a NanoMed."

Chasin hurled something in our direction, and Evy caught it without looking.

"How—" I gaped at her.

She ignored me, tapping rapidly at the screen embedded in the new device. After a moment, she glanced up and saw me watching. "Nano-Med," she said. "It's based on the same technology as they use for cosmetic changes. I can use it to close the wound."

She finished working on the device then pressed one end against Everest's side just above the white coating. The box bleeped, and she looked at the screen. "NanoMed away." She flicked her holo-ring and pulled up a screen. "It'll beep again when it's done, but I can monitor progress from here. The nanobots will repair most damage, but they can't pull out the projectile. That will have to wait until we can get him into a med pod. Or maybe the Gagarians have something else."

"Where are the other two?" I asked. "Levi and Seraphina?"

"Levi is over there." She nodded at Chasin as she got to her feet, her eyes scanning the clearing. "He's got a head injury and a couple of broken bones. Seraphina isn't here—I was hoping she was with the other rover?"

I shook my head as I stood. "No."

"Then they must have taken her." Evy's voice echoed through my audio implant with the next words. "Rico, status."

"We've just reached the lake," Rico replied. "We'll be with you in ten. Shabina is reporting no movement on our six."

"Excellent," Evy said. "Marika?"

"No movement here, either," Marika said. "There's a mess of footprints on the eastern edge—temperature scan shows that's where they came from and where they went. And rover tracks."

"So, they didn't have grav-lifters?" Evy mused.

"What about Seraphina?" I asked.

"Don't know," Marika said. "They could have loaded her on the rover. Or she could be on foot. No way of identifying individual footprints."

Ice water rushed down my spine, and my head felt light. Good thing I was sitting.

Evy glanced down at me. "She's not dead," she said confidently. "They left these two. They wouldn't bother taking a dead body." She turned to scan the path we'd been following. "Thor, Aella, what you got up there?"

Aella's voice came through the audio as Thor reappeared around a boulder near the far end of the clearing. "Nothing to see here. Just more trees. Can't tell if there are any footprints, but my thermal scan only shows wildlife here."

Voices approached from behind us. Wronglen challenged, and after a muttered conversation, the supply train and rover came into the clearing. Rico had attached grav-lifters to the four corners of the rover, and it flew above the path at double the previous speed. The passengers clung to their vehicle, eyes wide. Zina grinned as the vehicle dropped to a few centimeters above the ground, then settled gently.

Zane leaped out of the rover and raced toward us. "What happened?"

Evy gave him a rundown while the others checked on their friends.

Eric tapped Everest's sealant cocoon. "What is this?"

"He had a wound," I explained. "That stuff stops the bleeding while the nanobots fix stuff."

His pale face went even whiter. "What kind of wound?"

"Projectile weapon," Evy said.

"Where's Seraphina?" Zane asked.

"Gone," Evy said shortly. "Who did this? Do you have factions within your exploration team?"

"Gone?!" Zane rubbed his hands over his head, as if he wanted to pull out the hair he didn't have. "What is with you people? We aren't from Gagarin! This was done by the Hellions. They're a gang of marauders who live in the caves a few klicks from here. They target our villages as well as travelers. But they've never been bold enough to attack by day. I wouldn't have let Seraphina go ahead if I'd known…" He trailed off.

"A gang? How big?" Evy asked.

"We're not sure," Zane said. "We think they have about forty."

"Weapons?" Evy snapped.

"Bows and arrows, mostly," Eric said, still crouched beside his friend. "Some have guns—projectile weapons—they've taken from us."

"No energy weapons or stunners?"

"Where would they get those?" Joss scoffed. "We don't have that tech."

Without warning, a cloud of people in grav-belts whirled in over the trees and dropped to the grass, weapons out.

CHAPTER SIXTEEN

Dad touched down, his support team fanning out around the clearing. "Evy, sit rep."

While Evy explained to Dad and Zane, the explorers scanned the ground, muttering among themselves. I flipped through the channels on my audio but couldn't find the one they were using—probably encrypted. As I watched, a team of four activated their grav-belts and drifted along the path where Marika stood guard. She fell in behind, and they disappeared into the trees.

"Is Everest going to be okay?" Peter asked me.

"He'll be fine," I said, hoping it was true. "Evy used a NanoMed on him."

His eyes grew wide as I explained what that meant. "What kind of repairs can they do?" he asked.

"Anything, really," I said. "It can't pull the projectile out of his body, but it can stop the bleeding until we can get him to a med pod."

"What about Levi?" he asked as we moved closer to the old man.

"He has a bad concussion, but he wasn't hurt elsewhere. I set the program to repair damage in the cranial region," Chasin said. "The NanoMed stops internal bleeding. We'll get him into the med pod, and he'll be better than before. I mean, it doesn't look like he's had any rejuv, so the med pod can repair damage due to aging as well as injury. Like, if he had cataracts or any other age-related issues, those'll be fixed."

"That's...amazing," Peter said. "Can it repair diabetes?"

"Dia-what? I'm not sure…" Chasin flicked his holo-ring and pulled up a screen. He swiped a couple of times. "Oh, here it is. Yes, pancreatic malfunction is simple. Just have to reprogram the cells to do their job. I hadn't realized Gagarin was so far behind on medicine." He bit his lip, as if realizing he shouldn't have shared that information with the enemy.

"We aren't from Gagarin, so I have no idea what medical tech they have," Peter said in disgust. "I wish someone would believe us!"

"All right." Dad's voice rang out through my implant and across the clearing. "We're going to transport Levi and Everest back to base for medical care. Beta team, you'll escort them. Once they're healed, you'll bring them to the Gagarin camp."

Several of the Gagarians shouted, but Dad held up a hand. The yells subsided to mutters. "Alpha team is tracking the attackers. The rest of us will move together to the—" he glanced at Zane "—to the village with the supplies and the rover. Questions?"

No one moved.

"Good. Beta, secure your patients," he said. "Evy, organize the march."

A team converged on the rover. They removed the grav-lifters from Zane's vehicle and unfolded two stretcher pods. While they loaded Levi and Everest into the pods, Rico strode up to the rover.

"Who's the expert on this vehicle?" he asked.

"I am," a timid voice said. Tiah peeked out from behind Zane, her hand raised. "I helped build it."

"Great." Rico felt under the front end. "Help me do a system check. Maybe I can give it a little more zing. It's too primitive for my equipment. How's it even open up?"

A flush spread over Tiah's brown face at his criticism, but she grinned when he asked the question. She tapped a small hatch on the rear seat and reached inside. The back seat folded away from the vehicle, revealing the internal parts.

I knew nothing about solar-electric vehicles, so I went back to watching the beta team. They had moved the two men to the stretcher pods and pulled a blanket-like cover-up over their bodies. With a flick of the controls, the covers popped up into rigid canopies. Then they attached the grav-lifters to the front and back.

"Who's coming with us?" Chasin asked.

Dad blinked. "Beta team. Weren't you listening?"

"Yes, sir," Chasin said. "I mean them." He nodded toward the Gagarians grouped around the stretchers. "They'll want to send someone, right?"

Dad considered the group. "They can send two. But no weapons."

"Sir." Chasin nodded and grabbed two spare grav-belts from the supply train.

"Thanks for the offer," Zane said. "Eric and Jake will go with them."

"Dad," Joss objected. "Those two will get into all sorts of trouble."

"No, they won't," Zane said.

"Siti will take care of them," Dad said. "Right?" He caught my eye and tipped his head toward Eric.

"I wanted to see the village," I muttered.

"When our guests are recovered, you can come to the village with them," Dad said.

"Yes, sir." I didn't do my cute salute this time so he'd know I was disappointed.

He ignored me. "Move out."

I started to show Eric how to control the belt, but Chasin stopped me. "We've got them tethered to the pods. They said they don't have this tech; and it's faster to trail them than train them." He gave me a meaningful look then checked both boys' belts. "They're ready. When we lift the pods, your belts will lift, too. Then we'll pull you to the base."

Eric kept one hand on Everest's pod, barely glancing at the ground as they rose. Jake's eyes widened in delight as Levi's pod pulled him upward.

I flicked my controls and locked onto the pod, too. As it continued to rise, I slid in beside Jake. "These are kinda fun, aren't they?"

He glanced at me, then his eyes slid away.

"Wait till we're out of sight of them." I jerked my head at Dad and the rest of the group. "Then I'll show you some tricks."

A grin spread across Jake's face then he bit his lip.

"It's okay," I said. "It won't hurt Levi. Your belt is doing all the work of lifting you; it's just taking directions from the lifter on the pod."

We rose above the treetops and streaked forward, heading to camp at top speed. Our legs flew out behind us, and Jake laughed. Eric glanced back and scowled.

"Everest will be fine," I called over the wind. "Relax and enjoy the ride."

Once the clearing had disappeared behind us, I showed Jake how to do some acrobatics. Eventually, Eric let go of the pod and joined us. We tumbled and twisted above the trees, giggling like children.

"Siti." Chasin's voice sounded tired through my audio implant. "We're approaching camp. Time to act like an adult."

Heat washed over my face. "Yes, sir," I muttered.

"Don't call me sir. I work for a living," Chasin replied with a grin. "And don't worry about it—we all do that stuff when we get a chance. But it's time to behave now. Don't want anyone complaining about our lack of professionalism."

"You're right. Thanks," I said, flicking off the connection. "Boys, time to settle down."

By the time we reached the plateau, Eric and Jake bobbed along beside me as if they'd been members of an explorer team for ages.

Someone opened the gate, and we slid in. The two guards assigned to us dropped to the rock and headed for the armory. Chasin kept the stretchers a meter above the ground and pulled us toward Beta Mod.

I hadn't been inside Beta yet. It was exactly like Alpha, where Li and I had set up her workspace, except instead of labs there was equipment storage and medical. I showed the boys how to turn off their grav-belts, and we followed the pods into the building.

While I helped the boys remove their grav-belts, Chasin pushed the injured men to the back of the room. He retracted the covers and lowered the stretchers into the med pods.

"What's he doing?" Eric demanded, thrusting the belt into my hands and striding to the back of the room.

"That's the med pod," I said. Jake and I stopped by the first pod. A clear opening near the head allowed us to see Everest inside.

"It's a more sophisticated diagnostic and treatment tool," Chasin said.

"The NanoMeds are great field medicine, but they don't cure. They stabilize until we can get you back to one of these." He stroked the hood as if it were a favorite pet.

"You can watch everything here," he went on, tapping a screen on the side of the device until it glowed. "See? It's scanning his body and identifying irregularities. There's the projectile, and you can see the blue markings where the NanoMed repaired damage to the liver and intestines. They also cleaned up anything that spilled out during the injury. A damaged intestine can leak into the peritoneal cavity and cause infection. NanoMed takes care of that. But it can't remove the metal."

He tapped the screen again. "There's some odd brain wave activity."

"I thought you said his head wasn't injured," I said.

"It wasn't." Chasin tapped the machine again. "He passed out due to blood loss from the wound. There was no visible trauma to the head. And this isn't reading as trauma. It's just unusual brain activity. That's okay. The med pod will analyze and correct it."

Jake grabbed my arm. "NO!" he cried. The word seemed to echo through my mind. He dropped my wrist and grabbed Eric's.

Eric yelped, staring at Jake. "Are you sure?"

Jake nodded.

"Stop the machine," Eric commanded.

CHAPTER SEVENTEEN

"Stop the med pod?" Chasin asked. "You're crazy. We need to get this projectile out of him."

"That's fine, but don't fix his brain," Eric said, panic seeping into his voice. He grabbed Chasin's arm. "Don't touch his head!"

Chasin gave him a narrow-eyed look and tapped the screen again.

"Did you turn it off?" Eric asked.

"Yes," Chasin replied.

"Show me!" Eric pointed at the screen. "Show me you turned off the brain repair."

"Okay, calm down." Chasin poked at the screen, and a visual of the whole body appeared. "See this yellow line? That shows we're focusing on everything to the right—from the neck down. Not touching the brain or brain stem. Good thing there's no paralysis."

"What about him?" I asked, pointing at Levi's pod.

"He's got a concussion—pretty serious." Chasin crossed the room to the other pod. Eric and Jake followed behind. "We had to repair his brain. This area," he pointed to an image of a brain, "had significant blunt force trauma. There was some bad inflammation here and here. And, as I mentioned, we fixed his cataracts. You can see the report here. Looks like he had some sinus issues as well. And that odd brain wave thing your friend has. I've never seen anything like it before."

Eric and Jake exchanged a look.

"It's already done?" Eric asked softly. "Whatever caused the odd brain waves?"

"Appears so." Chasin nodded. He pulled up a screen. "I'm just a tech, so I'm not an expert in brain function. I couldn't tell you what repair affected those brain waves. But his scans look perfectly normal now. Why, what's the problem?"

Jake and Eric looked uneasily at each other again. After a moment, Jake shrugged.

Eric scratched his head. "Everest and Levi have some, er, abilities," he said. "That may or may not have something to do with those brain waves."

"What kind of abilities?" I asked.

"I don't think I'm supposed to tell you that," Eric said.

"Secret brain abilities?" I asked. "Like, they can melt our faces with their minds?"

"Don't be ridiculous," Eric said.

"Then what?" I asked.

"You'll have to talk to Seraphina. It's not my secret." His eyes went back to Everest's pod. "You're sure you've got his, uh, isolated?"

"Yes, sure," Chasin said. "He's sedated, of course, but that doesn't cause any long-term effects. Other than monitoring his vital signs, the pod is only working on the gut injury."

"Good." Eric looked around the room, then grabbed a stool and rolled it to the pod. "I'm just going to watch. How long will it take?"

"Probably a few hours," Chasin said, glancing at the display. "I'll be monitoring from here." He crossed the room and sat behind a desk. With a couple flicks of his fingers, a series of screens appeared above the desk. "You want a comfier chair?"

"No, I'm good," Eric said, leaning his forehead against the clear part of the pod.

I glanced at Jake. "You wanna see the camp?"

Jake nodded.

"You might want to check with the boss." Chasin put his feet up on the desk.

"Roger." I changed channels on my audio and called Dad. "Hey, Dad, it's me."

"Report," Dad said.

"Uh, we got the two Gagar—Levi and Everest are in the med pods. Chasin says they're going to be fine. They have some odd brain wave anomalies. And I want to show Jake around the camp."

"Anomalies?" Dad asked. "Tell Chasin to call me."

"What about Jake?" I asked, but Dad had already disconnected. I turned to Chasin. "He wants to talk to you. Didn't answer my question about the tour."

Chasin shrugged. "Just don't show him anything classified." He chuckled, then his face straightened. "Yes, sir."

"Like I have access to that," I muttered as I opened the door. "Come on, Jake, I'll show you the camp."

He smiled, his eyes flicking to mine then away again.

I AVOIDED the labs but showed Jake the barracks and supply room. We sampled snacks at the chow hall and played with the gliders currently in residence. He took a particular liking to a black and green striped one name Lonnie, and the owner promised to let him know if Lonnie ever had a litter. Not likely, since CEC-approved gliders were all female. While they were definitely eco-neutral, we didn't need to be overrun by the cute little guys.

We'd just rounded the rear of the shuttle so Jake could get a look inside when he stopped suddenly. He looked as if he were receiving a message on his audio implant. Maybe I had trusted Zane and the others too quickly when they claimed they hadn't come from Gagarin. It was common knowledge Gagarin had stolen and copied our implant tech.

"May we go back, please?" he asked in a stilted voice. Jake spoke very little, and the few things he said came out sounding rehearsed—as if he'd memorized a different language but didn't have a real understanding of what it meant.

"Sure," I said, turning toward Beta mod. It wasn't until we reached the door that I wondered at my certainty the infirmary was where he wanted to go. He hadn't specified, and he could have meant he wanted to return to the plaza to play with the gliders.

He pushed open the door and trotted toward the infirmary at a quick pace. When we opened the inner door, loud voices assaulted our ears.

"—you let them do this to me?" Levi wailed. "You took everything from me!"

The old man sat on his litter, glaring up at Everest, his feet dangling over the side.

"Maybe it's them," Everest said, tipping his head in my direction. "Remember, they have some kind of shielding."

The old man pinned his eyes on Jake. "You heard him, didn't you?"

Jake shrunk in on himself. Everest stood and put a hand on the boy's shoulder. "Don't take this out on him, Levi. It's not his fault." He stood behind Jake in support, but I could see his legs tremble and the weight he put on Jake.

"Get back on that cot," I growled, bearing down on Everest. "What's he ranting about? Where's Chasin?"

"He and Eric went to get something," Everest said. "Drugs?"

I nodded. "Even with nano tech, some injuries can require meds. Why was the old man yelling?"

Levi sat with his head in his hands, quiet now. He glanced up at my question, then looked at Everest and closed his mouth.

"It's personal," Everest said. "We need to get home. How soon will we be able to travel?"

"I'd have to ask Chasin," I said. "I'm not a med tech." I looked at all three males. They clearly wanted to discuss something without me in the room. "I'll see if I can hurry him along."

Their voices raised again before I got the door shut behind me. I flicked my holo-ring and clicked on base surveillance. Drat. I didn't have access to the infirmary. I'd have to find out later what they were arguing about.

THE EARTH CONCURRENCE

I found Eric and Chasin in the pharmacy. "Here you are! Everest wants to know when they can head out, and I'm anxious to get back to the mission."

Chasin glared at Eric. "I am, too. Eric had questions. Lots of questions. Shall we?" He gestured to the door for us to precede him.

"What are Everest and Levi arguing about?" I asked Eric as we waited for Chasin to lock the pharmacy.

Eric glanced at me and looked away. "It's private."

I tried a different tack. "Do you have integrated comm circuits?"

The redhead's eyebrows furrowed. "I'm not even sure what that means."

I gave him a disbelieving stare. "Integrated comms?" I tapped my jaw. "Radios inside your head?"

His eyes went wide, and a delighted smile crossed his face. If he was faking, he was good. "You have those? I wish! We have bulky handsets." He touched an awkward box attached to his hip. "Speaking of, I should probably call Zane, but I can't get a signal."

"It's the dome," Chasin said, opening the outer infirmary door.

"The dome?!" Eric's face went pale. "How—?"

"The force field around the base," Chasin went on, not noticing Eric's odd reaction. "It blocks everything except what we bring in through our comm nodes."

"Oh." Eric went pink then settled back to normal. "Your protection bubble."

"Exactly," I said. "I can take you to the perimeter and ask them to open a gate."

He shook his head. "I'll just wait until we leave. It won't be long, right?"

Chasin knocked on the door, hard, and opened it. Total silence greeted us. Chasin's lips twitched. "As soon as we get these into your friend, we're on our way." He held up a small card with an array of little bumps. "If you were staying here, we'd just inject a pain nano, but when patients are outside the dome—I mean force shield—we prefer to use pills. Safer to carry, easier to apply."

He handed the card to Everest. "Take one of those by mouth each day at this time." He flicked his holo. "About three pm. When they're gone, you should be back to normal. Until then, take it easy. No heavy lifting. No strenuous work."

Everest turned the card over in his hands. "Each of these bumps is a pill?"

"Yeah, they pop out like this." Chasin showed him how to pop out a pill and handed him a water pac. "They're pain relief and antibiotics. You should be fine, but your wound was exposed to the air for some time."

Then he turned to Levi. "These are for you. Different medication, equally important. You had a severe concussion, and we don't want any neurological problems."

Levi slapped the card out of his hand. "Get your evil out of my face." He stomped to the door. "I am leaving. The rest of you can come with me or stay here for all I care."

"He's not going to get very far," Chasin muttered, leaning down to pick up the pills.

CHAPTER EIGHTEEN

We found Levi at the edge of the base by the path to the Gagarin camp. Laughlin, on duty again, or maybe still, refused to open the gate.

"I don't have authorization," she insisted in a bored voice.

Levi railed at her, raising his cane. Laughlin took a half step back and pulled her stunner. "Drop the weapon!"

"Explorer Laughlin!" I called as Eric, Everest, Jake, and I hurried over. "He's with us."

"Tell him to drop the weapon, Princess," Laughlin snarled.

"I prefer 'imperialness,' remember?" I said, my eyes narrowing. I turned to the old man and put out a hand, palm down. "Levi, please lower your cane. Explorers are trained to take threats very seriously. I don't think getting zapped with a stunner is in your best interest, considering your recent head injury."

As I spoke, Everest hurried past me. He stood next to Levi, concern written on his face. But he didn't do anything—he just stared at the older man.

"Open this damned fizzy thing and let me out!" Levi yelled. "You can't keep me captive!"

Everest unfroze with a jerk and put a hand on Levi's shoulder. "Relax. Let's go home."

Levi swung around, his cane still raised. "Did you feel that, boy? Nothing!"

Jake darted forward and pressed his hand on Levi's arm. The old man deflated almost instantaneously. Everest grabbed his arm, keeping him from collapsing on the rocky plateau.

"Eric, give us a hand." Everest looped an arm around Levi's waist and moved him away from the glowering Laughlin. "Where to, Siti?"

Eric took Levi's other side, turning the man toward me. His face had gone slack, and his eyes sagged almost shut.

"What's wrong with him?" I asked. "Do we need to take him back to the clinic?"

"He needs to get home," Everest said. "I don't—do you have a rover?"

"We do, but it's slow." I turned and led them back toward the clinic.

Chasin met us mid-way across the yard. He took a quick look at Levi and reached for his scanner.

I put a hand on his arm. "He wants to go home. I don't think scanning him is going to tell you anything new, and it's going to upset him further."

Chasin's eyes narrowed, but he nodded. "Transport pod?"

"Can you—" I made jerky, twisty motions with my hands.

"They can be configured for sitting upright," he replied with a little grin. "I'll grab one and meet you at the beach gate."

"This way," I told the boys. "We're headed home." I hurried to the edge of the cliff and caught Anivea's eye where she stood guard. "We're supposed to go—"

"You'll have to wait for escort," Anivea said. She held up a hand when I started to protest. "Commander's orders. Team is enroute now."

I sighed and turned to the boys. "Why don't you let Levi sit on the shuttle step?" I pointed to the craft. While we waited for Chasin and his transport pod, I showed Everest how to control the grav-belt. He and Eric played with the altitude controls, bouncing up and down while Jake sat quietly next to Levi, leaning against the old man. I started to suggest he give the guy some space but realized Levi was deriving some comfort from the contact.

Chasin arrived and unfolded the pod into a chair with arms. Everest and Jake helped the old man into the chair. Jake kept one hand on Levi at all times.

"I didn't realize Jake and Levi were so close," I muttered to Eric.

Eric jerked a little, then looked at Levi. "They aren't. Jake's just, uh, a calming presence."

"What does that mean?" I asked.

Eric shrugged. "What I said."

Chasin explained how to arrange the restraints so Levi wouldn't fall out and demonstrated the cover. "It can be lowered to protect him from the wind. We can set it to clear or opaque—just depends on the passenger's preferences." He raised an eyebrow at Levi, but the old man ignored him.

Everest looked at Jake and nodded. "Leave it clear." Jake nodded back. Strange.

"Your ride's here," Anivea said. The space beside her fizzed blue then cleared. Thor drove his air bike through and landed next to the shuttle. The two explorers who'd guarded us on the way back to camp—Ralph and Catrian—reappeared to join the group.

"I'm here to take you to the commander," Thor said with a grin.

"I thought you were independent journalists," I said.

"I don't mind doing a favor once in a while," he replied.

"Especially if it gives you access to an exclusive story?" I narrowed my eyes at him. "Not sure this is going to get you anything interesting."

"We'll see." He grinned again. "People are unpredictable. You never know what they might say. Or do."

"Pity you missed the fight," I muttered.

"What's that?" he asked, his eyes sharp.

"Levi staged a ninja attack on Laughlin," I said with a straight face. "Sorry you missed it."

Thor glanced across the camp, but Laughlin's position was out of sight. Then he looked at Levi, slouched in the transport chair. "Yeah, right." He turned to Chasin. "Tether that thing and let's get moving."

We tethered our belts to the air bike, and Thor lifted off. Our little train headed out, ignoring the trail and cutting straight across the landscape. "We're only about twenty minutes away by line-of-sight," Thor said via the audio implant. "Those Gagarians sure took a round-about way."

I nodded absently, my attention on "those Gagarians." While Eric showed Everest how to flip and spin, Jake stayed by the transport pod, occasionally reaching out to touch Levi. Sunlight glinted off the transparent cover, making it hard to see the old man. I let my tether out slowly, dropping back until I was next to the pod.

Levi sat slumped in the chair, his body relaxed. His eyes were open, and he gazed at the land speeding by below us. Every few moments, he'd freeze, then look at Jake. The boy put a hand on the old man's arm, and he relaxed again. What was going on there?

"We're going to take a short detour," Thor said over the audio. "Commander wants us to check out something." The bike banked left and settled into a new course.

"What's going on?" Eric shortened his tether and slid next to me.

"Nice work," I said, nodding at his belt.

He grinned. "Easy peasy. Where're we going?"

I shrugged. "Commander asked for a detour and fly-by."

Eric froze. "Fly-by of what?"

"Didn't say," I replied. "Or at least Thor didn't tell me."

"I thought Thor was a journalist," Eric said. "Why's he getting orders for the team?"

"Good question." I glanced at the explorers accompanying us. Catrian was the highest ranking of the three, but she was a first-termer. I activated my comm link. "Did the commander ask you to detour?"

"Thor said—"

"Thor isn't in your chain of command, is he?" I asked.

"*Perod!* I'm too used to taking orders—" Her voice cut out.

I smiled and shrugged at Eric.

"Commander okayed it," Catrian said, her voice subdued. "Thanks for reminding me to check, ma'am."

"Siti," I reminded him. "I'm not an officer."

"Not yet, but you will be," Catrian said.

"Hopefully," I agreed. "What did he say?"

"He said if it's important enough for Thor to check it out, we should go. Having the Gagarians along should provide some protection."

"Really? They were the victims of that attack, not us."

"Yeah, this whole thing is too weird." Catrian nodded at Eric, who had maneuvered next to Everest and was now whispering to his friend. "They don't look happy about the detour. I wonder if this is the cave system the attackers supposedly came from."

We approached another cliff. This one had vines growing here and there, and it towered high above the nearby trees. Off to the right, I could see a clearing that might be the village, but I ignored it. Something was not quite right about that cliff.

"Is that a window?" Ralph pointed.

Light glinted off something near the top of the cliff. "Maybe they built into the cliff," I said. "Back in the day."

"That's the Dome," Eric said, slipping in beside me.

"What?" I asked. "How is that cliff a dome?" I made a curved motion. "Aren't domes supposed to be, I dunno, round-ish?"

Eric laughed. "That's what I thought, too. It's officially the Roth Research Center, but we call it the Dome. Like the BioDome from the early twentieth century. Self-contained research center."

"All I see is the window," I said. "Is this where the attackers—what did Zane call them—the Hellions? Is this where they're hiding?"

"No. Their cave is over that way." Eric waved to the north.

"Wait, that's a manmade structure." Ralph pointed at a short, blocky building squatting at the base of the cliff. A ramp sloped down into the building, and a ladder climbed up the side. A tall wall encircled the buildings, ending at the cliff on each end.

Thor made a wordless noise. The bike dropped like a rock, taking the tethered transport pod and the rest of us with it. Levi woke from his stupor and screamed.

CHAPTER NINETEEN

"Thor, abort!" someone—I think it was Chasin—yelled. Ralph and Catrian, who hadn't been tethered to the bike, chased after us.

"The boss said fly over, not land!" As we fell, I heard Chasin yelling into his comm feed. "Sir, the journalist is going crazy! He's landing at the site."

Dad's voice came over the audio, loud and angry. "Thor, abort! If you land without sufficient security and with passengers in tow, I will report you to your superiors."

The bike continued downward.

"You'll be sent home in disgrace and you will NEVER be embedded in another CEC expedition," Dad said. "You know I have the chops to make that stick."

The bike leveled off so suddenly we all bounced off an invisible floor and bobbed up a few meters.

Eric whooped and grinned. "That was terrifying!"

"Yeah, you loved it," Everest replied.

We bobbed about two meters above the blocky building. Wooden chairs stood atop it, like someone's backyard patio. The ramp was clean and well-maintained, and the solid apron in front of the building had been recently swept free of the tree needles that lay scattered about the dirt arc between a high wooden barricade and forest. A paved path led away from the building and into the woods.

Catrian moved in on Thor, spitting out a low monologue. Thor tried to interrupt, but she kept talking. Jake adjusted his belt controls and moved closer to the transport pod. Chasin closed in on the other side.

"Is Levi all right?" I asked over the comm, not wanting to upset the boys.

"Physically, he's fine," Chasin said. "Heart rate is elevated—to be expected after a stunt like that. He's mad as hell, too."

Jake hung silent in the air, his hand on Levi's forearm. I moved closer. The tension seemed to slowly drain out of the old man.

"What is Jake doing?" I asked Eric.

He and Everest hung back, watching from a slight distance. They exchanged a look—one I was getting tired of seeing. Deciding how much to tell me. This diplomatic stuff stank.

"You might not have noticed, but Jake has a calming, uh, aura," Everest said. "He's very sensitive to emotions, and there's something about him that…"

When he trailed off, Eric stepped in. "He's really good at defusing emotional situations. Kind of a superpower."

I eyed them. "How does he do it?"

The boys looked at each other again and shrugged. "You'd have to ask him," Eric said. "But he's not very good about explaining."

"Sorry, guys," Thor muttered. He sat atop his bike, shoulders hunched, eyes down. Chasin floated nearby, his eyes locked on the journalist. "I kinda forgot you were back there. I don't normally have passengers." He waved at the structure beneath us, and his voice grew more animated. "But this is big news! This building is old but still functional. That's huge!"

"Let's get moving," Catrian cut him off. "If the boss allows, you can come back later. Keep the speed down to twenty percent." She swung her arm overhead, then dropped it, pointing in the direction of the path below.

"Twenty percent?" Thor muttered, shaking his head. He pushed his throttle, and we eased forward.

Ralph took the lead, with Thor and the rest of us right behind. Chasin had obviously untethered and followed under his own power. He stayed by Jake and Levi for a while, then looped over the group and slid back by me.

"We'll be there in ten minutes," Chasin said aloud. Then he switched to internal comm only. "Levi was terrified and furious. Did you see what the kid did to him? He just deflated."

I tipped my head at the boys. "They say he has a calming aura. Maybe some kind of pressure point? Is there something in the arm that would do that?"

"I'd like to learn that trick," he replied.

"Maybe Jake can teach you." I chuckled. "If you can get him to explain. He didn't talk much to me."

We flew over the thick trees. The path was invisible below us, but according to Chasin, it was fairly direct. About two klicks away, the trees ended, and a wide-open space lay along the river where it emptied into the lake. At one end of the clearing, small buildings lay in a neat grid. This section ended at an open square with larger buildings on three sides. The fourth was a green space that sloped down to the river. On the right of the square, the main road curved with the river, and more small buildings lined both sides of the street.

Beyond the smaller buildings, a few larger ones stood along the banks of the river. A high wooden wall encircled the entire settlement, and fields of green stretched beyond that. A four-meter-high double gate stood open in the wall where the path emerged from the woods. Just inside the gate, a smoke-damaged building squatted. A crew of men and women appeared to be building a new roof.

"They've been here a long time," I said, looking at the massive settlement. "Those buildings are made of wood—trees! And those fields—even with modern equipment, it takes time to clear that much land."

"The team says they haven't found any evidence of modern equipment," Ralph said over the comm. "Everything is about the same level of tech as that rover."

"Maybe they repurposed the equipment after they cleared the land," Catrian suggested.

"Why bother with the fields?" Chasin asked. "They could feed the wood into a synthesizer to create food for a long-term base."

"Or land enough macro-blocks with the team to keep them fed," Catrian said.

"I thought food synthesizers were inefficient," I said, remembering my discussion with Li about Autokich'ns.

"For a short explore and report mission, we sometimes bring them," Chasin replied. "For longer stints, they make life a lot easier. But if you're colonizing, living off the land makes sense. These folks are here to stay."

"You guys are awfully quiet," Eric called to me. "Impressed by our village?"

I adjusted my tether and swooped closer so I wouldn't have to yell. "It's not what we expected," I said.

"Maybe because you expected a Gagarian camp?" Eric raised one of his sandy eyebrows. "We told you we aren't from there. This village has been here for—" He turned to Everest. "How long?"

Everest thought for a moment, then shrugged. "I'm not sure. My great-great—" he paused. "—seventh great-grandparents moved here after the eruptions up north. The air was too hard to breathe and the dirt too ashy. Lots of folks died then. Maybe two hundred, two-fifty years ago?"

I stared. "Two hundred and fifty years ago? And where did they move from? What eruptions?"

"Someplace called Idaho." Everest's eyes unfocused, and he stared off into the distance. "They lived in the mountains near a great river. But the eruptions destroyed a lot of land up there and caused famine across the continent. Weather changed; it got colder. Skies were choked with ash for years. When too many people died, they moved the rest of the town here. It's a bit warmer, and the winds started to clear the air enough to breathe and grow plants."

I stared. I could almost see the people with animal-pulled carts, trudging along dirt trails into a small clearing by the lake. I looked at the village as we approached. I must have a more vivid imagination than I'd thought. But that was a detailed backstory. The "remaining settlers" theory was looking more and more believable.

As we descended into the open square, I glanced at Eric. "How come you don't know all this, too?"

"I'm not from here." He pointed at the paved plaza as we landed. His arm swung up, pointing back the way we'd come. "I'm from there."

CHAPTER TWENTY

Eric thought for a moment and grinned. "Actually, I'm from here too. Well, maybe more like over there." He pointed across the river.

Everest slapped Eric's arm. "Don't confuse the lady. He's from the Dome," he told me.

Levi struggled out of the transport chair, shrugging off Jake's grip. Everest tried to help the old man, but he swung his cane out, barely missing Everest's shins.

Everest leaped back, hands up. Levi glared. A crowd surged out of the large building, both Gagarians and explorers. A woman with long dark hair and almond-shaped eyes took Levi's arm. He struggled briefly, and they glared at each other. The woman's eyes widened, and she glanced at Everest. He nodded and the three of them started across the plaza, moving slowly and carefully.

What was that all about?

An older woman behind me called out, "Jake!"

A smile crossed Jake's face, and he ran to her, using a long, loping skip. Grandmother, perhaps? I looked at Eric. "You got family here, too?"

"My mom and sisters," he replied. "They're probably working." He looked up at the building behind Zane and Dad. "See, second floor, third window on the left? That's Mom's office." He waved, and a woman, barely visible through the thick glass, waved back. "She helps administer the village."

"Shouldn't she be down here at the meeting?" I asked.

"Nah, Zane and Mara can handle it." He smiled sadly. "She doesn't like conflict."

"Unlike you." I grinned savagely.

"Eric was born for conflict," Peter said as he wandered up.

"Hi, Peter. Is that your grandmother?" I asked, nodding at Jake and the woman.

Peter and Eric followed my nod, and both did a double-take. "No," Peter said slowly. "That's my mother."

I looked at the woman again. She looked ancient—way older than my dad. "Really?"

"She was awake for an extra twenty years." Peter's voice was flat.

My audio implant pinged. "Serenity," Dad said. "Come here, please."

Zane and my father stood on the wide steps in front of the building. A woman with dark curly hair and dark skin stood beside Zane—she looked enough like the twins to be their mother.

I excused myself and hurried up the steps. "You called, sir?"

His lips pressed together, suppressing laughter or annoyance—I wasn't sure which. He nodded to Zane and the woman. "If you'll excuse me a moment, I need to speak with my daughter." He took my arm and hustled me down the steps and across the plaza. He stopped when we reached the middle of the open lawn. "I'm glad to see you got here in one piece. What happened at the camp?"

"We took Levi and Everest to medical, then I showed Jake around the camp," I said.

"What about the old man?" he asked. "Something happened, but they won't tell me what."

"I'm not sure," I said slowly. I stared off into the distance, trying to remember. "Jake wanted to go back to the clinic. It was like he got a message via an internal comm."

"They say they don't have implants, but we know the Gagarians use them," Dad said. "Go on."

"Chasin should be able to confirm that, right?" I asked. "I mean, the med pod would have noted any non-organic modifications during the scan."

He clapped me on the shoulder and grinned. "Yes! Excellent. Wait here while I call Origani." He turned away, flicking his holo-ring. Even standing right next to him, I couldn't hear anything he said over the comm—just a low murmur.

I gave up trying and gazed across the river. It was wide here—about twenty meters I guessed—but moved swiftly toward the lake. Late afternoon sun glinted off the water, and something in the woods across the river. I squinted but couldn't identify anything but trees and rocks.

"No modifications," Dad said, snapping me back to our conversation. The vertical lines between his eyebrows were deeper than usual, and his jaw clenched. "At least nothing we can identify. How did the boy know to return to the clinic?"

"Maybe he just felt it was time?" I suggested. "We'd been gone more than an hour. Is that standard for med pod scan and repair?" Until this mission, I'd led a sheltered life and had no personal experience with med pods.

"It varies considerably, depending on the injury," Dad said. "We'll leave that one on the back burner. Continue your report."

I tried not to grimace. Report, like I was just another explorer. "We returned to the clinic, and Everest and Levi were arguing. Eric and Chasin had gone to the pharmacy. I think Eric was trying to keep Chasin out of the room."

"We can review the recordings," Dad said.

"Recordings?" I hadn't been able to review them, but obviously, Dad would have access.

"Every moment is recorded," Dad said, misunderstanding my question. "We're on a historic mission, but that's standard procedure. That room—and every room in the camp—is under constant surveillance. Surely, you knew that."

I cringed mentally. Obviously, the clinic would be recorded, but I hadn't thought about the other rooms in the mods. I mentally ran through the last few days, wondering what I might have said or done that could get me into trouble. Or just embarrass me. "Yeah, I knew it, but I didn't *know* it, ya know?" He gave me a blank stare. "I mean, it hadn't really sunk in. Hey, Thor and Aella don't have access to those recordings, do they? They said I'm fair game."

"Don't be ridiculous," Dad said. "We don't give the press access to mission recordings. But he's right, you're on this mission, you're fair game. I thought you knew that."

I waggled my hand in a tilting motion. "I knew, but…"

"You didn't *know*. Got it." He rotated his hand in a 'continue' motion.

"Um, Levi was mad. He said we took something." My brow furrowed. "There was something else… Oh, yeah. He and Everest had these weird brain wave signals. Eric got really excited and insisted Chasin modify the med pod program to *not* affect them. But Levi's was already running."

"Could they have an organic communications device?" Dad stared at me. "I know our labs are constantly working toward a less intrusive system, but is it even possible? And maybe our med pod broke Levi's." He tapped his fingers against his thigh in a complicated rhythm.

I smiled to myself, remembering that drumming from my younger years. That was his thinking noise. I waited quietly, not wanting to interrupt.

"That's got to be it," he said. "We need to learn more. If Gagarin has developed organic comm, we need to know."

"Dad, I don't think they're from Gagarin," I said.

He jerked as if I'd woken him. "Don't be ridiculous," he said again. "Where else could they have come from? Liwei isn't as advanced."

"I think they're from here," I said. "That facility over there—" I waved toward the cliff. "They call it the Dome. It's old. And they told me there's deep sleep pods in the basement. Some of them were down there for centuries."

"I've heard the story," Dad said, with an indulgent smile. "They make it sound reasonable, but we know deep sleep doesn't have that kind of range. I might believe fifty or even a hundred years. But five hundred?" He barked a hard laugh. "They're from Gagarin."

"But this village looks old, too," I protested.

"They built it to look old." Dad dismissed my concerns. "We have the tech to do that—if we wanted to bother. No, these are Gagarian colonists, trying to take Earth out from under us." He turned to survey the people still loitering in the plaza. "They've been here a while—I'll give them that. Possibly several decades. Or maybe they brought families. We just need to find someone who can't keep their mouth shut. There's always someone."

He turned and looked at me, his face speculative. "I think you and Marika could be very useful. Evy is getting together a small team to help them investigate the attack."

My eyes widened. "You want us to go with them?"

He laughed. "Of course not. You aren't trained for that kind of mission. I'm not even sure what kind of mission it is. Seraphina returned while you were at our camp. She says they left her for dead, and she followed them. That seems suspicious. I want to know what's going on here."

He tapped his thigh again. "Evy's going to set up camp outside their barricade, but I want you two to stay here. Talk to as many people as you can. Find someone who will tell you the truth. Maybe one of the kids." He clapped me on the shoulder. "That'll be your secret mission. Make me proud, Daughter."

"You aren't worried about them taking hostages?" I asked.

He laughed. "Please. You've seen their weapons. "

"But if they are Gagarians, won't they have more modern weapons hidden?" I tried to think what I'd do in their situation.

"I'm not worried. I'll be here, too—they've offered me a room. But I'll be busy with their leaders. You find out everything you can from the younger folks."

"What if I can't—"

"You will." He interrupted me. "I have no doubt you can find the truth." He urged me up the shallow grass slope, back to the plaza.

Zane and the woman waited for us there. "This is my wife, Katrina Thomas Torres," Zane said, his hand on the dark woman's back.

She bumped my fist with her knuckles. "Call me Katy."

"Katy, Zane," Dad said. "I'd like to take you up on your offer of hospitality. Marika, Siti, and I will stay here with you for a few days."

"Where is Marika?" I asked. "She was with the team following the attackers."

"They returned with Seraphina," Dad said. "But Marika wasn't with them. She came with us." As if conjured by his comment, Marika appeared on his other side and gave me a little finger wave.

"We'd be happy to have them," Katy said. "There are beds in the dormitory. Don't worry," she said to Dad. "They'll be safe there."

"I wasn't worried," Dad said. "Marika is a highly trained explorer. She can keep Siti out of trouble."

"Dad," I muttered under my breath. Way to make me look bad.

Zane's lips twisted in a little grin, then his face went serious. "In the meantime, what will your explorers be doing?"

"Exploring, of course," Dad said. "It's what we do. We won't meddle in any, er, local politics." He winked broadly, as if it were an inside joke.

"We'd be happy to have you meddle in local politics if you can get the Hellions off our backs," Zane answered. "But we'd appreciate it if you'd avoid the other villages. They aren't as used to higher technology as we are. No Dome nearby."

"Ah, yes, the other villages," Dad said. "Perhaps you can give me a map of areas to avoid. I wouldn't want to spook the natives." He didn't make air quotes around the last word, but I heard the sarcasm in his voice.

Zane didn't, or he chose to ignore it. "I'll get you a map."

"Stay out of trouble, Siti," Dad said as he followed Zane into the building. "We don't need any more excitement."

CHAPTER TWENTY-ONE

Katy smiled. "Come on, girls. I'll show you the dorm. Do you have any gear?"

"On the supply train." Marika pointed to the row of lift platforms now sitting in the middle of the plaza. "We can come back later and get them. I'm sure you're busy."

"Let's get them now," Katy said. "I don't have anything urgent."

"Does she not want us to wander around alone?" Marika asked through the comm channel as we followed Katy across the plaza. She was as good at speaking without moving her lips as my dad.

I shrugged. "Dunno," I muttered.

"What did you say?" Katy stopped to look at me.

"Where is the dorm?" I asked. Marika was saying something on the comm, but I couldn't focus on two conversations at once. I glared at her and gave a quick shake of my head.

Katy pointed. "Down that road. Third building on the left. Boys on the ground floor, girls upstairs. Well, men and women," she corrected herself. "Anyone who isn't married can live in the dorms. Couples usually get a place of their own. Zane and I live over by the lake, close to the barricade."

We stopped by the supply train. Rico sat atop the pile of crates, watching people come and go. He looked relaxed, but his eyes roved over each person who passed, assessing threats, mentally testing defenses. At least, I thought that was what he was doing. Knowing Rico, he was probably calculating the odds for later betting. He grinned when he saw us. "Boss says you're staying. Wha'chu need?"

"Overnight packs and our personal gear," Marika said.

Rico nodded to the second platform. "Personal gear is over there." He held out two flat rectangles, each the size of a tablet. "Here's your comfort packs. You need bedrolls?"

I took the packets and glanced at Katy.

"We have bedding and towels." She smiled. "Bunkhouse laundry is a standard chore for the eight to twelves."

"Siti, come grab your bag," Marika called from the next platform.

I trotted over and took a backpack from her outstretched hand. My name was printed on a tag. "These have uniform items plus underwear and sleep gear. Toss one of those comfort packs in—that's toiletries." She grabbed one of the packets and dropped it into her pack, then sealed it shut. "Everything you need for a week-long sleepover."

"No food?" I asked.

"Boss isn't worried about food anymore." She shrugged. "As long as we eat the same things they eat, we'll be fine." She waited for me to close my backpack, then hoisted hers over her shoulder and walked back to Katy and Rico.

"Five hundred years?" Rico laughed. "Good one, missus."

Katy's eyes narrowed. She appraised Rico for a moment, her gaze taking in the weapon strapped to his hip and the blaster laying within easy reach. "How long are the rest of you staying?"

"We'll set up a campsite just outside the barricade," Rico said.

Katy's forehead wrinkled. "Outside? That seems like a dangerous plan. The Hellions could come back. They're up to something—they've never attacked during the day before."

"We have protection." Rico patted his blaster. "And a force shield. They can't get us. And we can respond a lot faster out there." He glanced at Marika. "You got what you need?"

Marika hefted her backpack. "All here."

"Great. I'm off, then." He swung his legs around, so he sat on the front edge of the cart and picked up the tablet. "We'll be right outside the gate if you need us."

The train rose off the ground then moved forward at a walking pace.

"Where's the third one?" I asked Marika as we followed Katy across the plaza.

"The third platform?" Marika asked. "It's already outside. That one has the field generator and the tent pods."

"Why'd they bother bringing the other two inside?" I asked. As we walked down the dusty street, people stared curiously at us, nodding and waving to Katy.

Marika shrugged. "Show of force? I dunno. It's above my pay grade."

The buildings on the plaza were stone, but the smaller structures were made of long, smooth, brown cylinders stacked into walls. They overlapped at the corners, and metal roofs covered the buildings. It gave the town a uniform look, even though each building had its own unique design. Some had carvings in the walls, especially over the doors and windows. Glass was thick and greenish, wavy in some places. The doors appeared to be heavy wood.

I brushed my fingers against the wall as we entered one of the buildings. "Is this wood?" I stopped and stared at the wall, seeing it anew. "These are trees?"

"Yes," Katy said. "Cut from the forest outside the village. When they cleared the fields, they used the wood to build. These log houses have been here for several generations. Aren't they beautiful?"

"But why logs?" I caressed the smooth wood again. "Why not use extruders to create plastek buildings?"

"Well, for one thing, I have no idea what plastek is," Katy replied. "The village was built using what they had. We've continued to use logs as the village grows because we have to clear more land to feed more people. If we didn't need the farmland, we'd come up with a different way to do things, but so far…"

I gave myself a mental head-smack. These folks were trying to convince us they were native to Earth. Of course they'd use native materials and techniques. Or maybe they really were natives, and this was the way they'd done it for centuries. Both seemed equally impossible, so I decided to try to stop making judgements and just absorb as much information as I could.

The front door opened onto a large room furnished with more logs. Seating made of logs with thick cushions of brightly colored woven material lined two walls. A table covered in green cloth and smooth, brown fabric took up a good portion of the middle of the room. Brightly colored balls lay scattered across the table, and long, straight sticks stood in a rack nearby. Braided rugs covered part of the floor, and a couple of shelves held battered looking— "Are those books?" I asked, crossing to the shelf.

"Sure are," Katy replied. "Mostly reprints of classics from before the Desertion, but some of the stuff on the lower shelf is Dome-produced literature." She grimaced as she said it.

"May I?" I put out a hand but didn't touch. At Katy's nod, I carefully withdrew a volume. "We don't use paper books at all. I've only seen them in museums."

The front cover had a simple line drawing with the title in large block letters: Pride and Prejudice. "I've read this!" I said in surprise.

"It's a classic." Katy paused by the steps to watch me. "Good to know it's still being read in the colonies."

"I hated it," Marika admitted. "I mean, there's no action. No fight scenes, no chases, no dramatic standoffs. Just a bunch of people having tea and gossiping. Ugh."

I bit back a smile and slid the book onto the shelf. "You're more of a Yhudi Vehar fan," I suggested.

"Too old," Marika said. "I like DeVar."

"I haven't heard of him," Katy said. "Her?"

"They," Marika said. "They're from Armstrong."

"Ah," Katy said, starting up the steps. "Maybe you'll share one with me. I'd love to read something new."

"I thought DeVar was big on Gagarin," Marika said.

Katy paused on the stairs. Her shoulders straightened, and she looked back over her shoulder, her eyes narrow. "Could be. Never been there."

We climbed the steps to a long wood-paneled hall with closed doors on both sides. "We're set up with two to a room," Katy said, pointing out the amenities as we walked long. "The showers are here, toilets there. The last room on the right is guest quarters—that's where you'll be staying. There's a small sitting room across from you—if you prefer some quiet. The main room downstairs can get loud in the evenings."

She pushed open the door, revealing two single beds made of the ever-present logs. Each had a fluffy, white pillow and a brightly colored blanket with geometric patterns. A small chest of drawers stood at the foot of each bed, and a window let in sunlight. Lacy curtains fluttered before the open pane.

Marika dumped her bag on the chest on the right, leaving me the bed on the left. "This is beautiful," she said.

Katy smiled. "The men's dorm is below, beyond the sitting room. Meals are provided in the village hall on the plaza. Dinner's at six—you'll hear the bell. There's also a small kitchen downstairs, with a few snack items—in case you don't want to traipse all the way across town for breakfast. Most of the kids living here have jobs in town or work in the fields. There's also a courtyard in the back. They have parties there sometimes."

She pointed to the window. "You're facing away from the barricade—you should be safe enough if the Hellions try anything. We have guards posted at night."

"Do they attack often?" Marika asked as she opened her pack and started moving items into the drawers.

"They're kind of new." Katy leaned against the door jamb. "They've attacked the village three times in the last six months. Before that, nothing. Mara says they've always had the occasional bandit, but no organized gangs like this." Her lips tightened.

"Why the barricade?" Marika asked. "You didn't build that in the last six months. If there was no one attacking before that, why did you need it?"

"We've been building it for two years," she replied. "When we—people from the Dome—started moving outside, some were nervous. The town council decided to build the wall—both for protection and to train us newbies. None of us had done much woodworking." She chuckled. "When the Hellions launched their first attack six months ago, we finished it up in a hurry. Luckily, it was a mild winter, and we were able to get it up fast.

We must have hurt them pretty bad in that first attack—they didn't try again for several months, and by then, we were ready."

"But maybe we can flush them out with your father's help." She glanced at me.

I raised my eyebrows—I wasn't going to commit to anything. "What do you know about these Hellions?"

"Not much," she said. "There are people who don't want to live in a village. Some of them think they should be able to take whatever they want. We think someone is recruiting those people for their own cause. They've holed up in a cave complex not far from the Dome. They attack traders—stealing food and equipment."

We finished unpacking, and Katy led us back downstairs. "I need to get back to work. You girls can stay here until dinner or explore the village."

"I'd like to see the Dome," I said, watching her carefully.

"I'll get one of the boys to take you over," she said. She paused, then leaned a little closer. "The inhabitants of the Dome are a bit suspicious of outsiders. They know about you—or at least their leadership does. But don't be surprised if you get some weird looks."

Marika and I nodded, even though I wasn't sure what she meant. "Eric said he's from the Dome."

"Oh, a lot of us lived there," Katy said. "Zane and I met in the Dome, and the kids were born there. Eric, Pete, Jake—lots of the people you've already met lived there. But we aren't Dome people anymore."

"What about Tiah?" Marika asked.

"Tiah is a Dome person," Katy agreed. "I forgot she went to meet you. Most of them won't come outside."

We followed Katy out into the street and back toward the plaza. As we walked, I noticed more of the log buildings. Many of them were gray and weathered. They'd been here a long time. The stones of the plaza also looked old and thick. But the dorm had been newer—the logs a warm yellow-brown. Part of the recent expansion?

Liam poked his head out of my pocket. I'd forgotten he was there—after Jake and I played with him at the camp, he had a snack and passed out.

"What is that?" Katy asked.

I let Liam climb onto my hand and held him out. "This is Liam."

He leaped off my hand and flew at Katy. She jumped back with a squeak then flung up her arm. Liam landed on her wrist and scampered up to her shoulder.

"Liam!" I hurried to her side. "Sorry, I need to train him to behave better. He won't hurt you." I grabbed him around the middle and pulled him away from her shoulder.

"He's blue." She reached out to stroke his fur. "Where did you get this creature?"

I told her about sair-gliders and their usefulness to explorer teams. When she stopped petting, Liam jumped to her wrist again and climbed up to her shoulder.

"I don't think he'd make a very good guard animal," she said as he snuggled into her neck. "Unless he bites on command." She looked a bit worried, as if she hadn't thought about that danger until the words came out of her mouth.

"They don't," Marika said. "They aren't usually as friendly as this one, though. Most of them are much more territorial. Must be her unusual upbringing."

"What do you mean?" Katy coaxed Liam onto her palm so she could get a good look at him.

"I found him on the ship," I said. "He doesn't seem to miss whoever used to care for him, which is unusual. Supposedly, they're one-person animals. Even weirder—whoever lost him hasn't come forward to claim him."

"Might be one of the ship's crew," Marika suggested. "They aren't supposed to have pets onboard."

"They have cats," I said.

"Those are working animals." Marika shook her head. "And they belong to the ship, not individuals. The CEC allows gliders. They've gotten the team out of hot water more than once."

"That sounds like a story I want to hear." Katy held Liam out to me. "But right now, I have some animals of my own to take care of." At my raised eyebrows, she continued, "I'm the village veterinarian. But here are Peter and Eric. Boys, can you take these ladies over to the Dome?"

"I was going to help with the recon," Peter said.

Katy shook her head. "Zane is taking Tim and his group."

Peter looked away.

"We're allowed to show them the Dome?" Eric asked.

"O'Doul said they don't mind," Katy said. "Show them where we used to live—maybe they'll believe us."

"Can do," Eric said.

"Great. See you all at dinner." She hurried away.

"Where's Joss?" Marika asked as we followed the boys across the plaza and onto the wide main road.

"He's got guard duty tonight," Eric said. "He's having an early supper."

"But you all just got back to camp." I tucked Liam into my pocket again. "Doesn't he get a break?"

"He wanted to do it." Peter rolled his eyes. "He likes guarding stuff."

Eric laughed. "He likes flirting with girls who admire the guards."

Marika smirked. "I'm sure the girls enjoy flirting with him, too. Aren't there any girl guards?"

"Yeah, but most of them are too smart to fall for his crap," Peter muttered. I'm not sure Marika heard his response, but Eric snorted.

As we strolled up to the wide-open gates, Joss popped out of a building built into the barricade. He must have been changing—he held his shirt in one hand, and the late afternoon sunlight glinted on his muscled shoulders. "Marika! You wanna stand guard with me?" He wiggled his eyebrows suggestively.

"Is that what you call it here?" Marika asked, her voice sultry. "Standing guard?"

Joss's teeth gleamed in his dark face. "No, but I like it. I'm going to use that. I just thought you might hang out for a while. So we could…talk."

Marika fluttered her eyelashes and triggered her comm device. "I'm going to see what I can learn from this tasty hunk," she said on the comm channel. "You go with the pale boys and see what they're up to." She gave Joss a sultry smile. "I'd love to hang out."

I fumbled with my own comm and glared at her when I couldn't activate it.

"Have fun at the Dome, Siti," Marika called over her shoulder as she pulled Joss away. "See you later."

"Fine," I muttered under my breath. I took a deep breath and smiled at my escorts. Linking one arm through each of theirs, I pulled them toward the gate. "Let's go see this Dome."

CHAPTER TWENTY-TWO

We walked down the wide road leading away from the front gates. The stone turned to dirt a few meters from the walls, and we entered the thick woods. The tall trees blocked the sunlight, making the road difficult to see. Peter set a quick pace. I thought about using my grav-belt, but that wouldn't be fair to the boys.

"You aren't worried about those Hellions attacking us?" I asked.

"They've never attacked by daylight," Eric said.

"Until today," Peter and I answered together.

"Good point." Eric patted the bulky weapon hanging from his shoulder. "That's why I have my little friend."

"I know that quote!" I said in delight. "You watch *Ancient TeVe*?"

"It's from an old movie." Peter glanced at me. "What's *Ancient TeVe*?"

"Vids from old Earth." I gave them a knowing smile. "I guess, for you guys, it isn't ancient, right?"

"Depends on what vids you mean," Peter said.

I rattled off a list of the shows I'd watched with Dad. The boys recognized most of them.

"Planet Defenders doesn't ring any bells," Eric said.

I thought about the show. "You might be right—that one is from

Armstrong, right after the Exodus." These guys knew their stuff. Time to try another subject. "What was the deal with Levi?" I asked.

Eric glanced away, his lips tight. When he didn't reply, I turned to Pete. "Can you tell me?"

Peter cleared his throat. "We're not supposed to talk about it. Not our story to tell."

"Okay," I said. Maybe he was just a crazy old man. They wouldn't want to advertise that. "Tell me about the Dome instead. What's the story there?"

"I thought I told you?" Eric said. "We went in there when we were kids—we were, what, fourteen?"

"I was fifteen," Peter said. "You were fourteen. Then we went into suspended animation. Eric came upstairs five years ago; Jake and I were two years later."

"He used to be older than you, and now he's younger?" I asked Eric.

Eric grinned. "Awesome, right?"

Peter rolled his eyes. "He never lets me forget it. Anyway, Zane and Katy were younger than you when we first met them. But they didn't go downstairs—into suspended animation—right away. Then they were awake again in the middle—maybe a hundred years ago? That's when Zina and Joss were born. When we finally came upstairs, they were older."

"Much older," Eric said. "Pete's mom did the same thing. A lot of the scientists did five-year stints, just to keep things running. Some of them did more." He glanced at Peter.

The other boy's eyes narrowed. "Yeah, some did more." They weren't telling me something.

"That's what they do on the Corps ships," I said. "Lt Wronglen? She was about our age when we left Grissom. She had to work a couple of five-year shifts, and now she's old. The explorers sleep all the way—so we're fresh and ready to do our jobs when we get here."

"I think they got the idea from the Exodus ships," Peter said. "Anyway, not too long after I woke up, we found out it was safe to come outside. Everest and the rest of them were already here."

"Is everyone who lived in the Dome in the village now?" I asked.

"Heck, no," Eric said. "There were ten thousand people in the basement—"

"Ten thousand?!" I repeated in shock.

"Give or take a few hundred," Eric said.

"Ten thousand people slept for five hundred years." I stared from one boy to the other. "That's...unprecedented."

Eric's brows lowered. "Not like we had a choice. We got left behind."

"With no food supply, no air filters, nothing." Peter glared.

I gulped. The Exodus was ancient history for me, but if they were to be believed, it was a recent tragedy for them. "I'm sorry. I didn't know. No one who's alive now knows."

"Do you believe us now?" Peter asked.

"I think I do." I wasn't sure my dad would buy it, but I was starting to believe.

The dirt road transitioned to stone again. Light shone through the opening a few meters ahead, glowing like the exit of a tunnel. We stepped out of the gloom onto a wide cleared stretch. It arched around another high barricade, matching the wall at the village.

Tall gates stood open, revealing a semi-circle of white. It wasn't stone, but it wasn't plascrete, either. Probably some ancient material, based on the crumbled edges and multiple patches. The straight side of the semi-circle butted up against the low building we'd seen from the air. The ramp extended downward, tunneling into the building. About half-way down, a light shone on an open gate. Another one at the bottom revealed a second opening.

"Here's the Dome," Peter said. "Come on inside."

We shuffled down the ramp, through the gate, and stopped at the opening. This one looked like an airlock, with the hatch removed. We stepped inside. The hatch at the other end and a regular door on the side stood open. Eric poked his head through the side doorway. "Hey Simon. Is Tiah around? We've got a visitor."

"She's working," a voice replied. "But she'll be off soon. I'll message her to meet you in the canteen."

Peter gestured toward the open hatch. "After you."

I stepped through, my feet clanging on the open metal grid floor. A shaft lay below us with stairs winding around a central opening. "That's a long way down."

Peter pointed at my belt. "You gonna take the easy route?"

"If you can walk it, so can I." I narrowed my eyes at him, then started down at a brisk pace. My legs started aching after the fourth switchback. "How deep is this thing?"

The boys looked at each other and shrugged.

"You don't know?" Eric stared at Peter. "I thought you knew everything about the Dome."

"I prefer not to remember this part," Peter's lips pressed together. "But there are five living and working levels and a bunch more below."

"Try not to remember what?" I asked.

Eric shook his head. "Old story. Our return to the surface was a bit…dramatic."

I smiled conspiratorially, but both boys ignored me. We reached another door, but this one was closed.

"The temps don't trust the outside air," Eric said.

"The guy upstairs seemed fine with it," I said.

"Security is mostly younger folks." Peter opened the door. "They're more flexible."

"They still won't go outside." Eric snorted. "Come on."

We stepped into a dingy hallway. Threadbare carpet covered the floors, and flimsy-looking doors stood at regular intervals in scuffed wall. At the far end, another door opened into a hallway. "People lived here for five hundred years?" I stared at the dismal corridors in disbelief.

"This was originally office space," Peter said. "Storage now. The living spaces are better. But yeah. The temps…I guess they didn't know anything better."

"Doesn't explain why they stay," Eric muttered.

We clattered down a couple more stairways and through some heavy doors. A rush of warm, fragrant air hit me. A beautiful meadow covered with short green grass stretched away to a small pond. A creek meandered between rocky banks, under a bridge and into a tunnel. Vines climbed up columns, with huge flowers and wide leaves hanging from them. Warm light shone down, birds sang, and children played on the grass. Clouds of exotically colored butterflies fluttered by.

"But we're underground," I whispered.

Peter grinned. "This is the park. Center of the Dome." He stepped onto the grass and turned to point over my head. "There are apartments on three levels. When we first arrived, we lived up there." He nodded to the tunnel. "Manufacturing and agriculture are through there. We can check them out later. It's almost shift-change. The canteen is over there."

He led us along the walkway circling the park to a large, cheery room. Small tables sat in orderly rows with four chairs to each table. A smattering of people wearing boxy shirts and baggy pants in faded colors occupied a few of the chairs. Some nodded or waved to the boys as we entered.

"Let's wait for Tiah here," Peter said, taking a seat.

"These people are all—they all look like her," I muttered.

"Five centuries with a limited gene pool will do that," Eric said.

"Like you know anything about genes." Peter smirked.

"I'm a parrot," Eric replied. "I just repeat what I've been told. Professor O'Doul said it often enough. I wonder if he's around?"

"Where would he go?" Peter asked.

"Outside?" I suggested.

Eric laughed. "The temps don't go outside."

"Except Tiah." Peter glared at Eric.

The redhead nodded. "She's different. Always was."

"You know why that is," Peter said. He turned to me. "Tiah has a—one of her legs is shorter than the other. The temps don't like anyone who's different."

"We think they just," Eric paused to draw a finger across his throat, "got rid of anyone who wasn't normal."

"You mean they killed people?" My chest tightened.

Peter held up a hand. "That's just speculation. And it's ancient history. But Tiah was treated badly as a kid because she was different. That's why she connected with Jake. Because of his autism."

"What's that?" I asked.

"Autism? It's why he's different," Peter said. "He doesn't talk much. He gets kind of stuck on topics sometimes. He doesn't always remember things we think should be easy, but he'll remember details no one else does."

"It's a lot better than when he was little." Eric nodded.

"Or we understand him better than we did then," Peter said. "Lena—I don't know if you've met her. She and Jake do almost everything together. She helped him learn to communicate better."

"I just thought he was kinda quiet." I thought back to our visit to the camp—he didn't do or say anything unusual.

"Exactly," Eric said. "But when he was little, he'd have tantrums."

"Everyone does when they're little," I said uncertainly. I hadn't spent much time with children.

"Yeah, but—" Eric started.

Peter cut him off. "Doesn't matter. He's good. But temps and ancients didn't mix much when we all lived here. And since we moved out, none of them have wanted to come outside." His head waggled side-to-side. "A few went outside, right at the beginning, but most of them won't. They think it's dangerous out there."

"To be fair, it is," Eric said. "Hellions, wild animals, invaders from other planets." He winked at me.

"We aren't invaders!" I said.

"Kidding!" Eric smiled, but the smile didn't quite reach his eyes.

More people had wandered into the canteen. They all had the same tan skin and dark hair, with thick eyebrows and a hooked nose—some more than slightly. As we talked, they lined up near the back of the room. A chime rang out six times. On the last stroke, the rear doors of the room opened, revealing a food line. Servers in white uniforms and hats started dishing out food for the people in line.

"Hi, guys." Tiah appeared by our table and gestured to the line. "Do you want to eat? I have guest passes."

"I'm starving." Eric jumped to his feet.

"You're always starving." Peter smiled at the girl. "Thanks. They said you were already back at work."

"I wasn't really working. I went to manufacturing to talk to them about the rovers. That guy—Rico?" She raised her eyebrows at me, and I nodded. "He had some fantastic ideas for upgrades." She showed us where to collect trays, and we went through the line.

"This smells great," I said, although the food wasn't nearly as pretty as Ahuja's creations.

"This is all grown inside," Tiah said with pride. "We get most of the meat from the village. Beef require a lot of grazing. But the produce is grown here."

We didn't talk much while we ate. Peter occasionally greeted people who entered, but neither Tiah nor Eric did. Not a very friendly bunch.

"What happened with Seraphina?" Tiah asked as we returned our trays to the kitchen. "Did they find her?"

"She's okay," Peter said. "She wasn't captured. She followed the Hellions to their cave but couldn't get inside, as usual. She's working with the—" he glanced at me "—the commander on a plan to take them down. They're doing recon tonight."

"When did you hear that?" I asked. Dad hadn't mentioned a mission tonight. In fact, I'd gotten the idea the whole plan was in the early stages.

Peter said, "Jake told me. On the way over here."

"How did Jake tell you that?" My eyes narrowed. "You *do* have integrated comm! I can't believe I almost believed you about growing up here!" How could I have been so gullible? "I'm going back." I shoved back my chair and stormed out of the room.

"Siti." Peter caught up to me and grabbed my arm, pulling me to a stop. "Look around. Gagarin didn't build this Dome. It's been here five hundred years, just like we said. And we lived here."

I swung around to glare at him. "Then how did you talk to Jake?"

Peter looked away.

"You can't explain it, can you?" I flung out my hand. "This stuff is old—I'll give you that. But that doesn't mean people have been here all along. You just got here before we did, cleaned the place up, and moved people in."

"No," Tiah said. "I was born here. In this Dome. So were most of these people." She pointed at the groups staring at us from the canteen. "Why do you think we look so much alike?"

"I didn't talk to Jake—he talked to me." Peter turned to meet my eyes. "Jake is telepathic."

CHAPTER TWENTY-THREE

"That is the stupidest thing I have ever heard." I stomped my foot. "How dumb to you think I am?"

"No, really." Peter looked pleadingly at me. "We don't know how it works, but most of the outsiders developed some kind of mental connection. For some reason, Jake has it too—maybe it's tied to his autism. No one else seems to have gotten it."

Eric shook his head sadly. "I got nothin'."

"Right." I crossed my arms over my chest. "Not only did you deep sleep for five centuries, but you're also psychic."

"Not me," Peter said. "Jake can talk to me. If he's close, and I really focus, I can reply. Sometimes. But I think it's more about him reading my answers than me sending anything. Some of the villagers can transmit to me if they're close. Everest, for example. But most ancients can't hear unless they're touching us. Jake and I have a weird connection. Strong. Maybe because we're brothers."

"Isn't that special." I pulled my arm away and continued toward the stairs.

"When we get outside, I'll prove it to you," Peter said.

"How are you going to do that?" I swung around. "I can talk to Marika or Dad or anyone else on the team and claim it's a psychic connection. But it isn't. It's tech." I tapped my head behind my ear. "Audio implant." I flicked my holo-ring, but without a booster nearby, it didn't respond. And this deep in the ground, even a booster might not work. "Okay, maybe not in here. I can't connect."

"I can't hear Jake in here, either." Pete's eyebrows went down. "Too much dirt and rock, maybe."

"Didn't Mara say only Lena could hear anyone inside?" Eric asked. "And she only heard Jake." He looked at me. "Lena's crazy powerful, but she talks less than Jake. The whole thing is weird."

"And you say all of the villagers have it?" My eyes widened. "Is that what happened to Levi? Those weird brain waves were your psychic abilities, and our med pod 'fixed' them?"

The boys exchanged a look, but neither said anything.

"If your med pod can turn off that ability, it should be able to turn it on, right?" Tiah's eyes lit up.

"Maybe," I said slowly. "Seems reasonable. I'll have to ask Chasin when we get back to camp."

"No," Eric said. "They don't want your people to know about this. You can't tell anyone."

I tapped the CEC logo on my uniform jacket. "You know who I work for, right?"

"Please, Siti." Peter touched my arm. A warm spark frizzled up it. "Don't tell them. I know you have to report, but can that part be off the record? At least for now?"

"It's not like they'd believe me anyway," I muttered. Although, with Chasin's record of the unidentified brain waves, they might. I took a deep breath. "I won't mention it for now. It's just hearsay anyway."

"Great." Peter turned away. "Let's finish our tour."

They took me across the park and through the tunnel. It opened out into a cavernous room. Vast fields of grain and other plants filled the room. I stared. "We're still underground?"

"Yup," Eric said. "Look at the lights."

Banks of yellowish lights filled the ceiling high above us. I waved my hand. The lights cast hundreds of weird shadows on the path. "And those are bright enough to grow plants?"

"Obviously." Tiah gestured to the fields.

"They were brighter when we first arrived," Peter said. "And more concentrated. But over the years..."

I grunted but didn't answer. I wasn't sure what to believe at this point, so I'd just listen—and record—everything. I wished I'd gotten that weird psychic conversation on vid. Then I wouldn't have to break their trust directly. *You work for the CEC, Siti. They shouldn't trust you.*

Except I didn't. I wasn't an explorer. I wasn't even sure I wanted to be one. I was just along for the ride as the commander's daughter. The team never let me forget that. Even Dad—he might have asked me to do some snooping, but he didn't trust me.

Of course, I'd given him plenty of reasons not to trust me. Maybe it was time to straighten up and prove I could be as reliable as any other explorer.

I tried activating my comm again, but it was still dead. Now that I thought about it, Marika had said something about comm links when outside of camp. In case the booster—which they hadn't issued me—wasn't connecting. But they hadn't issued me a comm link, either. Probably because they expected me to stay with Marika all the time. Not my fault my babysitter had a soft spot for hunky boys.

Eric showed me the farm, where smaller animals lived. "We used to have a few cattle and a *lot* of goats, but most of them moved to the village. They do better with more space. The bunnies and chickens are fine here, though."

Tiah nodded. "We trade tech for meat. Each part of the community concentrates on what they do best."

"Sounds kind of socialist," I said.

"You must not have studied history," Tiah said. "Socialism means everything is owned by the government. Everything here is owned by us."

"But who is the government?" I asked.

Eric groaned loudly. "If I wanted to talk about politics, I'd visit Professor Rinette."

Peter held up both hands in surrender. "No, please! Let's go to manufacturing."

Tiah showed us the workshop where they built the rovers.

"This is really old tech," I said. "Maybe you can trade with us for newer stuff. What do you have that we might want?"

"I've been trying to think of something we could trade," Tiah admitted. "But you're so far advanced…"

"We can trade them access to Earth," Peter said. "Maybe we'll let you stay if you give us good tech."

"I think that's exactly what my dad is trying to avoid," I said. "Oh, crap. I shouldn't have said that."

"Now we both have secrets we shouldn't know," Eric said. "You keep ours; we'll keep yours."

"Wait, are you saying that's why he's so convinced on this Gagarin thing?" Peter asked. "If we're from here, he has to negotiate with us over the planet. If we're from Gagarin, he has an equal claim?"

"Yes and no," I said. "Planetary politics aren't that straight-forward. Whoever reaches a planet first can lay claim. But Earth is different because we came from here."

"And if we never left, that throws everything out of whack." Peter nodded. "That makes sense. Hey, we should head back."

"So you can share the secret you promised not to tell?" I grabbed his arm.

"First, I didn't promise." Peter pulled his arm free. "Second, it's getting late, and we need to get home in case the Hellions decide to come scouting again."

"Right," Eric said. "We might be better off to stay here tonight."

"I need to report in," I protested.

"So you can share the secret you promised not to tell?" Peter threw my words back at me.

"Because they expect me to report in," I said. "But I said I wouldn't mention it." For now.

"Well, let's get a move on, then," Eric said.

When we reached the entrance stairs, Tiah stopped. "I'll come see you tomorrow," she said.

"Really?" Peter looked surprised. "You'll come outside again?"

"It's nice out there." Tiah looked equally surprised. "I might try to bring some others with me, if you don't mind."

Eric's mouth dropped open. "Temps who want to go outside?"

She laughed. "You all are still alive after three years, so it's looking like a safer bet. And I want to expand our trade to other villages."

The boys stared at her.

"What? I can't have ambitions? I've studied commerce. Multiple revenue streams is the way to go." She crossed her arms over her chest.

"You silenced Eric. Nice job." I held out my fist, and she bumped it with a grin.

"Only for a minute!" Eric cried.

"We'd better go." Peter nodded at the clock in the park. "It's getting late."

"See you tomorrow, Tiah!" I followed Peter and Eric up the steps.

CHAPTER TWENTY-FOUR

My implant pinged as we approached the village. Message from the commander. "Report ASAP."

"Oops." I grimaced at the boys. "My dad doesn't sound happy. I'm going to stop by the camp before I come inside."

Peter stopped, but Eric continued toward the gate.

"You're staying in the dorm?" Peter asked. "Do you want us to wait for you?"

"I think I can find it." I gestured at the huge gate standing open a few meters from the camp.

"We'll tell Joss and Felice to let you inside." Peter turned and backed toward the town. "They're closing the gates in a few minutes."

"How do you know?" I asked, trying to keep the conversation going. I didn't really want to talk to my dad. "Did Jake tell you?"

"They close it at sunset." Peter pointed over my shoulder. I turned to see the red and pink streaks across the sky. "That's soon."

I breathed in. The sunset was spectacular. "We don't get colors like that on Grissom."

"No pretty sunsets?" he asked. His voice was soft, and he'd moved closer, standing behind me.

"Oh, they're pretty enough, but not as bright." I tried to remember my science classes, but nothing came to mind. "Something to do with the atmosphere, I think. Our colors skew more bluish."

Peter sighed. "I'd like to see a sunset on another planet. I was supposed to go to Sally Ride. Have you been there?"

"Yeah." The air had grown chilly, and I crossed my arms across my chest. "It's crazy. One massive city. Amazing—don't get me wrong. But completely different from this."

"When we came to the Dome, I figured I'd be stuck on Earth forever," he said softly, almost as if talking to himself. "But now that you're here...I wonder if I could join your explorer team?"

"You'd have to go to basic training on Grissom," I said. "Or the academy, if you want to be an officer. I'm going next year. Well, I might." Why had I said that? Just because Dad wanted me to go to the academy didn't mean I was going to do it.

"Next year?" He sounded surprised. "How are you going next year? Won't it take twenty years to get back?"

"No, we have jump capability." I turned to look up at him. "It took twenty years to get here because there weren't any beacons. Once the *Glory* gets those in place, ships can jump here. We'll be able to get to Grissom in a few days."

"Seriously?" His eyes widened so far I could see white all the way around the brown pupils. If he was faking, it was a masterpiece of acting. "Days? That's...wow."

"Siti!" My father's voice echoed across the clearing. "Report!" He stood just outside the force shield protecting the small camp. It nestled against the town wall, just as our main camp hugged the cliff face. His foot tapped the stone-paved road as he glowered.

"I gotta go." I held out my fist. "Thanks for the tour."

He bumped mine. "I'll wait for you inside. Show you to the dorm."

I backed away. "I don't know how long this will take."

"It's okay. I'll wait." He waved and turned away.

I hurried across the wide road to my father.

"What did he want?" he barked before I could open my mouth.

"He took me to see the Dome," I said.

"Why didn't you report on schedule?" He waved at Rico, standing guard, and a gate opened in the force shield. We marched inside.

"I didn't have a comm link, and we were outside the booster's reach." A message from Marika pinged. I ignored it.

"Where's Marika?"

"She stayed here to talk to Joss." I shrugged. "We decided to divide and conquer."

"She's supposed to keep you out of trouble. And if you go out of booster reach, you're supposed to take a comm link. Didn't she tell you that?"

"I, uh—"

"Never mind. I'll talk to her later." He led me to a table and chairs near the wooden wall. "Sit. Tell me what you learned."

I told him about the Dome—how old it was and how everyone inside looked alike. "I really think they might be telling the truth," I said. "Their manufacturing is primitive."

He shook his head. "We knew that facility existed. It wasn't a secret. It's why we landed here, and it's why the Gagarians built their village here. So they could access the data inside the facility. They've moved people inside to convince us they never left. They can play their little game, but eventually, we'll find proof. We just need to keep looking."

His eyes unfocused, and a moment later, Flynn appeared with a flat, palm-sized rectangle. Dad took it and nodded his thanks. "This is a comm link." He flipped open a pocket on my jacket sleeve. "Goes in here. It will boost your comm signal so you can report in. If you leave the village, keep it on you."

"Oh, that reminds me. I have vid!" I swiped my holo-ring and pulled up the files. "From inside their Dome. It's pretty amazing." I flicked the file and swiped it to him.

"I'll review it later." He stood. "For now, let's get back inside. They close the gates at night."

"Peter said Joss would let us in." I jumped to my feet and followed him across the camp. "We could always go over, if we had to." I tapped my grav-belt.

"Don't." He held out a hand as if to stop me. "We don't need to remind them of our capabilities. As long as they think their wall will keep us out, they'll feel more secure and might let something slip."

He nodded at Flynn, and the force shield opened.

"If they're Gagarians, they won't forget," I said. "They have the same tech. You can't have it both ways, Dad."

His lips pressed together. "You're right. Their charade is so well-done it's making me complacent. They aren't primitive indigenous people; they're crafty Gagarian agents. Still, it doesn't hurt to downplay our capabilities."

We stopped before the double-high gates, shut tight against the night. Above, a couple of heads peered over the top of the wall, and someone shouted. A person-sized door opened to let us through.

Dad nodded. "They've really gone all-out to imitate the ancient methods. Look at the woodwork. And a smaller, more defensible opening for night-time access. It's cleverly done."

"You still don't believe us?" Joss slipped out of a narrow stairwell to stand beside us. Behind him, Marika lurked in the dark, as if to avoid Dad's notice.

"It's very convincing," Dad said. "Siti, have a good night. I'll see you tomorrow."

I nodded and took a step away. I knew when I'd been dismissed.

"Marika, report."

I bit my lip to hide a grin. Marika's eyes narrowed, but she stepped around Joss and joined the commander. "Here or in your quarters, sir?"

"We'll walk." He pivoted sharply and strode toward the town square.

"You need an escort to the dorm?" Joss asked with a wink.

"I thought Peter was waiting for me."

"He was, but his mom needed him," Joss said. "He said he'd try to come back…"

"It's fine." Joss was cute but seemed like too much effort somehow. "I know where I'm going, and your Hellions can't get inside, right? Besides, don't you need to be up there?" I pointed to the top of the wall.

"It's early. Felice can cover for me." He turned and raised his voice. "Can't ya' Felice?"

""Leave the girl alone," a female voice called down. "She said she can get home on her own."

I grinned. "Thanks, Felice!"

She leaned over the hip-high railing along the top of the wall and raised her fist. "Solidarity, sista!"

Joss rolled his eyes. "I know when I'm not wanted." His wink belied the aggrieved tone, and he disappeared up the narrow stairway.

CHAPTER TWENTY-FIVE

I crossed the plaza. In the dusk, the uneven stone paving made walking more difficult. I thought about using my grav-belt. I could hover just above the stonework… but Dad had specifically forbidden it. I might be inclined to ignore the rules from time to time, but I knew better than to flout Dad outright.

I entered the narrower street that led to the dorm. Faint music filtered to me, and soft lights glowed in some of the windows. A few people strolled along the street. They all nodded or waved to me, but none of them spoke.

Outside the dorm, lights flickered on the side of the building. I looked closer. Actual flames burned inside thick glass jars attached to the wall.

"Oil lamps," Peter said, startling me.

"I thought you went home?" I glanced over my shoulder to meet his eyes.

"I went to see Mom, but I live here." He pulled open the front door. "There's probably a party going out back, if you want to join." He crossed the dark living room toward an open door. Light streamed out, creating a bright path on the floor.

"Who lives here? Besides you, I mean. Not that you're, not—" I broke off, my face heating.

Peter stopped in the doorway and glanced back, his lips quirking up. "All the younger people." He rattled off a long list including Eric, Everest, and the twins.

"Not Jake?" I asked.

"He's only thirteen," Peter said. "He'll move in a couple of years. If he wants. He might stay with Mom. If she's still…" He cleared his throat and crossed the small kitchen in three steps. "Door to the courtyard is here."

When he pulled the door open, the music I'd heard earlier swelled. A long, narrow paved area—about ten meters wide—stood between the building and the inside of the town wall. An open flight of steps led up to the platform that ran along the inside of the barricade. Seraphina sat on the bottom step, plucking the strings of a large curved instrument. A man sat farther up the steps with a different instrument tucked under his chin as he dragged a stick across strings. A girl I hadn't met sang in a strange language.

"What's she singing?" I asked.

"It's called *Fill-iù Oro Hù Ò*," Peter said. "I think it's originally from Ireland, but it's changed over the centuries."

"My translator doesn't recognize the words." I flipped my holo-ring and pulled up diagnostics. "It says 'unknown—more input required'."

"Does that thing work on a stored database or does it translate on the fly?" Peter asked.

My eyes narrowed. "How do you know about databases?"

"I grew up in the twenty-second century, not middle earth." He laughed. "We had computers."

Like Dad had said, the pre-industrial appearance of the town had lulled me into thinking their tech was from the same period. It made sense, given their story. But it also made the Gagarian theory plausible. I wished I knew what to believe.

"Attack!" A shout went up along the top of the wall, cutting through the music.

As one, the partygoers dropped their glasses and instruments, streaming toward the building. I jumped back into the kitchen, hoping to avoid a stampede.

"Stay inside," Peter said, pushing me farther into the building. "We'll be back." He hurried away.

Around me, people moved quickly but without panic. A rush of people poured into the building. Within minutes, the first of them returned, trickling back into the courtyard. I followed Seraphina out of the building.

At the bottom of the stairs, she turned. "Stay there!" She thrust a hand toward the dorm. "You'd be in the way on the wall." With another hard glare, she ran up the steps two at a time.

I stood in the courtyard, feeling useless. A constant flow of villagers hurried up the steps beside me, all of them bristling with guns, bows, even spears. Eric slung his enormous weapon over his shoulder and grinned as he loped up the steps.

"Siti, stay inside." Peter reappeared beside me. "Please. If you get hurt, your father will blame us. We don't need that."

"I—fine." I looked up at the wall. Heavy footsteps echoed on the wooden planks as they ran along the platform near the top. "Where are they going?"

His eyes darted upward. "They're attacking along the rear entrance, near the fields. I gotta go. Stay inside."

He raced up the steps and away.

The empty courtyard seemed to mock me. "I'm not trained to fight," I whispered, but it just smirked. Fine. I'd go inside as I'd been ordered.

"Siti, where are you?" Dad said through the comm.

"I'm at the dorm. Don't worry, I'm going inside."

"No, don't." The comm went silent for a second, then his voice came back. "Use your grav-belt. Get up high enough to see what's going on and record."

"Won't Thor and Aella do that?" I slapped my forehead. Why'd I give him a reason to send me inside to safety? I flipped on my grav-belt, and my feet lifted off the ground.

"I need as many internal sources as possible," he said. "Most of our people are too far away or busy. Get up there. But stay out of range of the attack. Out." The comm went dead.

I increased altitude and slid silently up the side of the building. Once above the barricade, I could see the cleared space around the village and the thick forest a few hundred meters away. Below, in the streets, more people surged toward the far side of the village.

I flipped on my recording device and engaged low light mode. My field of vision shifted to gray scale. Bright light flared over the tops of the buildings. I swiped my acceleration tab, and my grav-belt pushed me toward the light. The sounds of shouting and a crackle of flames reached my ears. I flew faster.

Gong!

I gasped as pain slammed into my toes and shins. I'd hit the edge of a metal roof. Below, heads snapped upward, and I dropped close to the building, curling into a fetal position.

No one shouted, but I waited for a few more seconds to be sure I hadn't been spotted. Then I straightened and rose a few meters higher. I drifted over the buildings, silently gaining on the people running below. When I reached the last rank of buildings, I dropped into the shadow of a chimney, leaving my belt on neutral.

I stood on the roof of the grain mill. A huge wheel turned idly in the stream flowing under the wall a few meters away. A man with a bow stood beside the stream, focused on the water. Before me, a small square lay between the end of the street and the closed gates. A dozen villagers stood on the meter-wide platform running along the inside of the wall. The outer barricade came up to chest height, providing good cover for the defenders.

Beyond the wall, a small building burned, smoke belching from holes in the roof. Grain lay trampled in the fields, and a troop of dark figures fired flaming arrows at the wall.

The villagers picked off the attackers with their projectile weapons. Shouts of pain echoed across the ravaged field as one after another fell. Some of the attackers dragged their comrades to safety, but most of them left the crumpled forms on the field.

A rover barreled down the dirt road between the fields. It skidded to a halt, spinning half-way around before stopping. The attackers converged on the vehicle, leaping onto the stripped-down machine. The wheels spun, dust billowing up, and it trundled away, the last of the attackers jogging in its wake.

"That's it!" a voice called out. "Get the fire brigade out to mop up."

As I debated whether to stay put or drop down and help, another rover rumbled over the rough cobblestones below. This one had reels of hose on its sides and a tank in the back. A team of the defenders gathered around the fire cart and another took up defensive positions as the gates slowly opened.

"Clear!" someone shouted. The firefighters and their escort jogged toward the burning building. A figure riding on top started squirting water high into the air. The water crashed down onto the burning structure, sizzling and hissing.

Something glimmered to the north. I swung around, looking over the rooftops toward the dorm. A glint of light caught an arrow as it flew, slamming into the guard standing near the steps to the dorm. Without a sound, the body toppled back off the platform.

I screamed, "Attack! From the north!"

Confused voices shouted directions. People flailed around the plaza, as if trying to locate the threat. I flicked my grav-belt and dropped like a stone.

They scattered as I fell among them. I misjudged my drop and crashed into a woman. "Sorry! Don't shoot!" I flung up my hands as dozens of weapons swung at me. "It's me, Siti! Someone shot the guard!"

"Down on your knees, invader!" a voice snarled.

Fear washed over me in an overwhelming, cold wave. I dropped to my knees, slamming them into the rough stones. "Don't shoot me!" I whimpered.

"That's Siti!" Peter's voice cut through the angry yells. "She's not a Hellion! Stand down!"

The fear left me as quickly as it hit, leaving a sick emptiness in my stomach. I lifted my head. "They're attacking again," I whispered. "They shot the guard by the dorm."

"Tanis, do you hear me?" Zane's voice cut through the muttering. I lifted my head to see him talking into a small rectangular device. "Tanis!" He looked up, making eye contact with me. "No response. Eric take a team to the north wall, now!" He tapped the device and spoke again. "Renault, report!"

Peter pulled me to my feet, his hands clamped around my upper arm. "Come on, show me where you saw the attack!" He grabbed my hand and dragged me away from the plaza.

"I was up there!" I stumbled behind him, pointing upward. "When the fire truck went outside, someone shot the guard. She fell off the wall."

"Over the wall, or inside?" Peter darted down a narrow path between two buildings.

"Inside," I gasped. "Hang on, we can get there faster." I pulled my hand from his and flicked my grav-belt settings. "Come here, put your arms around me."

"What?" He gaped at me.

"Oh for—" I threw an arm around his waist and pulled him close, hitting the lift button on my belt. We lurched upward, his weight dragging my arm down painfully. "Hang on! Put your feet on mine. I can't hold you by myself!"

His arms clamped around my shoulders, and we rose above the houses. "There!" I flicked the controls, and we crossed diagonally above the nearest building. I angled us toward the wall, picking up speed as I grew more confident in my ability to not get us killed. We bounced from roof to roof, our feet scraping across the tops of several buildings.

"Look out below!" Peter yelled as his dangling boot knocked a clay shingle off the building below us. "Maybe we should go a little higher."

"You aren't strapped in. If I drop you, I want you to have a chance at survival."

He gasped as we drove directly toward a tall structure.

"Plus, we're almost there." I swerved around the end of the dorm. Peter's weapon swung on his shoulder, toppling a flowerpot from the balcony railing.

"Good thing we're ahead of everyone else," he muttered.

We lurched over the fence behind the dorm and dropped into the courtyard, shaking the petals from the flowering vines. While I shut down the belt, Peter scrambled across the space to the crumpled form laying in the shadows of the wall. He pressed his hand against her neck. "She's alive!"

"I have a med-kit." I stumbled to him. "In my room."

Peter glanced up at the wall. "No time. I've called for help. We need to hold them off!" He lunged to his feet and bolted to the stairs. "Come on! I need you!"

I glanced at Tanis, laying still and silent on the stone, then up at Peter.

He stopped on the steps. "If we don't hold them off, we'll all be dead. Please, I've called Mara. Come help me."

I yanked the emergency blanket out of my belt pouch and spread the thin fabric over Tanis's body. Then I scrambled up the steps behind Peter.

At the top of the wall, I chanced a glance over. Three long rope ladders hung down the side, their tops secured with a modified grappling hook. Three or four ragged men climbed each ladder. "They're almost up!"

"Stop right there, or I will shoot you!" Peter called. "At this distance, I can't miss."

"Hah! Is that little Pee-pee Russell?" The owner of the raspy voice laughed from his perch atop the nearest ladder. "You won't shoot! Pee-pee is too scared to shoot us!"

In my monochromatic night-vision, Pete's face went ghostly white. "Juan?" he asked in disbelief. "That can't be you."

The thin, straggly man climbed another rung. "It can be and is." He laughed, breaking into a hacking cough. "A vision from the past, eh, Pee-pee?" His hand grasped the top rung of the ladder.

Beyond him, the men on the other ladders continued to climb. Peter stood stock still, staring at Juan.

"Stop now, or I'll shoot," I growled.

Juan did a double take. He stared hard at me for a minute, then a malicious smile crossed his face. "Hey, Tran! Pee-pee got a girl to defend him."

A high-pitched giggle cut through Juan's words.

My eyes narrowed. Dad said to observe, but there was no way I was putting up with a bully. I yanked my stunner out of its holster and slammed it into the hand that had just grasped the top of the wall. "Enjoy your fall, creep," I muttered and squeezed the trigger.

CHAPTER TWENTY-SIX

Juan's eyes bulged, and his hand seized on the wall, tendons popping out of the back, nails biting into the wood. The acrid scent of burned flesh and fresh urine singed my nostrils. I pulled the stunner away and flicked his fingers off the wall. With a gargled yelp, Juan fell from the ladder, slamming into his friends on the way down.

I didn't stay to watch. I pushed past Peter and pointed my stunner at the man atop the next ladder. "It's just as effective at a distance," I called. "Try me!"

The man lifted his hand in an obscene gesture. At least I assume it was obscene, although it wasn't one I recognized. I took a half-step to get a clear line of sight and fired.

Lightning lanced out from my stunner, and the man convulsed. I let off the trigger, and he fell, taking two others with him. They hit the ground with satisfying thuds and yelps. I swung around to target the middle ladder. The men had already scrambled half-way to the ground, so I let them go. "Pull up the ladders."

Peter still stood by the first ladder, staring down at the men clinging to it.

"Pull it up! If we take it, they can't use it again!" I fired at the men below him, even though I knew they were at the edge of my range. Then I holstered the weapon and began pulling up the ladder closest to me.

"You got 'em on the run!" Everest cried, thundering up to us along the platform. "Nice work Peter! What did you do?"

Peter jerked as though woken from a deep sleep and reached for the ladder. "She did it, not me." Head down, he pulled hand over hand on the rope ladder.

"They're taking the ladders!" someone called from below. A chorus of shouts went up. Men ran at the wall, leaping for the dangling rungs. The ropes burned my palms as someone yanked.

"Duck!" Everest cried. He launched himself at Pete, taking the younger man to the platform. A volley of arrows flew over them. I dropped the ropes and threw myself into the lee of the wall.

"Siti, report!" Dad called through the comm.

"Sorry, sir, busy right now," I muttered. "We're under attack on the north wall."

"You were to observe, not get involved!" he yelled.

I flipped off the comm. "Shoot them!" I cried at Everest as he pulled himself to a crouch. "We can't let them get away with their ladders."

Everest and Peter both popped up and fired over the wall. I crouched behind it, pulling my ladder up again, rung by rung. If I could just get it out of reach... I poked my head over the wall to look.

"The cavalry's here!" Joss yelled, and gunfire ripped out of the darkness, targeting the men below. Screams and yelps rewarded his efforts. Behind him, Eric carried his bulky weapon. He fired rapidly, shot after shot ripping into the night.

Below, the men turned and ran, abandoning their ladders. A few more arrows angled up at us, but they fell short as the attackers retreated.

"Nice work, boys," Joss said, clapping Everest and Peter on the back.

"She's the one who saved us." Peter jerked his chin at me as he reeled up the ladder. "I was useless."

"No, you weren't," I said. "I couldn't have done it on my own."

"We need to get the specs for that lightning gun." Peter changed the subject. "You should have seen it. It put out blue sparks and took those guys out."

"Non-lethal weapons for the children," I said, patting my stunner and rolling my eyes. "They won't let me have a blaster."

"I doubt they'll let us have one either," Joss grumbled as he dumped a ladder onto the platform.

"How's Tanis?" Peter peered over the wall as if he'd suddenly remembered. Then he relaxed. "She's okay."

"How do you know?" I dropped my ladder and edged past Everest and Joss.

"Mara told me," he said. "With Jake's help."

"We got this section," Joss said. "You guys go down."

Peter, Eric, Everest, and I hurried down the steps, Eric grunting under the weight of his strange gun. In the courtyard, Jake and a woman crouched near the prone guard. The woman turned as we approached and smiled at us. "Arrow wound is superficial. It was enough to throw her off-balance, and she fell off the platform. Broke a couple of bones in the fall, but she'll heal. This blanket is amazing." She fingered the thin survival material.

"Standard issue," I said. My comm alert blared. "I gotta talk to my dad." I hurried through the building and into the street. I flicked my holo-ring to activate the locator and followed the gentle pull on my ring down the street toward the main plaza.

Maybe this would be easier if I got the initial report out of the way before I reached him. I took a deep breath and flicked the comm button. Before Dad could speak, I launched into my report. I explained about the guard being shot and how Peter and I raced to the rescue. "When we arrived at the dorm, the invaders were climbing the wall. I helped Peter fend them off until additional guards could assist." I smiled a little smugly at my official sounding finish.

The pause was deafening. Then came the storm. "You used a CEC grav-belt to recklessly transport a Gagarian agent. You handed CEC equipment over to another Gagarian agent, and you immersed yourself in a Gagarian internal issue! What were you thinking?"

I gaped at the empty road in stunned silence. "I was thinking I'm staying in that dorm, and if these Hellions snuck into the city, I'd be dead."

"You have to learn when to get involved and when to stay out of the way," Dad snapped.

I turned the corner and headed across the plaza. My father stood on the wide steps of the official building. He waited until I climbed up beside him to continue. "You alerted the locals. That should have been enough." He shook his head, but I couldn't tell if it was condemnation of my actions or acceptance of my incompetence. "This town has guards on the wall for a reason."

"I told you, the guard was down." I lifted my chin. I wasn't going to let him tag this as a failure. "There was no one on that part of the wall. The others didn't arrive until after we'd stunned the first invaders. If I hadn't acted, they would have had a dozen men inside the town before anyone arrived."

"And we have a full encampment right outside." Dad flung a hand toward the front gate. "You could have retreated there in safety. That's what you should have done."

"And just let my friends be killed?" I cried.

"Your friends?" Dad's eyes narrowed, and his voice dropped to a deadly whisper. "These people are not your friends. They are enemy agents, intent on stealing Earth away from the United Colonies."

I crossed my arms over my chest. "They're Terrans who were left behind and survived on their own for five hundred years."

He shook his head, and this time, the disgust was clear. "You've bought into their story. It's time to return to the base. I'll have someone escort you there in the morning. As soon as Hydrao returns, you'll go back to the ship."

"Dad, no!" I tried to grab his arm, but he pulled away. "Please, just listen to them. They're telling the truth. Go see their Dome! Talk to the people there. They can't possibly be Gagarians."

He held up a hand. "Enough. Come with me. You're done here."

"But my stuff is in the dorm," I protested.

He glared at me, his lips pressed tightly together. "Fine. There's no room for you in the camp anyway. Take me to the dorm. If it's secure, you can stay there the rest of the night. Then back to camp in the morning."

I led him down the street, my head hanging low. A mob had converged on the dorm. Most of them were soot-stained and looked exhausted. They slumped on the couches in the common room, or leaned against walls, staring vacantly at nothing.

Mara came down the stairs and stopped on the third step up. "Tanis is going to be fine."

A soft cheer went up around the room.

"She's broken a few bones, but the arrow wound will heal." Mara smiled at the tired young men and women. "You have all done well. The water heaters are boiling, so there should be plenty of hot water. Go get showered. We've got a double complement on the wall. You all need to get some sleep."

Zane stepped onto the tread below Mara. "And we'll celebrate tomorrow. Nice work, everyone. Go get cleaned up." As the residents got to their feet, muttering and groaning, he spotted Dad and me standing just inside the front door. He made his way through the throng, patting shoulders and knocking fists as he went.

"Can we speak outside?" He gestured to the door.

Dad looked him up and down, then turned and stepped out the door. "Siti, with me."

I glanced around but didn't see anyone I recognized. "Coming."

Zane stood under the lamp beside the door, the light glinting off his head. Dad stood a meter or so away, arms crossed over his chest.

"I'll thank you to keep my daughter out of your internal troubles," Dad said. "We didn't come here so she could be killed in a Gagarian civil war."

Zane crossed his own arms. "I know you're getting tired of hearing this, but we are not from Gagarin. The men who attacked our village are locals who have been evicted from their own village—probably for theft or antisocial behavior. They are led, we discovered tonight, by a pair of men from the Dome. Peter identified the Mylinchek brothers. They, like us, spent the last five centuries in deep sleep in the basement of the Dome. I would like to take you over there tomorrow, to show you, so you can stop this stupid Gagarin business."

Dad's nostrils flared in shock. No one called the hero of Darenti Four stupid. "We arrived on an empty planet to find it already settled. The only place you could have come from is Gagarin! You've done it before; you'll do it again. But we will not cede Earth to you!"

Zane rubbed his head. "I'm too tired to have this conversation again. Why don't you have your ship do a scan of the planet? You'll find settlements all across the globe—too many to be Gagarian. They'd have had to land hundreds of years ago. I assume that isn't possible?"

"No," Dad said. "They—you didn't have the resources to mount an expedition to Earth that long ago. Maybe thirty or forty years, at the most. We've been watching."

"There you go." Zane rubbed his head again. "Take a look at your satellites and ask your analysts how long it would take to settle this many people. Then we'll talk."

"I'd love to do that," Dad said. "But the *Glory* didn't launch any visual sats. Earth is a known quantity. We didn't need detailed pics for the initial landing. They'll be back in a couple of days, and then you can be sure we will do exactly what you suggested. In the meantime—" He turned to me. "I would like to know if it is safe to leave my daughter here for the night. I can easily move her to the camp." He raised an eyebrow, challenging the other man.

"It's as safe as it can be." Zane heaved a sigh. "We've doubled the guard, and I think we inflicted enough damage to keep them from trying again tonight. She'll be in the same building as our best-trained guards, so even if they came over the wall, she'd likely be safe enough. She seems to be quite capable of taking care of herself. Plus, she can use that anti-gravity device to fly away, right?"

"If she was smart," Dad muttered.

"Hey!" I glared at Dad. The crazy events of the night combined with the strange revelations of the day put me into a dangerous mood. Normally, I wouldn't contradict the commander in front of the troops. But Zane wasn't one of his, so what the hell? "I am smart! I helped hold off that attack, and I'm tired of you treating me like a little girl!"

Zane bit back a smile, but his lips quirked up on the ends. "Siti was instrumental in preventing a tragedy. We appreciate her assistance."

Dad's narrowed eyes glared from the tall man to me and back. "You're welcome." He turned on his heel, then glanced over his shoulder. "Stay out of trouble this time, Siti. Good night."

We watched him march up the street toward the plaza.

"Is he always so friendly?" Sarcasm dripped from Zane's voice.

"I think he was scared I'd get hurt." I yawned. "I'm sorry he's being so stupid about this Gagarin thing."

"Why can't he see the truth?" Zane took a few steps away, then swung around and stomped back. "It's obvious! There are too many of us! We don't have your tech. If we're from Gagarin, where are our ships?"

"I think he's so wrapped up in this theory, he can't let it go," I said slowly. "He's twisting the facts to match his conviction."

"Doesn't seem like a good habit for a commander or an explorer," Zane muttered. I didn't think he meant me to hear him.

CHAPTER TWENTY-SEVEN

The next morning, I woke with the sun. I hadn't set my personal protection shield to automatically dim, since back at camp, we slept in a windowless block. But here, the sun glared in through the open window.

Marika sat up and yawned. "What time did you get in?" She had been asleep when I'd finally gotten to bed last night. Or early this morning.

"I dunno, one? Maybe one-thirty. You?" I gathered my clothes and toiletries.

"Twelve-thirty. Everyone went to bed as soon as your dad left." She scrubbed her hands through her curly red hair, leaving it even wilder than usual.

"Speaking of Dad—did you hear anything about a plan to infiltrate the Hellions' caves?" I sat on the bed, my shower items in my lap.

She shrugged. "They did some recon. Not sure they discovered anything. Why?"

"I forgot to ask Dad last night. Not that he'd tell me." I grimaced. "I have to go back to the base today. He didn't like me getting involved in the attack."

"He'll cool down." She swung her legs off the bed. "Probably change his mind."

"He doesn't do that," I said.

She stood and grabbed her own gear. "Maybe not with you, but he's very flexible when he's on an assignment. You just have to convince him sending you back would be detrimental to the operation."

"How do I do that?" I asked. "And how do you know so much about my dad? This is your first assignment with him."

"One of the things I've learned in my long career is how to read people." She winked on the word long. "Our commander is always going to put the mission first."

"Even ahead of his only child?" I followed her toward the showers.

"That is a bit of a wild card," she said. "You need to show him you're as safe here as in the camp and that you can be an asset to the team. You've already made a connection with Peter and Eric—get him something juicy from that connection, and he'll let you stay." She pushed into the shower room.

I stood in the hallway, staring vacantly at the closing door. I knew something that might make me valuable to the mission. But telling Dad felt like betraying Peter's and Eric's trust. I raised my chin. I was a CEC explorer—or might be soon. My duty was to the team. And I couldn't help Eric and Peter if I was sent home in disgrace.

PETER, Zina, and Joss waited for us in the common room. The twins looked tired, but Peter's face was haggard, with dark circles under his blood-shot eyes.

"Finally!" Eric burst out of the small kitchen, a sandwich in his hand. "I thought you'd never get here!"

"And that you'd starve in the meantime?" Marika raised an eyebrow at his sandwich.

Eric waved up and down his body with his free hand. "All this takes a lot of fuel."

Zina snorted. "I'd say 'all that' is already full of something. Let's go." She pushed the door open and dropped it in her brother's face. Joss caught it with a practiced air and held it for the rest of us.

We crossed town to the community building, the others trading jokes and barbs. No one mentioned last night's attack. Was that because the attacks were so common or because they were blocking it out?

We grabbed trays and served ourselves from a buffet that stood along the back wall. "You know, it's funny how everyone in the universe serves food the same way," I said.

"Buffets for the win!" Eric piled more eggs on his plate and topped it with a mountain of bacon.

"Is this real food?" Marika asked as she poked a spoon at a large rectangular tray of porridge.

"What else would it be?" Zina took some toast. "That's oatmeal. Made from oats grown in the fields the Hellions trampled last night. Enjoy it while it lasts."

"Will that attack affect your food supply?" I asked as we crossed the room to join Jake and a little girl at a mostly empty table.

"Of course. But not until next year." Zina stepped over the bench and sat. "That grain wasn't fully grown. I think we can probably get some surplus from the Dome or trade with another village—unless the Hellions have destroyed their crops, too."

"Do they attack everyone?" Marika watched the others eat for a moment before picking up a piece of bacon with her fingers.

"They've hit a few villages farther up the river," Joss mumbled through a mouthful of something. "We're the closest to their camp, though, so we get hit the most often."

"Zane said that guy I stunned—Juan—is their leader." I glanced under my lashes at Peter as I said this.

His face went still, and he stared into the distance while he chewed and swallowed. "Leader seems like too lofty a word for Juan. He's a bully. He used to pick on me when I was a kid. Back in Utah." He gulped some juice and started coughing.

Eric pounded him on the back until the coughing stopped. "You okay, mate?"

"Not really," Peter said. "That thug used to torture me as a kid. If I'd known he made it to the Dome, I would have—" he broke off. "He shouldn't have gotten—they should have given his place to someone else. I thought he died five hundred years ago. It's what he deserved."

The others stared at Peter in amazement. Jake put a hand on his brother's arm, and Peter's face relaxed.

"Dude." Eric shook his head at his friend.

"How would you feel if you suddenly found out your tormentor was a Hellion?" Peter spit the words out. "That instead of being five hundred years dead, he's alive and able to inflict pain and terror on you—or someone else?" He shoved the bench hard enough to jostle all of us and climbed over. Jake reached for his arm again, but he shook off his brother. "I need some air."

We all stared as he stomped away. "Is he going to be okay?" I asked.

Eric shrugged. "Dunno. He never talked about that guy before, but I get what he's saying. I'd be pissed if my dad had gotten back into the Dome."

"Was he a bad guy?" Marika asked. I shot her a look. "What?" she asked through the comm.

"Subtle," I muttered. Her shoulders made a tiny shrug.

"He was a bad guy." Eric shoved more bacon into his mouth.

I looked at the twins. Zina held up both hands. "Before my time."

We ate in silence for a while.

When I looked up from my oatmeal, Jake's eyes met mine, then slid away. He'd scooted along the bench into Peter's open seat, his little friend sliding along next to him. His eyes flicked to me several times as we ate, but he said nothing.

A bell clanged eight times, ringing through the building. All around the room, benches slid back, scraping against the wooden floors.

"We gotta go—time for work." Zina picked up her tray and climbed over the bench. "You two are fine, but the rest of us have a schedule."

Marika glanced at her holo-ring. "I gotta get to the camp. Siti, I'll see you later today." She followed the rest out the door.

I started to rise, but Jake's finger tapped my hand.

"Did you want something?"

He held out his hand, palm up. The little girl did the same.

"You want me to hold your hands?" I dropped back onto the bench. When they nodded in synch, I put my hands into theirs.

I gasped. This was nothing like the comm link the CEC team used. I got images, feelings, smells, sensations, and the occasional word. The little girl's name was Lena. She and Jake were friends for many years, and she had helped him learn to do this. She was curious about me because she couldn't sense me. Jake thought it might be my personal shield stopping the brainwaves.

Or something like that. The meaning was clear, but there was no way to explain everything they transmitted in words. I yanked my hands away.

"How did you do that?" I grabbed the closest glass and chugged the water.

"Peter told you," Jake said. His eyes flicked to mine again.

"That was—there's nothing—do you do that all the time?" I stared at the boy, aghast. How could anyone tolerate that much coming in all the time?

He held out his hand again, but Lena pulled hers away. She leaned against Jake.

Slowly, I extended my hand and placed the tips of my fingers in Jake's palm.

He smiled—at least I felt a bit of amusement through the touch. This time, I got words. *Lena would like you to remove your bubble so she can sense you.*

"Can she read my mind?"

No, that's why she wants you to remove the bubble.

"You mean my personal force shield?" I reached toward my holo-ring, which I wore on the hand currently touching Jake's. "It's against CEC policy to turn it off outside the camp."

Just for a few seconds. There's no danger here.

"That's what you say," I muttered. "How do I know you won't lobotomize me with your weird brain waves?"

Jake and Lena giggled. *We don't do that. Look inside. We're friendly.* Something opened, and I felt a sense of welcome, safety, warmth.

I pulled my hand away again. "That's what you'd say right before you sucked out my brain," I said.

Jake's eyes widened and Lena's face paled.

"I'm just kidding." Mostly kidding.

They were just kids, though. What could they do? They weren't controlling anyone else, as far as I could see. I thought about what my dad would say about removing protective gear in the presence of "Gagarians."

But Dad was the hero of Darenti Four. A designation he'd earned by taking a big risk. If I remembered the stories correctly, he'd done exactly what I was contemplating, in a show of peace. I nodded. "I'll do it. But only for a moment."

Lena slid off the end of the bench and scooted in beside me. She put out her hand again, and I took it. My palm enveloped her tiny fingers, making me feel like a giant. I flicked my left thumb against my holo-ring and pulled up the interface. One-handed, I flicked the personal field off.

Lena went completely still, her eyes going wide. They darted to me, then to Jake, and around the room, inventorying the few remaining diners. They came back to Jake, and she yanked her hand away from mine.

"On!" she whispered as she darted away from me.

I flicked the interface and turned my shield back on. "What's wrong?" I leaned across the table, reaching for Jake's hand again.

He shook his head, staring at Lena. Confusion then surprise crossed his face. His eyebrows went up, and hers went down. Then he turned and touched my hand.

She can't hear you unless she touches you. With the bubble off, she can't hear me.

"Are you saying I interfere with her psychic abilities?" I asked. "That without the filter, my, uh, brainwaves cancel hers out?"

He nodded and shrugged. *Yeah?*

CHAPTER TWENTY-EIGHT

"Just hers, or yours, too?" I asked as we walked out of the community center. "Do I cancel out your ability to hear her?"

Jake put his hand on my arm. *I couldn't hear her as soon as she touched you.*

"Yeah, but she pulled her hand away before I put my field back on. Could you hear her then?"

His hand fell away from my arm. I stopped and turned. He glanced at me and shrugged.

"Siti! Here you are," Dad said.

"I was just coming." I turned to face him. "As soon as Jake and I finished our conversation."

Dad glanced at the two kids and turned back to me, obviously dismissing them. "I want you to stay here a little longer. I've reconsidered the situation. Mr. Torres wants to show me the Dome, and the team is busy exploring the local area." Over the comm, he continued. "You keep working on those young people. Find out as much as you can. Maybe the kids will spill the secrets." His eyes flicked to Jake and Lena.

"They don't talk much," I said aloud. "But I'll try. What about the Hellions?"

"That's Evy's job, not yours," he said. "Unless you're in personal danger, no use of force is authorized."

"Yes, sir." I snapped to attention. I wasn't sure he read the irony in my posture.

"Excellent." He turned away. "I'll see you at dinner."

Marika was right. His willingness to change his mind over me seemed at odds with his stubborn insistence that these people came from Gagarin. I pulled my eyes from his retreating back and turned to Jake and Lena. "Where's everyone else?"

Jake touched my hand, and I got images of a clean-up crew out by the burned building, guard duty, and activity involving cows and horses. "Are those real horses?"

He nodded, and I got the impression he didn't think much of them.

"Tiah said she was coming over today. Do you know when?"

The kids looked at each other and shook their heads.

"Maybe I'll walk over there and meet her. You wanna come?"

More headshakes, this time more violent.

"You don't like the Dome." I tilted my head at Lena. "Have you been inside?"

She nodded and held up a finger. Once. Interesting.

Jake took my hand again. *The temps have an effect similar to yours.*

"Really? They dampen your abilities? But Tiah came with you to the meeting...oh." I remembered Seraphina sitting close to my end of the table with many seats between her and the others. She was trying to read us, without interference from Tiah. I laughed. It wouldn't have made any difference, if all the explorers were as "disruptive" as I.

"Anyway, I'm going to go over to the Dome. I'll see you later." I waved at the kids and headed for the front gate.

Zina and a woman I didn't recognize stood on either side of the platform above the open gate, watching. I climbed the steps and stood beside Zina. "Is this what you do all day?"

"As much as I can." Zina glanced at me, then her eyes snapped back to the surrounding land. The road leading toward the Dome swirled with green light in the bright sun, and the forest surrounding it had been cleared of underbrush. Sneaking up on the town from this direction would be impossible in daylight. And yet, they still posted a guard.

"Why do you have to guard during the day?" I asked.

"We don't, usually," Zina said. "But after last night's attack and the ambush by the lake…"

I nodded. "Are you going after the Hellions?"

"We've tried." She slapped the wooden wall, the sound ringing loud and hollow. "We know where they hide. But they seem to know when we're coming. The caves are empty—at least as far as we've dared to look. It's tricky—crawling around in a dark cave you know nothing about with hostiles potentially setting up ambushes? Not fun."

"Maybe they hear you coming." I tapped my forehead on the word "hear." "Zane said they've got people who were thrown out of other villages. Surely, they must have the same 'skills' as the villagers here."

She gave me a sharp look. "You know about that?"

"Jake and I had a little conversation this morning. Apparently, I act as a dampening field." I tapped my collar. "Or my protective shield does."

'Your protective…oh, that transparent bubble you wear?" She focused on my collar. "Is it produced by your jacket?"

"Yeah, there's a generator in the hem." I tapped the slim band around my waist. "But the power pack is on my belt. Not the grav-belt but this one. The uniform bends it, I guess you could say. It forms to my clothing with a looser field around my head and hands. When we pick up something, we aren't really touching it—the field makes contact."

"Cooool," Zina said. "How did you talk to Jake, then? He doesn't do the out loud thing."

I rubbed my forearm with my left hand. "I'm not sure. He touched my fingers—or didn't because of the field. But it was enough to get through, I guess."

"How do you eat?" a female voice behind me asked.

I swung around. The other guard stood about a meter from me.

"This is Esabella." Zina nodded to the tall, blonde girl.

"You look like Everest," I said. "Only prettier."

"He's my cousin." When she grinned, her crooked teeth distracted me.

Back home, that smile would have been corrected before she reached puberty. I glanced at Zina, noting her perfect teeth.

"You're one of them." I mentally slapped myself as soon as the words escaped my mouth. "Sorry. I mean, you grew up out here, right?"

"Yeah, we're from the original village." The blonde raised an eyebrow.

"Can you do that mind thing? Like Jake and Lena?" I asked.

"No one can do that mind thing like Jake and Lena," Esabella said with a laugh. "I mean, we can all talk to each other without words, but we can't do what they do."

"Can you talk to me?" I asked.

"Not from here. I can't sense you at all." She closed her eyes and moved her head back and forth a couple of times. "It's like Zina is here alone."

I flicked my holo-ring. "What about now?"

Her eyes popped wide, like Lena's had. "That's creepy. She just—poof—disappeared. You're both gone. Dead space."

"I thought you couldn't read my mind," Zina said. "You guys always claim we're too muffled to understand."

"Oh, you are," Esabella said. "But I can 'hear' something. Like muttering or rustling. Whatever she did, though—now you're completely gone."

I flicked my holo-ring.

"And now you're back! The elders aren't going to like that!" Esabella exclaimed.

"Why not?" I asked.

"First you can take away Levi's gift, and now you can hide the ancients?" She gave an exaggerated shudder. "Not good."

"We didn't take away his gift," I said hotly. "We repaired his concussion. Maybe the injury did it."

"Nope, we've had head injuries before." She rolled her eyes. "Look around you—plenty of opportunities to get hit on the head. No one ever lost their gift before."

"If you can take it away, I wonder if you can create one?" Zina suggested. "I wouldn't mind having the gift. Dating a villager is tough when you can't read his mind."

Esabella laughed. "Tell me about it. I hate not knowing what Sergei is thinking unless I touch him."

"More guarding, less chatting!" a female voice called from below.

We looked down to see Katy, Jake, and Peter standing below us, inside the village walls.

"We're watching!" Zina made a show of turning away, her rifle aimed over the wall as she turned in a careful semi-circle. Esabella hurried to the other side of the gate.

"Sorry—didn't mean to get you in trouble!" I pulled a face at Esabella and bumped knuckles with Zina. "I'll see you later."

I hurried down the steps and caught up to the three as they strode along the path toward the Dome. "Can I walk to the Dome with you?"

They turned with a start. "I didn't hear you." Katy raised her eyebrows at Jake. He shook his head.

"It's something with my protective field," I told Katy. "Jake and Lena had the same problem."

Surprise washed over Katy's face. "They talked to you?"

I explained what we'd discovered that morning. "They said Tiah has the same effect. I wonder if it's true of all the, er, what do you call them?"

"Temps?" Katy suggested. "That's why we're going to the Dome. We've just put two and two together. We think the Hellions may be using the villagers' gifts to target us."

"What do you mean?" I asked.

"They always know where our defenses are the weakest," Katy said. "And they clearly knew the rover was alone and unarmed yesterday. Last night, they knew Tanis was far enough from the next guard to allow them a foothold by taking her out."

"Seraphina and Everest told us about Tiah," Peter put in. "We're wondering if we can make use of that dampening field to sneak up on the Hellions. They hear us coming and hide. We didn't realize how before, but they must have someone like Lena with a long range."

Katy turned speculative eyes on me. "Maybe you can help us, too. More than one dampener would be optimum."

I held up a hand. "I'm not allowed to get involved. But if Tiah can do it, what about other temps?"

"That's why we're headed over." Katy walked a little faster. "To find more help."

"How have you never noticed this before?" I asked. "You've lived across the way from these people forever."

Katy chuckled. "The temps never come out, and the villagers hate to go in."

"Besides, we always thought it was the building dampening their signal, not the people," Peter said. "They say we ancients are muffled, so we figured it was the same for everyone inside."

"They don't come out?" I asked. This still boggled my mind. The Dome was beautiful inside, sure, but staying in there would be like living in a ship—or a station—for your entire life. I shivered.

"It's a cultural thing," Katy said. "For generations, they've been told outside is unsafe. A few left when the Dome first opened, but they were rebels."

"Rebels like Tiah?" I laughed. "She didn't really strike me as being rebellious."

Katy sighed. "She's never been treated well by her own people. It still took her three years—and extraordinary circumstances—to build up the courage."

We broke out into the sunshine and crossed the dirt in front of the high wooden wall. The gates lay open, as they had yesterday, but today, two guards stood atop the wall. They waved and exchanged greetings with Katy and the boys and nodded politely to me.

"Who are they?" I asked as we headed down the ramp. "Not temps, right?"

"The village protects the Dome," Peter said. "It's part of our trade agreement. They provide tech and some foods we can't grow outside."

"Like coffee." Katy grinned.

"And chocolate," Jake said, surprising us all.

"Ah, important things." I nodded seriously.

"Exactly." Katy nodded. "Let's go see if we can find us some dampeners."

CHAPTER TWENTY-NINE

We tromped down the dim stairwell and into the livable parts of the Dome. Katy's shoulders tightened as we descended. The boys didn't visibly react, but a feeling of unease rolled over me, and based on our recent discussions, I guessed it was Jake's, not mine.

When we reached the park, all three relaxed a fraction. Tiah stood on the grass near the canteen, watching the butterflies.

"Tiah," Peter called and waved.

The girl looked up and smiled, crossing to meet us halfway. She glanced curiously at me. "What can I do for you?"

"We have some... questions," Katy said. She explained their theory. "We're wondering if you and possibly any other Dome dwellers—"

"Insiders," Tiah said. "We—they—decided we should be called Insiders."

"Insiders." Katy nodded. "Do you think any of them might want to help us with an experiment?" She smiled again, uncomfortably.

"Outside?" Tiah asked in alarm. "I'll come out, but…"

"Surely there must be others who are curious," Peter suggested. "It's nice in here, but there's so much to see out there."

Tiah shrugged. "Professor O'Doul is your mostly likely option. He's fascinated with the stars. He might be persuaded to go outside if he can actually look at them."

"Really? What about younger people?" Katy asked. "There must be others who want to get away from home? That's a pretty natural experience."

Tiah shrugged. "They live in the dorm—that's as far as they imagine going. Anyone who really wanted to go outside left three years ago."

"How many left back then?" Katy asked.

"A few. Mostly troublemakers." Tiah's nose wrinkled.

Peter grabbed Katy's arm. "We must be right. The Hellions have Insiders hiding them."

"What are you talking about?" Tiah demanded.

"We think—we know you block mental signals." Peter shrugged apologetically. The girl nodded, once, abruptly, so he continued, "We have tried several times to follow the Hellions. We follow them physically—we've never been able to pinpoint them mentally."

"When we've followed them before—the villagers always said they were too far away to hear." Katy's eyes narrowed. "But that wasn't it, was it?"

Peter looked at Jake. The younger boy's eyes darted away. Peter listened for a moment, then explained, "They weren't sure what was happening. Things move so fast after an attack—they thought—hoped it was just… they didn't want to believe—I don't know."

Katy stared at the boys. "We've tracked them—physically—to their cave complex. Then they disappear inside. And you weren't able to hear them. But really, you couldn't hear them the whole time?"

"Yes and no." Jake's hands twisted together as Peter translated. "They hear some of them—when they're spread out, they catch bits and pieces. But once we have them on the run, most of the group disappears. It sounds like they might have a couple of Insiders with them. Maybe their dampening field isn't very big, so we hear anyone who isn't close enough?"

"But when they bunch up to get into their cave…and once they're inside…" Katy left it hanging.

"You need my dad," I said. "We have equipment that could scan that cave system and locate life-forms. It doesn't rely on your woo-woo energy."

They all glared at me.

"What?" I held up my hands. "You have to admit it's pretty woo-woo."

Reluctantly, Katy and Tiah chuckled. A quick smile flashed across Jake's face and disappeared.

"If we have our own signal dampeners—" I jerked my head indicating Tiah. "Then what?"

"Maybe we can lay a trap for them outside the caves." Katy paced a few steps away, then came back. "We can move in before dusk and wait for them to come out to attack."

"Do you have any idea how big the cave system is?" I asked. "How many entrances?"

"No, but that's something Professor O'Doul can help with—and he won't need to leave the safety of the Dome." Katy grinned in triumph.

WE LEFT the Dome with a printed copy of the geological surveys done five hundred years before. "We don't have anything newer," O'Doul had told us. "It wasn't a priority."

"We probably didn't have the equipment, either," Katy suggested as we started down the road to the village. "I suspect some of these passageways have been blocked over the years. Maybe new ones opened."

"I know the *Glory* could do a scan like that." I snapped my fingers. "They'll be back in a couple more days."

Katy shook her head.

"We don't want to wait," Peter agreed. "People have been hurt. We need to stop this now. And maybe Mara can help some of those lost souls—if we can reach them."

"Help them?" Katy's voice cracked. "They've attacked us. They shot Tanis and Everest. They left Levi for dead!"

"Jake says they need help." Peter grimaced. "Only injured souls lash out like that."

"You can help them if you want," Katy said, her voice hard as titanium. "I just want them stopped."

The anger in her voice chilled me to the bone. Fair enough—her children were in danger every night. But the people who had been injured were Mara's people. I shook my head.

"What happened to Levi?" Peter asked. "Do you think it's permanent?"

I held up both hands. "I know nothing about the med pods except how to make them work. And even for that, I follow the tutorials."

"But you were there when it happened," he continued. "You saw what they did."

"I don't know. Chasin ran a brain scan and repair." I rubbed my nose. "He mentioned odd brain waves, and Eric got upset and told him not to do any repair on Everest above the neck."

Katy nodded. "That's what Eric told me, too."

We walked in silence for a while. The sky was overcast now, making the road dim under the thick trees. Tiah cried out and fell to the ground.

"My ankle," she said, clutching her leg.

"Is this your bad leg?" Katy asked, crouching beside the girl.

She nodded. "It's always been weaker. I've twisted it before."

"Can you walk on it, or should we carry you?" Katy asked.

"I...let me try to stand." She took Katy's hand and pulled herself upright. Peter stood nearby while she tried to put weight on it.

Something flickered down the road. I held up a hand and stepped around my companions to get a better look. A group emerged from the underbrush, moving quietly toward the village. Their ragged clothing blended into the trees. I flicked on my low-light scan. Weapons, lots of them. None of the men even glanced in our direction.

"Who's that?" I whispered.

All four heads snapped up. "I don't recognize them," Katy said.

"Neither do I." Peter's face tightened. "Jake, see if you can reach Esabella." He glanced at Tiah and away. Jake stood and started back toward the Dome, but I grabbed his arm.

"Wait." I flicked my comm and scrolled through the list, trying to remember who was at the village and who was in camp. I connected to Evy. "Where are you?"

"Siti? I'm about ten klicks from the village. Where are you?"

"On the road to the Dome. Someone is approaching the village, and they don't look friendly."

"Roger. Contact Flynn. He's there with the boss."

I signed off and called Flynn. His signal went to voicemail. Gritting my teeth, I left a message and tried Marika.

"What's up?" Her cheerful voice sounded loud in my ears.

"Hostiles approaching the village. From the Dome road."

"What?"

I repeated my statement, listing numbers and visible weapons. "We're behind them, staying in the shadows. We have an injured person."

"Right. I'll alert the gate guards and the boss." Marika's voice snapped into professional mode. "Who's with you?"

After a quick discussion, I signed off. "We've been instructed to return to the Dome."

"My family is in the village. I'm not hiding in the Dome," Katy said.

"Tiah can't walk." Peter patted down his pockets. "I don't have anything to strap her ankle with."

I rummaged in my belt pouches and came up with a roll of Supra-Thin bandage. "Try that."

"Why don't we use your magic flying machine?" Katy suggested.

My hands tightened around my grav-belt. "I can't just give my grav-belt to her."

"Your father used them to transport our people before when they were injured," Peter said.

"Yeah, but those were extras," I protested. "We didn't have to—they're considered essential safely gear. Explorers don't take them off outside camp."

"Fine," Peter said. "You and Tiah wait here. Katy and I will go help the village, and we'll come get you when it's safe. Just stay here in the shadows."

"Wait! I—"

"No, that's the best idea," Katy agreed. "I'm not going to be responsible for putting the commander's daughter in the middle of a civil war."

Zane must have told her about his conversation with my dad. "You aren't responsible for putting me anywhere," I said. "I can take care of myself."

"Right now, we need you to take care of Tiah." Katy pushed me toward the edge of the road. "Just get under those bushes. With Tiah's magic brain waves, they won't find you."

"But they'll hear you," I protested. "As soon as you're far enough away, they'll hear you behind them."

"Not if they have their own dampener," Katy said. "It doesn't work both ways."

"She might be right," Peter broke in. "They didn't even look at us. They must be listening, and they didn't hear anyone. Which means they don't have a temp—I mean an Insider with them right now. Maybe they meet up later, when they're closer to the target."

"Look." I unfastened my grav-belt. "I'm putting this on Tiah. We'll all go back to the village. We can sneak around the Hellions and get in through the rear gate." I looped the belt around Tiah's waist.

"What—I don't—" Tiah pushed the belt away half-heartedly.

I cut through her protests. "I'm setting it at ten centimeters, and I'll just pull you. Easier than trying to teach you the controls, and there's no one to tether to."

I tightened the belt as small as it would go, but Tiah was tiny. It hung loosely around her hips. I pushed it over her chest, to her armpits. "This isn't ideal, but it'll work." I flipped the control and set it to a decimeter.

Tiah whimpered as her feet lifted off the ground. "I don't like this."

"Sorry, they need you." I pulled a length of micro cable from my belt pouch and hooked it to a ring in the grav-belt. I gave it an experimental yank, and she drifted forward. "Like a balloon," I said with a grin. "But I don't have to worry about you floating away. Do you want to go higher?"

Tiah's eyes widened in fear. "No!"

"Probably not a good idea with them around, anyway." I jerked my head toward the village—and the Hellions approaching it. "We're ready —let's go."

We broke into a jog, staying single file in the center of the dirt road. Tiah bobbed along behind me. I glanced over my shoulder. She had her arms wrapped around her torso and her eyes clamped shut.

"Careful not to step on any loose branches," Peter whispered. "They can't sense us, but they'll hear us."

Katy shushed him.

A rough cough from around the next corner sent a shiver over my skin. We slowed to a crawl, pausing every few steps to listen.

Peter held up a hand and stopped. Katy and I froze. Tiah bumped into me, her toes tapping against my legs. I felt her wince against my back.

Peter turned slowly and motioned for us to come closer. As soon as he could reach, he grabbed Katy's forearm and mine, his grip firm but gentle. Jake took his other hand and Katy's. Peter's voice echoed in my head, as if a long way away. *They've stopped. Just off the road. Do you hear them? Move slowly.*

Katy and I both looked over his shoulder. The road curved ahead and sounds of low talking reached us.

I'm going to see—

I gripped his arm and shook my head. With my free hand, I pointed to myself. "They can't sense me," I mouthed.

Katy raised an eyebrow, but Peter nodded. I handed the cable looped to Tiah's belt to Katy and tiptoed around them. This would be quieter if I could use the grav-belt, but there was no point in dwelling on that. I stepped onto the thick pine needles at the edge of the dirt road and eased forward.

As I crept along, the voices got louder. Someone muttered something, and a couple of people laughed. I moved closer, ducking under a low branch. A glance over my shoulder revealed I was out of sight of the others. I stepped over a small branch and leaned around a thick tree trunk.

The road was empty. I froze, listening. The voices seemed to come from behind me. I turned my head, trying to get a better sense of direction. They must have moved off the road, through the underbrush here. I tiptoed around the tree, peering into the woods.

"What have we here?" The voice sent chills down my spine.

I scrabbled at my holster, but a hand clamped around my wrist before I could pull the stunner loose. The hand belonged to my victim from the previous night: Juan Mylinchek. In daylight, he was just as ragged looking.

His eyes were bloodshot, and his face looked puffy. Graying, patchy beard covered his cheeks, and his dark hair receded from his forehead. His clothing was ripped and stained.

"Oh, no, girlie, you ain't tryin' that again." Juan pulled the stunner away and peered at it. "How does this thing work?"

So far, no one else had joined us. Should I scream and alert both my friends and the rest of Juan's posse? Or should I try to disable him quietly? I swallowed hard. "It has an identity scanner," I lied. "I'm the only one who can operate that."

He eyed me sideways. "Identity scan? How? Blood? Optical?"

Crap. He was smarter than I'd expected. "Um, if you give it to me, I'll show you."

"How stupid do you think I am?" He shook my arm, hard. His grin revealed broken teeth, and his rank breath felt hot against my cheek. "You aren't gettin' anywhere near this thing. Tell me how it works."

"How stupid do you think I am?" I said back to him.

"I guess we'll see." He thumbed the control panel and it lit up. "Now we're gettin' somewhere."

"You don't want to do that," I said, my voice rising. "If you try to use it, it will identify you as a threat and shock you."

He twitched involuntarily, and I bit back a grin. Obviously, he remembered our previous encounter. "This says 'fully-charged.' Nothin' about identity."

"Of course not," I bluffed. "This is military issue defensive equipment. It's not going to have warnings printed on it like civilian stuff."

His eyes narrowed. "Why did you warn me?"

"Uh, because you're touching me. I don't want to get shocked, too." I shuddered as if I'd experienced that too many times already.

"Good." He took a firm grip on my wrist, pushing my sleeve up so we had skin-to-skin contact. Then he handed me the weapon. "Show me how to operate it."

I shrugged. "Okay. Like this." I jammed it against his neck and pulled the trigger.

Juan seized, his hand tightening painfully on my wrist. When I released the trigger, he collapsed in a heap.

"I lied." I yanked my new emergency blanket out of my belt pouch—I was going through these things like crazy—and shoved a couple folds of material into his mouth. Then I rolled him over and used some zip ties to secure his hands. I shoved him as far off the road as I could, trying to push him into the underbrush. But the thick foliage stopped me. I shook out the other end of the blanket and draped it over him, hoping the camouflage pattern might help hide him. Then I hurried back to my friends.

CHAPTER THIRTY

"There you are!" Thor pulled up beside me on his air bike.

"Keep your voice down!" I hissed. I glanced over my shoulder, but Juan's body was hidden by the thick shadows.

Thor's eyes sparkled. "What kind of mayhem are you up to?" He revved his air bike—which had no audible effect, so I wasn't sure why he bothered. "Hiding something from Daddy?"

"There is a cell of Hellion terrorists behind those trees." I pointed toward Juan. "I just took down their leader, and if they hear us, they'll kill us."

Thor laughed, loud. I smacked my hand over his mouth with a resounding clap and winced. "I mean it!"

He pushed my hand away. "You called for backup, right?"

My eyes widened, and I smacked myself on the forehead. "What—" I slapped my comm interface. "Siti to village camp. I'm under attack."

No one answered.

"Seriously?" Thor gunned the bike again, and it leapt into the air. "I need to get this on cam!" As he zipped away, a cloud of micro-drones dispersed from the back of his bike.

"Thor! I need help!" I wailed, but quietly, in hopes Juan's friends hadn't heard us.

A useless hope.

"Put your hands where I can see 'em girlie!" a nasal, high-pitched voice demanded.

I held my hands out from my body and slowly turned. "I'm under attack," I muttered as I turned. "I could use some assistance."

A huge man dressed in a filthy sleeveless shirt and ragged pants aimed a crossbow at my chest. Having seen what that weapon did to Tanis, my breath caught in my chest.

Blue tattoos covered his arms and shoulders, and several small stars lay scattered across his right cheek. His squinty eyes bored into me, and the resemblance to Juan was uncanny in someone so completely different. "Where's my brother?"

"I don't know what you're talking about," I said, my eyes darting over his shoulder. I dragged them away from the motley assortment of men and women behind him and tried to keep my breathing even.

The smell made that almost impossible. I'd have bet none of these people had been near a bath since they left the Dome three years ago. I gritted my teeth and took shallow breaths. "Are you Tran?"

He bared his few remaining teeth in what I assumed was a smile. "You've heard of me."

"Saw you fall off the ladder last night," I said, with more bravado than I felt.

His beady eyes disappeared into the network of wrinkles around his eyes. "You're the bitch who zapped my brother! Where is he?"

"Not my turn to watch him," I said.

The men and women behind Tran chuckled. He swung around to glare at them. I took off running.

"Stop!" A crossbow bolt slammed into the dirt beside me, burying itself to the ragged feathers.

I leapt aside and spun around in a crouch. My eyes flew to the edges of the road, looking for a break in the underbrush I could squeeze through. It was thick here. Vines with centimeter-long sharp spikes filled the space between trees in an impenetrable barrier.

"One more move, girlie, and the next bolt goes into your throat." Tran locked another bolt into place. Behind him, a wall of guns, arrows, and even a couple of rocks seemed to be aimed at my head.

I twitched my fingers against my holo-ring and sent an SOS signal to the camp. At least, I tried to send it. I didn't dare check my displays with all those eyes on me. "What about him?" I asked, looking upward.

"Who?" Tran snarled.

"The vid guy," I said. Of course, the coward was nowhere in sight. "Thor. He's got micro-drones recording this whole interaction."

"Drones? We got a solution for that, don't we Brain?" Tran glanced over his shoulder.

The people behind him shifted, and a pale man with lank hair shuffled forward. He held a small box in his hand. It looked like one of the communicators the villagers used. Brain? Maybe he was the smart one. He certainly wasn't the brawn.

"What's that?" I asked.

"EMP device," Brain said. "I built it myself."

"EMP?" The name sounded familiar, but I wasn't sure what it did.

"Electro-magnetic pulse." The man grinned. Unlike his companions, his teeth were straight and blindingly white. "It'll kill those drones."

I looked skeptically at the box. "You sure about that? Those things require huge magnets, don't they? Or coils or something. Have you tested it?"

Brain looked at his box, then up at the sky, and shrugged. "No time like the present." He flipped the switch.

Nothing happened.

He flipped the switch back and forth.

"How do you know if it's working?" Tran asked.

"The drones should fall out of the sky."

They all looked up.

"I don't see any drones," Tran said.

I eased backward a half-step.

"*She* said they're micro-drones. I think that means they're tiny." Brain jutted his chin at me. All the heads snapped down and their eyes bored into me.

"Gimme that," Tran snarled. He grabbed the box from Brain and hurled it at me.

I ducked, but it hit me in the temple. Pain exploded in my head, and everything went black.

A DULL THROBBING pounded behind my eyes, like a muffled bass drum. I lay still as awareness extended beyond my own skull. A mutter of sound, like people talking a long way away, reached my ears. Closer, an uneven dripping. Musty damp assaulted my nose. I sucked in a shallow breath, not wanting to alert any watchers that I was awake. Metal, stone, smoke.

I lay on a rough surface. Small bits of something bit into my back, becoming more unbearable the longer I lay there. My hands and feet were frigid with cold. In fact, my feet seemed to be bare.

Reassured by a complete lack of nearby sound, I cracked one eyelid open. Total darkness greeted me. Not just a dim room but completely black. Not even a chink of light around the edges of a door.

Suppressing a groan, I pushed myself to a seated position. The surface under my hand felt cold and dusty—stone, perhaps. I let my hand drift away from my body, exploring.

Definitely stone. Small pieces of rock rattled as I brushed my fingers against them. My hand met a roughly vertical surface, and I gathered my feet under my body. Using the wall for support, I pushed myself to my feet.

My head swam. I staggered and banged my head against a low ceiling.

"Ow!" I bit back the sound, fear keeping my voice low. I must be inside a cave, which meant I was likely still a prisoner. But my hands and feet weren't bound, so that was something. I reached for my holo-ring and discovered it missing. I'd hoped the Hellions weren't smart enough to know what it did, but maybe that Brain guy knew.

The throbbing in my head surged and waned in pulsing waves. I touched my forehead where it hurt the worst. No blood but a painful, swollen bump just below my hairline. That box had obviously hit me hard enough to put me out, so a head injury was a given. What were you supposed to do for a head injury?

My fingers went to my belt, seeking my first aid kit. Gone, of course.

The booster my dad had put into my shoulder pocket was also missing, as was my stunner and my other belt pouches. Only my uniform remained. I pulled back the collar and gave the translator a quick double squeeze—another emergency signal. If it could get through the layers of rock I was convinced hung above my head.

I turned—was that a less black darkness? My captors must be that direction.

Peter, Katy, and Tiah—not to mention Thor—must have alerted my dad to my capture by now. All I needed to do was stay alive, and Dad would rescue me. I snorted a little. By getting myself captured, I'd undoubtedly gotten the CEC to help the village with their problem.

Staying away from the Hellions was probably my safest bet. I moved slowly around the cavern, my fingers trailing against the wall and ceiling so I wouldn't crack my head again. After what felt like a lifetime, I reached an opening in the roughly circular room. I turned around and went the other way, hoping to find a second opening. Soon, I was back at the same spot. Or at least I thought it was the same spot. Hard to tell with all this darkness. But the only passageway seemed to move me toward a lessening of black.

Moving slowly to make as little noise as possible, I followed the passage. My fingers trailed against the rough stone, and I felt for each step with my bare toes. Every few meters, I stopped to listen.

The dripping noises seemed to fill my head.

My toes encountered cold dampness. The rock felt slick and slimy. I swept my foot along the ground, feeling for a drier patch. My toes were so cold, it was hard to tell what I'd touched.

I could stop here, or I could move on. I lowered myself down the wall, huddling in a crouch. Putting out a hand, I felt for the damp my toes had encountered. A trickle of water ran across the path and away—perhaps through a break in the stone? Impossible to tell.

I grew cold crouched there, so I pushed myself up and moved on. Stepping over the trickle, I crept along.

Were the voices getting louder? The darkness seemed to be easing. Before long, I could see movement when my hand slid along the rock wall. Definitely getting lighter.

Step. Stop. Listen. Step. Stop. Listen.

The passageway turned, and bright light stabbed at my eyes. I ducked back, hoping I hadn't been seen. My heart pounded in my ears, throbbing in time to the pain in my head. I breathed deep, as quietly as I could. My breath caught in my dry throat, and I struggled not to cough.

No one shouted or grabbed me, so I must not have been spotted. I leaned around the corner of stone and peered up the passageway.

About five meters away, the tunnel opened out into a larger cavern. Light flickered—much dimmer than I'd first thought. Perhaps a fire or a lamp of some kind. I crept up the slight slope and stopped just inside the mouth of the tunnel, my back pressed against the wall, grateful my CEC uniform blended with the shadows.

Two men and a woman sat in a circle around a small flame. I recognized them as part of the mob that had attacked me on the road. The tiny fire flickered within a thick glass globe, similar to the oil lamps in the village. The light hit the fingers of stone jutting down from the ceiling and up from the floor, casting uncanny shadows on the cavern walls.

"We shoulda just killed her," the thicker man said. "Dumped the body and continued with the plan."

"Juan was out cold," the woman said in a tired voice, as if she'd said this too many times already. "He'd never forgive us if he missed it."

"Why do we care?" the scrawny guy said. "I only joined the Hellions 'cause I was hungry. Don' care if Juan is mad. I want more food than he's been giving us anyway. Look at me!" He patted his stomach under the filthy, loose shirt. His stomach growled, loudly, as if in response. "Maybe it's time to strike out on our own."

"On our own?" the big guy snorted. "'Cause we were doing so well before."

"We've learned a few tricks—how to find loners." The scrawny guy scratched his head. "With Luisa here, we can hide from the other villagers and sniff out targets. Besides, you seen the weapons those aliens got? If we'da killed the girl, they'd come after us."

I squinted at the woman. Her skin color was hard to see in the dim light, but she had the same heavy, dark eyebrows and slightly hooked nose as Tiah—and all the other Insiders. If the men were former villagers, they would have the same mind reading abilities as Mara and Everest. Luisa would act as a dampener—to keep victims from "hearing" them until it was too late.

Could I sneak past these people? Even if Luisa wasn't with them, they couldn't use their "gifts" to listen for me—my personal defense shield prevented that. If it was still operational. Now that I thought about it, I wasn't sure what powered it. Was I still protected without my holo-ring? I had no way to check the interface, but surely, such a system would default to active and not off? It didn't really matter in this case—according to Lena and Esabella, without it, I was invisible to them.

They could still see me, though. Staying close to the rock wall, I stepped into the larger cavern. As long as I moved slowly, I shouldn't draw attention to myself. They were facing their lamp—their eyes would take time to adjust to the darkness. I just needed to stick to the shadows. I eased forward, crouching low and feeling for each footstep.

Snippets of their conversation filtered into my consciousness as I focused on my path. The Mylinchek brothers ran this gang through fear and hunger. The three seated here hadn't eaten in several days, as punishment for some unmentioned infraction. They'd apparently been tasked with keeping me in my little prison. I laughed silently. Clearly, Juan didn't understand the importance of keeping the troops fed.

I gained the far side of the cavern and slunk into another passageway. It sloped upwards slightly, and the lamp in the cavern behind me provided enough light to make my way without tripping. This tunnel was wider, with a smooth floor, as if it were frequently used. It curved to the right, and I paused for my eyes to adjust to the dimmer light.

After a few meters, it twisted to the left, and light from another source reached me. I slid along the wall, keeping to the shadows. More voices—louder and forceful—set my teeth on edge. I crept to the end of the tunnel and peeked around the corner.

More of Juan's gang sat around a large fire in the center of a wide cavern. The middle had been cleared of rubble except for the stones they sat on. Hammocks hung from the lower ceiling on the far side of the space, and someone stood over a makeshift grill. The smell of cooking meat drifted to me, making me nauseous. Smoke wafted up into the vast ceiling, hanging in a haze just above the gang's heads.

I crouched behind a boulder and listened.

"...her daddy is the big fish," Juan said. He sat between his brother and a short, curly-haired woman, with his back to me. "They can't get to us in here—we've proven how easy this place is to defend. He wants his little girl back, so we'll give her back. For a price. A few of those blaster guns. And some of those flying belts, to start with. What else we gonna ask for?"

"I want the flying bike," Tran mumbled over a mouthful of food.

"Yeah, and one of those shuttles," another man said. "I don't want to stay here on Earth. There gotta be better planets out there!"

"You know how to fly a shuttle?" Someone barked a laugh. "Hey everyone, Indigo knows how to fly a shuttle." Most of the others laughed.

"Make 'em give us a pilot, too," Indigo muttered.

"Don't be stupid." Juan hurled something across the fire, hitting Indigo in the head. The bone bounced harmlessly to the floor.

"Hey!"

"Shut up!" Juan picked up a rock, hefting it in his hand. When Indigo didn't respond, Juan continued, "We need power. I'm tired of living in the dark like a caveman. We'll demand one of those folding buildings Brain saw. And whatever they use to power it." He ripped meat off another bone with his teeth and chewed. "And food. I want something other than rabbit for a change."

"We'll take the wheat when it's ready to harvest." The man by the grill looked up. "I could do with an oven though. It'd be nice to bake bread."

"We aren't going to be here at harvest time," Juan said. "You think they're going to give us a bunch of stuff and let us settle here? No. We're taking what we can get and moving somewhere else. Somewhere we can build our own empire."

"They can fly," Tran said. "I wanna fly."

"You'll get your flying bike," Juan growled. "And one of their transport train things. We'll need it to move our stuff. You saw them dragging people around with those things."

"You think you can get all that for one little girl?" someone asked.

"She's his kid," the woman next to Juan said.

My heart stopped in my chest. I tried to suck in air, but my lungs didn't seem to work anymore. I knew that voice. It was Marika.

CHAPTER THIRTY-ONE

"Kassis will give you just about anything if you give his kid back," Marika said, her back to me. "But he's not gonna trade a pilot and shuttle for her."

What the hell? Why was Marika here? And why was she helping the Hellions?

"I say we get the shuttle," the idiot said. The others shouted him down.

"You gonna negotiate for us," Juan said.

"I can't do that," Marika said. "I can't blow my cover for you."

"Sure you can." Juan picked up a large knife and stabbed it into the meat on his lumpy clay plate. Firelight sparkled along the sharp edge. "If you aren't gonna help us, what good are you?"

"I can help you plan your negotiation," Marika said, her voice cold and hard. "I can suggest demands they will agree to. But I will not risk my cover to help you." A small blaster had appeared in her hand, seemingly out of thin air. She rose and backed away, moving closer to me.

I ducked lower, peering around the side of my boulder.

Juan stood slowly, his eyes darting from the weapon to her face and back. He slid the knife into the sheath on his belt and held his hands away from his body. "I want some of those."

Marika smiled. "I'm sure we can work out something. Now, let's talk. Just you and me."

Juan glanced at the crowd around the fire. "Out!"

"Where we gonna go, Juan?" Tran whined. "The aliens are outside."

The thin man pointed toward the darkest corner of the cavern. "Go out the back. They don't know about it. Leave Ferris and Levane on the front entrance."

"What about them?" a woman asked. She gestured toward the passage I'd come up.

"They aren't goin' anywhere." Juan grinned. "They got a job to do. And I'm not lettin' 'em run away until they can be useful." He mimed picking something off with his rifle.

The group chuckled as they shuffled to their feet. They lit makeshift torches and lamps from the fire and hurried away.

I thought about following them. If I could escape, Marika would have nothing to trade. But I needed to know what she was planning. I settled down behind my rock, my ears stretched.

"You can come out now, Siti," Marika said.

Crap. I froze, my heart pounding in my ears.

"She's down the cave," Juan said.

"No, she's not." Marika chuckled. "She's right there. With her emergency beacon blaring like crazy."

"What?!" Stumbling steps thundered toward me.

I took a deep, shuddering breath and stood. "What's your plan, Marika? Why are you betraying us?"

"Get her beacon off!" Juan lunged at me. I scrambled around the boulder, keeping it between him and me.

Marika laughed. "It's useless in here. The rock blocks the signal, except when she's in the same cavern." She grabbed my arm and pulled me around to face her. "Stay calm," she whispered as she reached for my collar. "I'll get you out of this."

I slapped her hand away. "Why are you doing this?"

Her eyes flicked over my shoulder, then back to mine, boring into me. Her free hand, no longer holding the blaster, flicked quickly through a series of movements. I rolled my eyes. She knew I hadn't studied the CEC signals.

Her hand snapped out and grabbed my collar. I tried to pull away, but her grip tightened like a vice. With her back to Juan, her fingers flicked a couple of times, then she yanked me forward, hard. "I turned up the gain," she hissed, her words nearly lost in the scuffle of our feet on the loose stones.

I stared at her as she dragged me to the fire. Which side was she on?

"Sit." She pushed me onto a boulder and sat on the next one. The blaster reappeared in her lap like magic.

Juan stomped to a boulder across the fire, his eyes fixed on Marika. "You turn off her beacon?"

"I told you, it won't help in here. The signal isn't strong enough to reach through the stone. And as long as she doesn't have her ring, she can't communicate." She stared him down. "But yeah, I fixed the beacon."

Juan raised his hand, looking at a ring on his pinky finger. "How's this thing work?"

"It won't work for you," she said. "They're tuned to the wearer. It doesn't recognize you, so it's dead."

"What if I cut off her finger and carry it around in my pocket?" Juan's hand slid lovingly toward his knife.

Marika barked out a laugh. "This tech is way beyond Earth stuff. It only works on living fingers. Unless you want to drag her around with you for the rest of your life, it's just a piece of jewelry."

For a second, he looked like he was considering it. Then he shook his head. "No. I want to trade her for stuff. But it's gotta be stuff I can operate without one of these, right?"

"Exactly." Marika nodded. "The supply train or drones, for example, can be operated with a tablet."

"Those," Juan said. "I want those."

Marika listed off a bunch of supplies: clothing, food, a shield generator.

"Weapons." Juan licked his lips. "You promised me weapons."

I opened my mouth to tell him no, but Marika kicked me in the calf. "I did." She nodded. "You'll get what you need."

"What's your plan?" Juan asked. "How're we gonna negotiate?"

Unintelligible shouts echoed through the cavern. Juan leaped to his feet and ran across the cavern. "Stay there," he shouted over his shoulder.

"Come on." Marika grabbed my arm again and dragged me across the cavern in Juan's wake.

"What are you trying to do?" I yanked my arm out of her grip, stopping at the mouth of the tunnel. "Why are you helping them?"

"My job is to cause trouble until the Gagarians arrive," Marika said. "They'll be here in two days. When you fell into Juan's hands, it made that job easier. The Hellions can't hold Kassis off forever. When I'm ready to leave, you'll be set free."

"The Gagarians?" I laughed. "You mean the villagers? They aren't really from Gagarin!"

She shook her head in mock disbelief. "I know. I don't know how the commander can be so stupid."

"You know they aren't—" I stared at her. "Who are you talking about?"

"I'm talking about the real Gagarians." She flicked her holo-ring to shine a light on the passage floor. She nudged me with her blaster. "Walk."

"The real Gagarians," I repeated in a dazed tone. "From Gagarin?"

"Where else would they be from?" Her low voice dripped with derision.

"But—"

"Come on, Siti. I thought you were smarter than that." She moved her hand, and the shadows bounced around the tunnel, making the footing uncertain. "Who do you think I work for?"

"The CEC," I replied promptly.

"Yeah, right." She snorted. "They pay crap. I'm a Gagarian agent."

I wheeled around to stare at her. "What?"

"Keep moving." She poked my stomach with the nose of the blaster.

"Where are we going?" I turned slowly, wondering if I could pull the weapon out of her hand before she fried me.

"We're going to negotiate with your daddy." She poked my back with the blaster this time. "Then you're going back into the hole until my ride gets here."

"What do you want?" I asked.

"I want my nation to have a say over Earth," she said. "My job is to stop the CEC from laying claim to the planet until Gagarin arrives."

"But no one can claim the planet if there are already people here," I protested. "We learned that in history class."

"History is written by the winners," Marika said. "That will be Gagarin this time."

Cold trickled down my spine. "What does that mean? What's your plan?"

"I don't have a plan," Marika said. "Aside from keeping Kassis busy. The rest is above my pay-grade." She grabbed my shoulder. "Stop here."

A narrow fissure opened in the side of the tunnel. If I ducked, I might be able to squeeze through—if I was crazy. "I'm not going in there."

"No, you're not. You're going to wait right here while I chat with Juan." She grabbed my arm and slid a long SnapTie around it. She thrust my arm into the fissure and pulled the tie through a gap in the stone, then wrapped it around my other arm. "That should keep you." She patted my shoulder and sauntered away, the light disappearing with her.

I leaned my forehead against the rough stone, trying to wrap my mind around what I'd just learned. Marika was a Gagarian spy. She didn't give a crap about me or the CEC or the mission. How would she make sure Gagarin 'won' this time? There was no war here, except between the Hellions and the village. Dad wouldn't care who won that war. How would that help Gagarin?

Exhaustion flowed through me, and I sagged against the tunnel wall. The rock scraped my arm, snagging the fabric of my uniform jacket. The gap she'd pushed the SnapTie through was too high for me to sit on the ground, so I leaned against the cold stone. Despair washed over me. The Hellions had made it very clear they didn't mind killing people. My chances of getting out of here alive had to be close to zero.

My eyes started to burn, and I blinked back the tears that threatened to fall. I needed to keep a clear head if I wanted to survive. Peter, Katy, and Tiah knew what had happened to me. Thor, too. Surely, my dad had followed us to the cave. He would have a plan to rescue me.

But what if he couldn't? Zane had said this cave was impossible to attack. They wouldn't risk anyone else's life. I'd have to trust Marika to get me out of here. And after her recent revelation, Marika wasn't inspiring any trust.

I blinked faster, but the hot tears spilled out anyway. At least no one could see me in the dark.

CHAPTER THIRTY-TWO

"Siti."

I froze, listening hard.

Nothing.

Great, now my imagination was playing games with me. I rubbed my damp cheek against my shoulder, scraping my arm again.

Wait a minute. The stone was rough. Maybe I could cut through the SnapTie. I twisted my hands, trying to touch my fingers to the rock.

"Siti."

"Who's there?" I whispered.

"It's Tiah," she said. A hand brushed my arm.

"How did you get in here? Do you have a knife?"

"Shh!" She put her cold fingers against my face, poking my cheek.

I nodded, knowing she'd feel the movement. Her hand slid down to my arm, reaching the opening in the stone. "Are you tied up?"

"Yes. There's a SnapTie holding my hands together around this piece of rock. Do you have a light?"

"I don't want to alert anyone." Her fingers snagged on the SnapTie, and something cold slid against my skin. "Hold still. I don't want to cut you."

"Don't worry about me. Chop away!" I tried to curl my fingers out of her way, but since I couldn't see anything, I had no idea if I was helping or hurting.

Something snapped, and my hand burned. "Ow."

"Sorry!" She grabbed my wrist. "Let me get the knife out of the way before you move." Her hand pulled away. "Now."

I dragged my arms away from the rock. The SnapTie hung limp from my left arm, catching on something as I pulled. I yanked hard, and it gave.

Blood dripped from the back of my right hand, but the wound felt small. I clapped my hand around the cut, wishing I still had my first aid kit.

"Come on," Tiah said. "This way." She slid her cold hand around my wrist and pulled.

"What about Marika? And Juan?" I whispered.

"Who cares?" Tiah pulled again. "We're going out the back."

"But they'll tell my dad they have me."

"Let's get away—then you can tell him you're free. Come on."

We crept down the passageway toward the flickering of the fire. When we reached the cavern, we paused. "The exit is over there." Tiah pointed, her eyes huge and scared in her narrow face.

My eyes caught on the hammocks hanging from the opposite side of the cave. Gear hung from some of them—including my utility belt. "I need to get my stuff. Wait here." I hurried across the room and grabbed the belt. No sign of my grav-belt or stunner. Crap.

As I ran back to Tiah, I strapped the belt around my waist. I was so focused on the belt, I stumbled into Tiah. She drifted away.

"Hey, you're wearing my grav-belt!"

"You gave it to me" She peered at me in concern. "I hurt my ankle, remember?"

"Oh, yeah." I rubbed the sore spot on my forehead. "Blow to the head." As if in response, the throbbing increased. I tried to ignore it. "Where do we go?"

"This way. Back exit." She shifted away from me.

"Wow, you got the hang of that thing really fast." I hurried behind her.

"You've been here a couple of hours," she said. "I had time to figure it out while we followed the gang."

"What about Thor? Didn't he bring help?"

"Thor? The guy on the flying machine?" She shook her head, the movement almost invisible as we left the glow of the fire behind. "He disappeared. Maybe he got shot down." The venom in her voice surprised me.

"Journalists are supposed to be impartial, I guess," I said doubtfully. "But since he has to ride back to civilization on a CEC ship, you'd think he would have helped us."

"We have to be quiet now," Tiah said. "There are more of those Hellions near the exit."

"How'd you get past them?" I whispered. A rumble of conversation filtered along the tunnel.

"I'll show you." She took my hand and led me through the passageway. The darkness thinned as we approached a larger cavern. She put her arm out, stopping me just inside the tunnel, and leaned close to my ear. "There's a drop-off. About ten meters. Rope ladder. I used the belt."

We inched forward. The passage ended in a narrow ledge overlooking another large cavern. A fire burned in the center, and smoke diffused the sunlight pouring in from a million tiny holes in the cave. The effect was dazzling.

A rope ladder hung from the ledge, leading into the darkness below. A slash of light streamed on the far wall, indicating an entrance a few meters away. People lounged in the sunlight, a few of them snoring. Another burst of conversation rumbled up to us, but we couldn't distinguish the words. I grabbed Tiah's shoulder. "They're down there."

She nodded and pulled me along the ledge. "Over here. It's darker."

I followed her into the deeper shadows, stepping carefully so I didn't dislodge the loose stone to alert the Hellions. "This ledge is getting awfully narrow," I hissed. Beneath us, a jumble of boulders lay along the floor of the cavern. Falling from here would ensure a broken leg—if I was lucky.

She glanced over her shoulder, then down. Her face went pale. "I forgot. We only have one belt!"

"I can use the ladder," I suggested.

Her eyes went wider, and she shook her head.

I looked back. Two of the gang headed toward the ladder.

"Is there anywhere to hide in that passage?" I asked.

She shook her head again.

"Fine, we'll go together. But let me drive. This might hurt your ankle." I stepped closer and tapped the belt interface. "Crap, the power is low. This could get ugly. Watch them. We need to move fast!"

I dropped the belt's relative altitude to zero, so Tiah's feet touched the ledge. Then I slid an arm over her shoulders. "Grab my waist," I whispered into her ear. "Now." I flicked the controls and pushed us away from the ledge.

She gasped as my weight fell on her shoulders, then the belt compensated. Badly. We dropped much more quickly than I'd expected. I pawed at the controls, trying to increase the lift as we dropped closer to the rock-strewn ground.

A hands-width above the ground, the belt compensated again, and we jerked to a stop. I dropped to the ground, stumbling against the rough surface.

"What was that?" a raspy voice asked.

"Probably just rats," another answered. "Or bats. Maybe snakes."

My eyes snapped to Tiah's face. Her eyes widened until the whites were visible all around. I pointed to the ground and lifted one of my feet. Comprehension crossed her face, and she smiled. Then she pointed at me. I shrugged, as if rats and snakes were no big deal.

Normally, they wouldn't be. I had my personal force shield—except I wasn't sure it was still running. And my feet were bare. There was always Liam. My hand clapped to my empty pocket. My face went numb—he wasn't there. Had the Hellions taken him? "I need to find Liam!" I whispered.

Tiah's head shook, vehemently. "He's outside. How do you think we found this entrance?"

My shoulders sagged in relief. Once again, a sair-glider saves the day! I leaned close to her. "How do we get past those thugs by the entrance?"

She jerked her head and drifted away. Trying to move as quietly as possible, I followed her over the rock-strewn surface.

A few meters along the curved wall, we reached a shadow-filled corner. Ducking low, Tiah disappeared into another small passageway. I crawled after her, pebbles scraping my hands and knees. Dust lifted, tickling my nose. I pulled my collar up over my face, breathing into my shirt.

My shoulders and hips were wider than the tiny Dome girl's. My arms scraped against the sides of the passage. The back of my head brushed against the roof, and the distant pounding returned to my temples.

Just when I thought I would scream, the rock tunnel opened into a small cavern, about two meters across and high enough to stand. Pinpricks of light fell like tiny spotlights on the rubble filling the small cave. Tiah used her hands to propel herself up the side of a small rockfall. "There's an entrance over this pile." A narrow space at the top of the pile gave her room to slither over. She turned and peered through the gap, her eyes ranging over my body. "It might be a bit tight."

I looked down at myself, then at her. "Not much we can do about that." I tested the first set of rocks. Confident they wouldn't slide under my weight, I started climbing. At the top, I stuck my head through the gap. "How much space is back there?"

"I can stand—if I could stand." She giggled—a tiny, nervous giggle. "But this isn't the worst part. The opening to the surface is small, too." She pointed toward a bright oval of sunlight.

I stared at it, my heart dropping into my stomach "There's no way."

"Sure there is. Look." Tiah lifted off the ground and sailed to the opening. Her shoulders scraped on the edges, but she twisted and slid through. A chorus of whispers greeted her appearance.

Something blocked the light, and Zane called out softly. "Are you coming? We can pass you the grav-belt if that helps."

"I can't get through that." I tapped the top rock on the slide before me. "I might be able to shift some of these, but what's the point? That hole's barely as big as your head."

"What about the other entrance?" Zane asked. "There's a guard, but we can draw him away."

"There are half-a-dozen men and women right inside the cave." I leaned on the rocks, thinking. "Is my dad out there?"

Zane's head shook side-to-side. "He's in front, talking to their leader. About a klick away."

"Can you communicate with him? Without my booster, my range is zero." I patted the shoulder pocket he'd stowed the device in just a few hours ago. Marika must have told Juan where to find it. "Plus, they took my holo-ring. And tell him Marika is working with the Hellions. She's a Gagarian spy."

Zane snorted. "Like he'll believe anything I say—especially about Gagarians. I'll send someone with a message." He turned away. "Joss! No, I'd better do it. Joss, you and Zina stay here. Help your mom set up the diversion. Pete, you're with me. The boss man seems to like you."

I squirmed into a more comfortable position. Rocks dug into my stomach and chest, but at least the top of the pile provided a relatively flat place to lie. It was also a single huge slab of stone, so shifting it to get over was definitely out of the question. I rested my forehead on the rock and waited for Zane.

A scuffling noise alerted me, and Tiah drifted through the hole again, bringing the emergency blanket I'd wrapped around Tanis last night. They'd cleaned off the blood, but the smoky smell remained. I wrapped it around myself, not realizing how cold I'd gotten until I felt the contrast.

"Thanks." I took the food and water she offered. Then she held out something else. "Liam!"

The glider leaped out of her hands and scrambled up my arm, chittering softly as he nestled into my messy hair. "You're such a good boy!"

"I thought you said all the gliders were female," Tiah said.

"They are—" Strange. I hadn't thought about it until now, but for some reason I'd assigned a male name and pronoun to Liam. I chuckled as I stroked his head. "I never checked. But you're right, they're all girls or we'd have an overabundance of gliders. I guess I should call her Liama."

Tiah grimaced. "Lisa?"

I tilted my head back and forth, considering. "How about Lia? What do you think?" I stroked the glider's head. "Are you a Lia?"

Liam's head shook in a decisive no.

Tiah's eyes widened. "Does he understand you?"

"No..." Nothing I'd read indicated any level of language comprehension, but... I chuckled. "They're smart, but not that smart."

Liam gave me a disgusted look that just made me laugh harder.

"Sh!" Tiah hissed.

I clapped a hand over my mouth.

Footsteps. Coming closer.

Tiah flitted away, and something fell across the opening, dimming the light in the small cavern. The tiny pools of light lay across the floor, like lacework. I plastered myself to the stone slab, hoping the shadows hid me. My breathing sounded loud in my ears. Behind the rock fall, Tiah shifted, and dust tickled my nose.

My personal shield should have prevented the dust from reaching me. Obviously, it wasn't working any more. I fought the sneeze for as long as I could, then buried my face in my arms.

The tickle exploded out of my sinuses. Ah-choo!

The footsteps stopped. Voices rumbled and stilled. Light flashed in the small opening leading back to the main cave. More voices, and then the footsteps left.

I waited.

Something shifted. They'd left a guard.

CHAPTER THIRTY-THREE

I LIFTED my head and turned to look over the rock fall. Tiah drifted up, her eyes only a few centimeters from mine. "There's someone out there," I mouthed.

She nodded, her eyes terrified. "Can they get through?"

I made a face. It would be a tight fit for Juan and a no-go for Tran, but the trio left in charge of guarding me could easily make it. "Get me a weapon," I whispered.

She nodded and flitted to the opening. The light streamed in as she pushed heavy fabric from the hole. After a quick conversation, she returned with one of the village guns.

The heavy pistol felt alien but comforting in my palm. I twisted onto my side to get a better look at it. The muzzle, handgrip, and trigger were obvious, but I couldn't identify anything else. "If I squeeze this, it fires?"

She held up a finger and zipped back to the hole. In a second, she was back, with a rectangular item.

She touched the gun. "Safety is off." She flipped a tiny lever. "On. Won't fire. If you run out of bullets, press this—" She pointed again, then tapped the bottom of the grip. "The magazine—" She broke off, probably noticing my confusion. She held up the new item. "This thing has bullets inside.

The empty one will fall out, and this one goes in." She described the motion with her hands.

"Let's hope I don't need that many bullets." The idea of shooting *things* into a person terrified me. "I wish I had my stunner."

"We don't have those. This is a good weapon. I helped make it."

I stared at her in amazement. "You made this?"

"I operate the drafting machines." She shrugged. "Someone had to learn it when all the ancients left the Dome, so I did. The computer cuts and makes the things, but I tell it how to do that. Most of our stuff is old designs, but when we come up with new ideas, we get to—" She broke off again. "I can show you later."

"Have you fired one?" I flipped the safety off and on again.

"No!" She looked horrified. "Why would I do that?"

I hid a grin. "Did Zane send someone to talk to my dad?"

"Peter and Jake went far enough so Jake could call Mara. She went to the cavern with your dad." She lifted up a bit to peer over my shoulder. "We should probably stop talking."

We'd kept our voices low, but she was right. They might suspect I was in here, but they didn't know, unless we gave ourselves away.

I laid there with Liam's tail curled around my neck, his tiny body huddled against my chest. Inside the emergency blanket, he put out enough heat to keep us both toasty warm. I relaxed against the stone slab and tried to ignore the throbbing in my head.

Something poked my shoulder, bringing me out of my stupor. Tiah peered over the rocks at me, her face harder to see now. It must be getting darker outside.

She leaned close. "There's a storm coming, but it will hold off until dark. Your dad is talking to that guy—Juan—near the front entrance. Some of the villagers are going to attack from this side. Lt. Evy is with your dad—they will come in through the front. They're going to squeeze the Hellions in between. You just need to stay here."

"Too bad it won't be that easy," Marika said.

My head snapped around so fast I clunked it against the stone, setting the pounding into high gear. Marika stood before the low entrance, my stunner in one hand and her blaster in the other. "I hope you had a nice nap. It's time to come down."

I slowly sat up, giving Tiah a "get out of here" look as I turned. Liam scrambled down my arm and into my pocket.

"Your friend needs to come out here where I can see her," Marika said casually, as if we were trying on dresses.

"There's no friend," I said, rubbing my head. "It's just me."

"I heard you talking," Marika said. "And I know you didn't have that emergency blanket when you were in the cave. I checked."

I shifted under the blanket, flicking the safety lever on the weapon. The extra bullet holder slid in my lap as I moved. I tried to grab it but missed, and it fell, hitting the rocks loudly as it went.

"What was that?" Marika demanded.

"I, uh, dropped something." I froze, hoping to give Tiah time to leave.

"Get your friend out here," Marika said again.

"She's long gone." I slid down from the slab, scooting down the rock fall on my butt. "She gave me the blanket and left."

"Get out here!" Marika called louder. "Or I'll shoot her."

"You won't," I said, just as loudly. "I'm your only collateral. You need me to trade with my father."

"I need you alive, but I don't need you in one piece." She pointed the blaster at my leg, half-hidden in the blanket.

"You must be getting desperate." I slid down a bit farther. "You aren't thinking clearly. How are you going to get me through that tiny tunnel with a big hole in my leg?"

Her eyes narrowed.

"Besides, if you think my dad is going to just let you go, you're crazy. He'll hunt you down if you hurt me." He'd hunt her down regardless, for messing up his mission, but she should have already known that.

"Good point." She slid the blaster into her holder and adjusted the settings on the stunner. Then she pointed it at my foot and pressed the button.

Blue lightning flashed out of the muzzle and hit my foot. Fire lanced through my leg, and every muscle seized. I screamed, louder than necessary.

"Move!" Marika barked. "Get into that tunnel. Now!"

Tears rolling down my cheeks, I dropped the blanket and raised the pistol to point it at her chest. "No."

"Oh, look. The princess has grown a spine," Marika said. "Isn't that cute. You know those projectiles won't go through my personal shield."

My eyes narrowed. That didn't sound right. Our shields were intended to protect us from little things—viruses, germs, bacteria. I didn't remember anything from the initial briefing about projectiles.

Marika smiled maliciously. "You don't think I have a standard shield, do you? Gagarin excels at military grade equipment."

"Right." I glared at her. "And it looks exactly like CEC stuff."

"Of course it does. I'm a spy, remember?" She jerked the stunner. "Drop the ancient gun."

I let the muzzle of the weapon drop a little and squeezed the trigger. A painful bang slammed into my ears, and my hand wrenched up. Marika cried out. The bullet ricocheted away, zinging around the small cavern. I dropped to a crouch, my stunned leg collapsing under my weight.

Lightning ripped out of Marika's stunner and slammed into my shoulder. Knives ripped up and down my arm. I yelped, and the gun fell from my nerveless fingers.

I wiped the tears from my eyes with my left hand.

"Move!" Marika barked, jerking her weapon toward the tunnel. "And don't even think about trying to pick up that gun. If I zap you in the head, it could cause permanent brain damage with that concussion you must already have. And then I can just wrap a rope around you and have Tran drag you out. That might be painful. Your head banging into rocks and stuff."

I left the emergency blanket on the stones and stumbled toward the tunnel. I tried to squat and ended up on my butt again when my leg gave way. "I can't crawl—my arm and leg aren't working right."

"You've got one good arm and a good leg," Marika growled. "Move." When I didn't, she raised the stunner. "Okay, rope drag it is."

I held up my working hand. "No, I'll crawl." I rolled onto my knees and started into the tunnel. My right arm hung useless at my side. Feeling had returned to my left leg—like dull needles poking into my calf and ankle.

"She's coming out!" Marika yelled. The narrow tunnel amplified the sound, ringing through my throbbing head.

Bright light stabbed into my eyes as I neared the cavern. Rocks gouged my palm and dug into my knee. I kept my head down, hoping to prevent more damage. On the far end, rough hands grabbed my arms and yanked me out of the tunnel. Tran's hot, rank breath blasted my face as he dragged me upright.

"They're going to try an assault," Marika told Tran. "We need to get her to the front, where she's visible. Can you carry her up the ladder?"

Tran grunted and flung me over his shoulder. My head barely missed the overhanging rock—my hair caught on something and yanked out a few strands. I flopped onto his back, hitting hard enough to knock the air out of my lungs.

Liam scrambled out of my pocket just in time to avoid being squished by my weight. He crawled under my hair and clung to my neck, chittering softly in my ear. Then he scrambled down Tran's back and disappeared.

Tran jumped, nearly dropping me in the process. "What was that?" he screeched in his high, froggy voice.

"Probably the rodent," Marika said. "She was supposed to leave that thing in the camp, but the princess never follows the rules."

"Rodent?" Tran's voice went even higher. "Like a rat? Get it off me!"

"It's gone."

"Are you sure?" He twisted around, squirming as if trying to see over his shoulder. I grabbed his shirt with my good hand and held on. I probably should have tried to get free, but my leg still felt like fire, and my arm was starting to come back—painfully. Plus, drums pounded inside my head.

"Just move," Marika snarled.

CHAPTER THIRTY-FOUR

Tran lumbered across the cavern, stumbling over the smaller boulders. My fingers clenched a fold of his filthy shirt as I prayed he wouldn't drop me. Another blow to my head would probably turn me into a drooling idiot.

From the corner of my eye, I caught a flicker of blue movement. Liam! He was following us through the cavern. I twisted around to look for Marika, but she was ahead of us. Ignoring the furious pins and needles, I held out my stunned arm. Liam scrambled up a spire of rock and threw himself at me.

He landed with his usual unerring accuracy then scurried up my arm and into my hair. I nuzzled his warm fur and tried to figure a way out of my newest predicament.

Tran stopped. "How am I supposed to climb with her?"

Marika sighed. "Don't you ever carry supplies up this ladder?"

"We bring 'em in the other way," Tran said.

"We got the elevator," a female voice said.

"Elevator?" Marika repeated. "In a cave?"

"Rope and pulleys," the woman replied. "Not fast, but easier than carrying stuff."

"No, she'll just jump off or something stupid like that." Marika slapped Tran's shoulder. "Up you go."

Crap. Time for a different plan. I could try squirming out of Tran's grip but didn't like the idea of landing on my head. Maybe I should just wait to see where they took me. Being compliant now might give me an opening later.

"Wait," Marika said as Tran reached for the first rung. "Let me tie her up first. This girl is trouble." She grabbed my arm. I resisted the urge to pull away. She slid another SnapTie around my wrists and pulled it savagely tight. "No wiggle room this time, princess. Up you go, Tran."

The giant made his way up the ladder. The ropes stretched with his weight, and my head and arms swung across his back. His body odor intensified, leaving me panting through my mouth in an effort not to smell him. My stomach churned, and a cold sweat soaked my shirt.

Liam chittered softly, his paws tangling in the fine hair at the nape of my neck. I winced.

We reached the top and Tran flopped onto his side, rolling me away. I should have been grateful he didn't squish me beneath his bulk, but by that time, I was desperately trying not to barf.

"Get up, princess," Marika snarled. "You can walk from here."

I moaned and rolled away from Tran. The air away from his cloud of stench cleared my head a little, and I pushed up to my hands and knees. The pins and needles had given way to a dull sparking along my nerves.

"I said, move!" Marika's blaster poked into my back.

I raised my head and glared over my shoulder at the little redhead. "I thought we were friends."

She laughed, a short, harsh bark. "Brown nosing the commander's daughter is useful. Doesn't make us friends. Get up."

I lifted my bound hands and grabbed the wall to steady myself as I climbed to my feet. My head swam. I sucked in a few deep breaths, glad Tran was out of range.

Marika barked another laugh. "Shall I have Tran help you?"

"Not unless you want to see me hurl." I gritted my teeth and swallowed again.

Near the brightly lit entrance, shouts went up. The people lounging around leapt to their feet, scrambling behind boulders and scrabbling for weapons.

"We're under attack!" someone yelled. Shots rang out.

"Move, princess!" Marika pushed me away from the drop off. "We need to get you out front where you can stop the violence. You don't want to be the reason your new friends get massacred, do you? Tran, stay here and hold them off."

I stumbled up the passage as fast as I could move. My stunned leg still felt weak, and I fell into a wall more than once. If she wanted me at the other entrance so badly, slowing down might be to my advantage. I bumbled into a wall and leaned against it.

Marika jabbed me with her weapon. "Don't make me stun you again."

"You're too small to carry me," I said, but my legs started moving again without me making a conscious decision to walk.

"You've been spending too much time with these Terrans. Grav-belts, princess."

"That would be easier for both of us," I muttered.

"Easier." She poked my shoulder with the stunner again. "But I'd have to stun you first, and I don't think your brain could take that much more damage. Just because we aren't friends doesn't mean I want to hurt you."

"Why are you doing this, then?" I slowed my steps a fraction.

"For the glory of the Gagarian Empire, of course." The words sounded like a quote.

"The Gagarian Empire?" I tripped over a rough spot, and my shoulder banged against a corner of rock. "Is there one?"

"Not yet, but we're working on it." She poked me with the stunner again. "Keep moving."

"How is this going to build the empire?" I gestured to the rocky cave around us.

"The United Colonies can't claim this planet," she said. "Earth belongs to all of us. And under the Inter-Colony Treaty of 2430, first come, first served."

That wasn't how I remembered it. The treaty specifically listed Earth as a "shared heritage site." I frowned. "What's the problem?" I asked, rubbing hair off my sweaty forehead. "Even if it was first come, first served, we got here at the same time."

"What? Who did?"

"Us. You arrived with us. Gagarin and Grissom at the same time. It's a tie." I stumbled into the cavern with the fire and leaned against a boulder to face her.

Marika's eyes narrowed. "That won't be how the commander will see it."

"Have you asked him?" I glanced around. This cavern seemed to be deserted. Maybe I could talk her around and get her to release me.

"Not my call." She jerked the weapon at me. "My job is to keep things stirred up until my team arrives. Then they'll claim to have been here all along."

"Dad will know that's not true." I groaned as I dragged my butt off the rock and took a few halting steps in the direction she indicated. "The *Glory* scanned the planet when we arrived. No sign of other ships."

"Not my call," she said again. "They've got a plan to cover that. My job is to keep things stirred up."

"You're sounding like a vid on repeat," I said. The thumping in my head picked up pace as we trudged up the gentle slope of the passageway.

"I don't make the rules, I just follow 'em."

"Only when they work for you," I muttered.

"Of course." She laughed, and this time, it was her normal, carefree laugh. "Best part of being a spy. Now shut up."

The thumping grew louder, and I realized it wasn't my head. "Weapon fire."

"I knew Kassis wasn't going to negotiate." She shoved between my shoulder blades. "Keep moving. You're his reason to back off."

We passed the place where she had tied me to the rock earlier and continued forward. Oil lamps burned in niches along the route, and the sound of low voices reached us. Around the next corner, Juan stood with a few of his ragged supporters.

"Gimme her!" He grabbed my arm and dragged me forward.

"What are you doing?" Marika cried. "We had a plan."

"Your plan ain't workin'. Makin' my own plan." He dragged me up the slope to the opening of the cavern.

We stepped out into a pool of artificial light. Dusk had fallen while we'd been inside, but Dad must have brought in a full assault team. The glare of the lights made my eyes water. Dark shadows moved in the distance, indistinct but comforting.

"I've got your girl!" Juan pulled me in front of him, the blaster he'd gotten from Marika pointed at my head. "Back off or she's toast!"

"If you harm a member of my crew, I will incinerate you," Dad said calmly. His voice echoed through the clearing and my audio implant. The sound of that internal voice brought tears of relief to my burning eyes.

"Siti, if you can hear me," Evy whispered through my implant. "Give me three fingers."

Leaving my hand hanging at my side, I curled my thumb and forefinger into my palm.

"Good. Are you injured? One for yes, three for no."

I gave her both signs.

A thread of a laugh rumbled in my ear. "Does that mean you're injured but mobile?" Evy asked. "One for yes, three for no."

I gave her one finger. I thought about using the rude one, but she was trying to help me.

"Great. Stay where you are for now. When I give you instructions, follow them exactly."

I dipped my head in a short nod.

"She's communicating with them, you twit!" Marika hissed from the safety of the tunnel. "Did you see her nod?"

"What?" Juan shook my arm hard. "Who are you talking to?"

"Get her back in here!" Marika dragged us both into the cavern. "We need a new plan. Is there another way out of here?"

"The high way," Juan said, looking up. "Rough climb. Not sure she'd make it—she's lookin' kinda flimsy."

"We don't need her if they don't know where it is," Marika said.

"I'm sure they did a geological scan by now," I said. "They'll have found it."

"No, they didn't." Marika grinned, the light glinting off her teeth. Her head shook slowly side to side in mock sadness. "Something happened to the scanning gear. A missing component that must have gotten loose in transit."

"Good thing we got an old scan from the Dome, then," I muttered.

Juan dropped my arm and disappeared into the darkness. "High way, people. Moving out!"

"Wait!" Marika grabbed my belt and dragged me after him. "We have the girl. We can make demands."

"You can make demands." Juan spun to confront her, his stolen blaster leveled at her chest. "Did you see what they've got pointed at us? They ain't negotiating. I'm done bein' your stooge. We're leaving. You can stay here and die."

"That wasn't our deal." Marika's own blaster appeared in her hand. "You don't think that weapon works, do you?" She laughed. "Biometrics."

Juan's eyes flicked to me. "She already told me that whopper."

"It's not a whopper if it's true," I said. "Stunners don't have bio, but blasters sure do. CEC doesn't want to put lethal weapons in the hands of primitive cultures."

Juan bared his nasty teeth at me. His eyes flicked from me to the lighted entrance behind me, then to Marika. He held the weapon up, sideways, his other hand open. "Fine. Point your gun at the girl and let's go make our demands."

Marika stared at Juan an instant longer, then swung her blaster toward me. At that instant, Juan hurled his at Marika. It slammed into her hand, and Juan bolted into the dimly lit tunnel behind him.

Marika swore softly, a string of foreign words pouring off her tongue.

I jerked my arm away. She whipped around to face me. "Don't even think about it, princess. We have mayhem to cause."

Weapons whined and spat deep inside the cavern. "Sounds like your friends have been busy. Maybe they'll do our work for us. We're out of here."

"Do you know where his 'high way' is?" I lurched as she pulled me into the cavern.

"No, but I know another exit. I made use of that scanning gear before I broke it." She dragged me past the still-burning lamps and into a side tunnel. Darkness closed around us. Marika must have activated her low-light system, but mine was off-line.

"Won't they trace you through your electronics?" I panted as she hurried me through the dark.

"The rock walls of the cave block most signals," she muttered. "If the scanning gear was working, they might be able to follow us. Move faster."

"I can't," I moaned. "I've been hit over the head and stunned twice. I haven't eaten since breakfast, and I hardly slept last night."

"Suck it up, buttercup." Marika squeezed my wrist. The bones ground together, and pain shot up my arm.

"Why don't you just leave me behind?" I wheezed. "If you're running away, you don't need me."

"I might need you on the other end," she said.

"You mean Gagarin?" I squeaked. "I can't go to Gagarin! I don't want to go to prison. I don't have any relatives there to bring me food or pay bribes to my jailers."

"What kind of crap have you been watching?" Marika sounded genuinely surprised. "We aren't a third world dictatorship. Prisoners are treated humanely. As the daughter of the villain of Darenti Four, you'd probably live better than me."

"You mean hero of Darenti."

"That's not what *we* call him." She shoved me forward and I stumbled to my knees. A light flickered on, illuminating the narrow passage. We'd reached a dead end. "Crawl." She pointed toward a low tunnel.

"I'm not going in there." I shivered. "There's probably snakes. Or bugs."

She fired her stunner into the hole. Blue lightning crackled around the rock, illuminating the tunnel for a few meters. "Not anymore. Crawl."

We crawled in silence. Every few meters, she stopped me and fired the stunner past, sizzling the next section long enough to kill anything in our path. "I didn't know a stunner could be used like that," I said.

"You learn lots of useful things on a CEC mission. Stop here."

I dropped to my butt and closed my eyes. The pounding in my head eased a little, but my mouth felt like a desert, and my stomach dipped and swung as if I were still hanging from Tran's shoulder.

"Here, drink."

Cold, smooth plastek pressed against my leg. I opened my eyes far enough to take in the canteen she held out. I grabbed it and tipped some water down my throat. "Why're you being nice now?"

She reached for the bottle, but I pushed her hand away and took another gulp.

"I won't be nice again if you don't share that," she growled, waving the stunner at me.

I handed her the bottle.

She sipped from the container and stowed it in the small backpack she wore. "My motto is to be nice when you can."

"You threatened to shoot me," I protested. "Several times! You stunned me and handed me over to a—a—a native savage."

She shrugged. "Nothing personal. That was just part of the job. You were a useful tool."

"I'm not a tool, I'm a person! I thought I was your friend until all this happened." My gesture took in the meter-high tunnel, my injuries, and her smug face.

"I like you, Siti, but that's not going to stop me from doing my job." She handed me a green packet. "Have some ChewyNuggets."

I wanted to throw them in her face, but my stomach flipped again. Maybe a little food would calm it. I ripped open the packet, tucking the loose piece into my pocket. I'd use it later to let people know where to find me, if the pounding in my head would stop long enough to let me think.

The first ChewyNugget hit my stomach like a rock. My stomach put up a fight, but the perfectly balanced nutrients worked their magic. I gobbled down the rest of the packet and held my hand out for more.

"Nope, my food has to last me until my team gets here." Marika handed the plastek bottle to me instead. "That's all you get."

I swallowed a little more water and handed it back. "Now what?"

"Now we go on." She nodded into the darkness. "Not far now." She leaned past me to fire the stunner again. The tunnel lit up. About a meter away, it ended.

"There's nowhere to go!" I cried.

"Oh, but there is." She re-holstered her stunner and fired the blaster at the rock wall.

I yelled, dropping to my chest and flinging my arms over my head. "Are you crazy? You'll kill us."

"Relax. Blasters don't ricochet like that primitive gun. Look." She fired again. The end of the tunnel burned red. The stone heated, then melted. She poured more firepower into the hot rock. At the center of the blast, the wall seemed to crumble into itself, like sand in the top of an hourglass. When she stopped firing, the rock drained away, leaving a black-edged hole that seemed to lead to infinity.

CHAPTER THIRTY-FIVE

I stared into the blackness.

"Move," Marika said. "It's cool enough now. This rock dissipates heat quite efficiently."

"But there's nothing there," I protested. My words echoed weirdly.

Marika rolled her eyes. "Of course there is." She shone her light through the hole.

The wall opened into a vast, smooth chamber. It looked man-made. Light glinted off markings on the far wall, but I couldn't tell if it was writing. Dark water lay beneath.

"Is that an underground lake?" I stared into the strange space.

"Swimming pool," Marika said. "It's empty after hours. Move."

"Swim—what?"

"It's the Dome's swimming pool. Too bad we missed the open swim. I hear they do it in the nude." She laughed and pushed my shoulder. "You can swim, right?

"I—of course." I crawled forward and stuck my head through the opening. Her blaster had burned through almost a half-meter of stone and a thin layer of some man-made material. "This is part of the Dome?" About two meters beneath me, water lapped against the wall. A narrow deck ran along the far wall and a wider one lay off to my right.

"Yeah, who'da thought they'd have a pool?" She laughed. "Apparently, they wanted to live in comfort for those five hundred years. There's a basketball court and tennis over that way. Now jump!"

She shoved, hard, against my butt, and I fell forward. Liam scrambled out of my pocket and launched himself as my feet hit the front edge of the hole. Legs and arms wheeling madly, I hit the water with a loud splash.

The water was warm and clear. I surfaced, spluttering. Lights flared on, illuminating the whole room. Liam clung to the wall above my head.

"Hey, auto lights." Marika peered down at me. "Nice."

"You're going to get your blaster wet," I called as I tread water below her.

"Grav-belt." She gave me a smug grin and slid through the hole. With a little wave, she drifted toward the wider deck. "Come on, we don't have all night."

"Maybe I'll just stay here. I haven't been swimming in ages." CEC gear was made to be lightweight, and my bare feet were finally helpful. The warm water stung in the abrasions on my arms and toes. I kicked, lifting my body into a back float. Better to float here for a while than be used as a hostage.

Marika crossed her arms. "I don't think so. I'm going to need my little princess-shaped human shield."

"If you shoot me, you'll kill me." I flipped over and paddled closer, feeling for the bottom. Most pools had a shallow end near the deck, right? "All this water acts as an excellent conductor."

"Your misinformation about weapons is adorable." She shoved her blaster into its holster and pulled out the stunner. "If I set it on low, you'll be fine."

My foot hit the bottom of the pool. I bounced off, moving a little closer so I could plant both feet. "Then what are you waiting for?"

"I don't want to have to wade in to drag you out." She rolled her eyes. "Look, I told you—I like you. I don't want to hurt you. But I'm not giving up my biggest bargaining chip until I'm sure I don't need it anymore." She waved the stunner at me. "That's you, in case I wasn't clear."

"No, I got it." Staying in the pool would get me stunned. It might slow her down, but it would definitely be uncomfortable for me. Getting out might help her, but surely, there would be other opportunities to get away? We were inside a facility full of people! Someone would see us, and I could run or shout or something.

The water seemed to have cleared my head. I looked Marika over. She seemed tired—exhausted even—but deadly. She had the upper hand here, and there was no one to rescue me. It was time to rescue myself.

I raised my hand out of the water. "I'm coming. Put that thing away."

"Not a chance." Marika stepped back from the pool, her stunner still aimed squarely at me.

I sloshed through the water and levered myself up onto the decking. I lay there, staring up at her. "Just give me a minute, okay? I'm not as fit as you."

Liam scurried across the damp deck and chittered at my wet hair. "Sorry, pet, not my fault. Blame her." I glared up at Marika.

"We were in the same Refit class. You're in great shape." My former friend leaned against the wall. "But I have time. My ride won't be here for a while."

"Your ride? You mean, off planet?"

"I wish. No, they won't be here for two more days. Now that my cover's been blown, I need to leave the CEC team, and I have an assistant for that." She rolled her shoulders. "That crawl through the tunnel sucked."

"Try getting shoved in a pool afterwards." Liam jumped to my shoulder as I rolled to my feet.

At the rapid movement, Marika scooted a little farther away. Was she worried about me? I hadn't exactly excelled at the hand-to-hand classes, but my extra centimeters gave me a slight advantage. Plus, I out-weighed her by several kilos. I filed that information away for later use.

"Let's get on with this, shall we? I'm getting cold standing here." I reached up to scratch Liam's ears.

She grabbed a towel off a stack near the door and threw it at me. "Maybe that will help. Now, you first, please."

Liam climbed down my back while I leaned over to wrap the towel around my hair, as if I'd just gotten out of the shower. I grabbed a second one when I reached the door. My CEC uniform dried quickly, so I didn't leave a trail of water behind me. I wiped my face again and draped the second towel around my neck. Maybe I could use it against Marika in some way.

We pushed through the door into a long dark hallway. Lights popped on as we moved. "That's going to blow any chance at surprise." I cursed myself as soon as the words left my mouth. Why was I helping her?

"I did my research. They have a curfew in here." We reached the end of the hall, and her voice lowered. "Everyone is locked safely away in their apartments at this time of night."

Well, crap. There went my plan to signal for help. Still, a scream ought to do the job, right?

"And if you make so much as a peep, I will zap you and tell them you're having a seizure. They won't know the difference."

Ugh. Time to come up with Plan B. Or probably closer to Plan L by now.

"Take a left, then up the steps." She prodded me with the stunner.

"How do you know so much about this place?" I plodded across the tiles to the stairway I'd been down twice before. "You didn't come over here."

"I studied the plans before we left Grissom."

"You knew about this place before we got here?" I stopped halfway up the first flight and stared over my shoulder at her. "How?"

She snorted. "Please. Everyone on the team knew about the Dome. We didn't think it would still be occupied, of course, but since my job was to cause havoc, I figured it was in my best interest to know all the possible resources. Scientific facilities usually have all kinds of trouble-causing agents." She motioned for me to keep moving.

"I'm still not clear on the timeline." I trudged up the steps as slowly as possible, hoping the delay would benefit me somehow. "Why didn't Gagarin just launch their own mission when we did? They could have gotten a full team here about the same time."

"There has been some political unrest back in the old homeland," she said dryly. "Missions to ancient planets require credits and the political will to do them. Both are currently in short supply at some levels. But my bosses weren't willing to give up control of this prize over lack of foresight on the part of the politicians. So, they embedded agents. Many before me, more still after me, I'm sure. As soon as they got word I'd made the team, I got my orders. They launched a small ship to follow as soon as they could."

"How do you know?" I rounded the corner at the top of the staircase and headed down the hallway.

"They told me."

"They told you they were *going* to launch a small ship. Twenty years ago." I opened the door leading into the office areas. I glanced back, but no one was in sight. The lights at the end of the hall flickered off. If we stood here long enough, they'd go off again, and I could attack. "You don't know that they launched it." I stood as still as possible. "You couldn't have gotten any messages after we left—we were in deep sleep, and then we were too far away."

She chuckled. "I'm not the only one on this mission. And the *Glory* set the jump beacons yesterday. Messages have been going back and forth since then."

"And you have someone on the crew passing you intel." I closed my eyes for a second. Then opened them quickly, so I wouldn't miss my chance.

Marika waved her arm overhead. "Nice try. You aren't going to get the drop on me. Keep moving."

I heaved a dramatic sigh and stomped through the office space. We climbed the last set of interminable stairs to the small landing by the security office. I peeked in as we passed, and one of the many almost identical Insiders nodded. "Are you armed? It's not safe outside at night."

Marika pushed me away from the door and waved her blaster. "We're fine, thanks for asking. Have a good evening, Saul."

"How do you know him?" I demanded as we left the Dome.

"Where do you think I've been 'exploring' all this time?" She grinned. "The mission has been somewhat flexible thanks to the crazy happenings around here. I've had time to snoop around a bit. Gather some allies."

How could she have found time to ingratiate herself with both the Hellions and the Insiders? Obviously, an enemy to be reckoned with.

We reached the end of the long ramp to the surface, and Marika grabbed my shoulder. "We'll wait here for my ride."

I leaned against the wall and crossed my arms over my damp chest. The night wasn't cold, but a breeze snuck through the open collar of my jacket and chilled me. Liam wrapped his warm tail around my neck and curled up against my ear. "Where are we going?"

She smiled sadly. "You're staying here. You'll be a liability out there." She glanced at the high wall surrounding the white half-circle apron. "I'm sure the good folks up on the barricade will help you get back to Daddy."

I looked up. "There's no one up there." Pulling away from the wall, I stepped out into the semi-circle of light. "The guards are gone. Even the one on top of the building."

"I guess they went to help with the raid," Marika said. "That certainly makes my escape easier. You'd better stay here, though."

"I can take care of myself." Crap. I'd totally forgotten about the battle raging in the cliff behind us. Had Zane and his team attacked from the rear? Was Dad inside, fighting the Hellions in the dark? He could be hurt—or even dead. Those projectile weapons were dangerous. I tapped my jaw, but my audio implant connected to nothing.

"It's so hard when the net goes down, isn't it?" Marika smirked.

I held out my hand. "Better give my booster back. You won't need it, but I will."

"You think I'm carrying a CEC booster around with me? They'd track me down in a second." She scanned the sky. "I left yours in the cave."

"I'll just have to retrieve it, I guess," I said, trying to sound cocky. It came out pathetic.

"You heard what Saul said." She held up the blaster. "It's dangerous out there. And Daddy is busy right now."

A flicker of light drew my eyes. Thor soared down on his air bike, grinning. "Quite the rumpus you kicked up over there."

"Thor, Marika is a Gagarian spy!" I threw myself at the bike as it landed beside us.

He laughed and pushed me away. "Tell me something new." He turned to Marika. "Aella was suspicious when I flew away. We need to move now."

"Sorry, princess, I gotta go. It's been fun." Marika patted my shoulder as she strode past. Liam snarled, and we both blinked in surprise.

She climbed onto the back of Thor's bike and clipped her belt to the retractable straps. Straightening, she caught my eye. "Don't go out there alone until daylight," she said, her voice serious. "I like you. I don't want you to get hurt and there are animals—human and otherwise—who will hurt you. I'm sorry we had to end up this way. You're a good kid."

"You're a bitch." I reached out and shoved her shoulder, hard, like a character in an *Ancient TēVē* vid trying to start a fight in a parking lot.

Her face hardened, and her stunner swung up to point at my chest. "I thought about leaving you free, but you've just sealed your fate. I can't have you running off to warn anyone."

Her finger tightened on the trigger. Liam launched himself off my shoulder and landed on the weapon, forcing the muzzle down. The blue lightning spiked harmlessly into the ground. Liam raced up Marika's arm.

Marika screamed and batted at her own head, flinging Liam away. He twisted in midair, then opened wing-like legs and soared back to me.

"He bit me!" Marika screamed. "Get us out of here!"

"I hope you crash into the lake!" I yelled as the bike lifted off the ground.

Thor laughed. "Not with me driving!" The air bike launched into the sky, barely missing the top of the wooden barricade as it swooped away.

CHAPTER THIRTY-SIX

Now what? I stood at the top of the Dome's ramp, debating my options. I could go back inside until daylight. I was sure they'd give me a corner to sleep in. I could camp out in the stairwell if they wouldn't. Or commandeer one of the lounge chairs on the roof. Although my clothes were almost dry, it would be hard to sleep with the temperature dropping.

But my father was fighting off Hellions, trying to get me back. I needed to at least let him know I was free. Maybe Saul could help me get a message to someone.

Liam chittered sleepily against my neck. "Yes, you're nice and warm but not really big enough. And you don't have a radio." An indignant chirp disagreed. I laughed and stroked his silky fur. "Yes, I know you would help if you could. You were a big help with the stunner."

Liam perked up. He scampered down my arm and leaped from my hand to the ground.

"Where are you going?" I chased him to the shadows of the wall at the edge of the cement apron in front of the Dome. He stopped, chittering loudly.

"Is that a stunner?" I bent down to pick it up. Marika must have dropped it when Liam bit her. "Good job, Liam!" I holstered the stunner and held my hand out. Liam jumped to my fingers.

Everyone said sair-gliders weren't sentient, but he knew I would want this weapon. And he'd prevented Marika from stunning me. I slid my hand down Liam's back and along his bushy tail. "You're smarter than all the other gliders combined," I whispered.

He pushed against my hand, nuzzling my fingers, and chirped his agreement. I tucked him against my damp hair and turned to survey the courtyard again.

A glint of light brought my head around to the south. Had Thor and Marika come back for some reason? I crouched in the shadows by the gate and pulled out my stunner. The battery level read medium-low, but it should be good for one or two more rounds. I dialed the effect up to "immobilize."

The bike dropped to the pavement, but only one figure sat on this one. "Aella? Is that you?" I called softly.

"Who's there?" She swung around, a blaster pointed in my direction.

Why did everyone have one of those except me?

"It's Siti. Don't shoot." I stepped into the light, dropping my stunner to my side.

"Where's Thor?" She lowered her weapon but didn't put it away.

"He and Marika took off." I pointed the direction they'd gone. "Can you get me back to my dad?"

Her eyes followed my pointing finger, then traveled back to my face. She seemed to register my identity for the first time. "What are you doing here? You were a hostage!"

"I got away," I said. "But I need to let Dad know I'm okay, and those thugs have my booster." I patted my empty shoulder pocket.

"You can't reach him right now anyway," she said. "He's inside that stupid cavern."

"Take me over there, will you?" I slid the stunner into my holster and closed the distance between us. "Please?"

"Did you talk to Thor?" She put out a hand to stop me from climbing on the bike. "Where did he go? Why's he with Marika? Have they got something going on?"

"Going on? They're Gagarian spies."

She stared at me. "Thor isn't smart enough to be a spy. Besides, they don't need spies on our team. They're all over this damn planet."

"No, those aren't Gagarians. They really live here." I glanced around the courtyard. "Can we talk about this while we fly? I need to let my dad know I'm safe."

"Climb on. Hook the retractable straps to your grav-belt." She twisted around to show me the straps.

"I don't have a grav-belt." I slid onto the bike and hooked the straps to my utility belt. It would probably snap if Aella rolled the bike, but it was the best I could do. "Keep it steady, and I'll be fine."

She shook her head and lifted off the ground. "Why do you think Thor is a spy?" Her voice came through my audio implant loud and clear. Apparently, we were close enough to link.

I explained what Marika had told me. "How'd you know he was here?"

"I didn't," she said, pushing the throttle to full speed.

I clamped my hands around her waist. "Sorry."

"No problem. I don't want to drop the boss's daughter, so hold on." She patted my hands where they clenched together above her belt. "After you disappeared back into the cave with that skanky guy, Kassis sent a recon team in after. Then Torres and a couple of the younger Gagarians—sorry, what should I call them?"

"They call themselves ancients."

She chuckled. "Well, Torres and a couple of his teen ancients showed up and said they'd talked to you. Then your dad told me and Thor to pull back. He didn't want us listening in on what they were doing. I guess he didn't want the greater universe to know he was working with Gagarians." She held up a hand. "He thinks they're Gagarians, even if you don't.

"Anyway, all of them—the CEC team and the, uh, ancients, went into the cave. Thor said he was going to get some footage from the other end, so he flew off to that back-door Torres described."

"You don't know what's going on inside?" I asked as we dropped through the darkness.

"Halt! Who goes there?" a voice yelled. Lights stabbed out at us as Aella landed the bike.

"It's me, Siti Kassis!" I called as I unlatched the straps. "I need to tell my dad I'm safe!"

"Who's that with you?"

"Aella Phoenix, G'lacTechNews." She flicked her holo-ring and swiped something toward the cave. Her ID, probably.

I climbed off the bike and hurried forward. "Please, can you reach my dad?"

The guard—Laughlin—of course it was Laughlin! She shook her head. "We've got no signal inside the rock."

"I'll go tell him."

Laughlin put her arm across the opening. "You can't go inside. And before you ask, I can't leave my post. When they send someone down, I'll pass the word."

"But if he knows I'm safe, they can all come out!" I protested. "They could get hurt stumbling around in there with those Hellions laying traps and stuff."

"The commander knows what he's doing," Laughlin said, her eyes narrowing as if I'd insulted her honor. "He said no one goes in."

"Ugh!" I threw up my hands and stomped back to Aella.

"And that means you, too, Aella Phoneix!" Laughlin yelled.

Aella held up her hands. "Wasn't even going to try." She lowered her voice as I drew near. "Already did. They really don't want any witnesses to whatever's going down in there."

Or they didn't want nosy media idiots getting in the way. I couldn't imagine my dad doing anything that wasn't suitable for media coverage. "Did you try drones?"

She shook her head. "Won't work inside those caves. The drone frequencies aren't that far off from our comm." I opened my mouth, but she cut me off. "Yes, I tried."

"We could go to the back exit," I suggested.

"I'm sure they've got a guard there, too," Aella said, but she started the bike.

I climbed on and reclipped my restraints. Then we sat there.

"What are you waiting for?" I asked.

"I don't know where this back exit is," Aella said. "Do you?"

I thought for a moment, trying to mentally retrace my steps inside the caverns. "I think it's over that way." I waved vaguely to the west.

"Let's go up and see what we can see." She launched the bike, keeping the ascent smooth and turning gently when we'd climbed away. "It's so dark—if they left a light, we should see it."

We soared along the cliff, keeping out of weapon range, watching for lights. Up here, the quarter moon provided enough light to see the rough stone running in a strangely uniform ridge for many klicks.

Something flickered on the table-like top. "What's that?" I pointed.

Aella's head swung up. "Someone on the top? I thought the back exit was along the base."

"It is. But when I was inside, Juan mentioned the 'high way.' It sounded like an escape plan."

"High way? Not a road but an actual *high* way?" She swung the bike into a smooth banking curve.

My hands clamped onto her belt again. Liam rubbed his face against my neck, as if to tell me we'd just fly to the ground if we fell off. Well, one of us would.

"I've cut the headlight," Aella said. "It looks like they're moving north. We'll land a bit beyond and ambush them."

"When you say ambush, do you mean attack them with our two whole weapons, or do you plan to fling pointed questions at their heads?"

Aella laughed. "I've got more than two weapons on this baby."

"Yeah, but we've only got four hands between us."

"I've got a fleet of professional grade news drones at my disposal." Aella swooped down, and our bike skimmed over the edge of the stone cliff and across the rough mesa.

"So, what, you're going to film them to death?" I tried to loosen my grip on her belt, but my fingers refused to relax.

"Have you ever been attacked by a swarm of flies? Drones are worse. They're agile and pointy." She landed the bike. "These even have a bit of a bite. G'lacTechNews doesn't like to send us into the field unprotected."

We climbed off, my legs stiff from the brief ride. Or maybe it was the crawling through the tunnels or getting stunned. I'd all but forgotten my head, but the pounding returned with a vengeance. "I don't suppose you have a med kit?"

She opened a compartment on the back of the bike. A swarm of drones flew out as she flicked and swiped at her holo-display. "Front compartment, left side."

I moved around her and found the compartment. It was a basic med-kit, just bandages and painkillers. I slapped a pain patch on my neck and sighed in relief as the throbbing dulled. Probably should have checked the contraindications before using it. I tipped the packaging, but the moonlight didn't provide enough illumination to read the tiny letters. With a shrug, I shoved the empty packet into my pocket.

Aella had finished with the drones and opened another compartment on the bike. She pulled out a blaster and handed it to me. "You know how to use it?"

"Point and shoot?" I hazarded.

She snorted. "Close enough. Don't pull the trigger unless you're willing to kill whatever you're pointing at."

A chill rolled down my back. Juan had threatened my life. He'd attacked the village and shot Tanis. But was I willing to kill him? "Maybe I should stick with my stunner."

Aella nodded. "Probably a good choice. Set it for max distance." She held out a small black square. "Here's a power block. You're probably low, and the sun won't be up for hours."

I slapped the magnetic connector against the stunner. I could almost hear it sigh with relief as the red light on the side scaled through orange and yellow to green. I tucked the block into a pocket. "I wonder why CEC doesn't issue these?"

"They have 'em." Aella pulled another stunner from the bike and handed it to me. "Loop that over your shoulder for when the first one dies. They don't expect you to stun that much stuff, though. And usually, CEC teams don't meet up with hostile humans."

"You seem to know a lot about CEC teams." I slung the second stunner across my back. Liam cheeped in surprise and climbed my hair. I reached up a protective hand. "Sorry, Liam."

"I did a tour when I was young." Aella slid a pair of blasters over her shoulder and pulled a piece of cloth out of another compartment. She threw it over the bike and flicked her holo-ring. The fabric shimmered and faded, making the bike virtually invisible.

I reached out to touch the bike. The fabric was slippery under my fingers, and when I pulled at a fold, I could see the shimmery stuff. "That is so cool! Does CEC have those?"

Aella snorted. "No way. Too expensive. And like I said, CEC doesn't run into hostile humans very often. In fact, this is the only instance I can think of."

"Why do you have all of this stuff?" I asked. "It seems over the top for a journalist."

"I've been in some hairy situations." Aella caressed her bike. "This was supposed to be an easy trip, but I'm always prepared."

She crouched behind the bike. "We'll use this for cover. I'll connect you to my booster. You try to contact your dad. We'll see if we can keep the Hellions penned in until we find out what he wants to do."

"Are you allowed to get involved in this kind of operation?" I glanced over the top of the bike. In the distance, lights flashed and bobbed. That had to be them.

"I'm not too worried about what I'm 'allowed' to do." She sat on the ground beside me and pulled her holo-screens up again. The cloud of drones wafted up and swarmed away from us. I peered over her shoulder. The drones' cameras created a three-dimensional visual net above her hand. "Besides, I control the news that goes off-planet right now. If there's anything I don't want them to know, it won't go back to HQ."

She flicked a control, and the view changed as the drones sped away from us. Their low-light cameras threw the stony mesa into stark relief. From a distance, the rocky top of the cliff looked smooth, but it was actually a patchwork of rough, rocky blocks. Gaps, ranging from a few centimeters to several meters, split the blocks. Some of them stood higher than others, creating a rough stairstep effect.

About half a klick from us, the drones swooped closer to the bobbing lights. The Hellions crouched in the shadow of a meter-high drop-off, staring back the way they'd come.

"I'm going to hover a few here and send the rest to find the exit." She swiped her hand through the net and split the view into two overlapping nets. On the right, the holo stayed in place while the other side zoomed away, skimming about a meter above the stone.

A dark slot came into view: a deep slash between two blocks of stone. The visual narrowed as the drones seemed to contract into a smaller cloud and slid down into the slash. They entered a large chamber and spread out. In the darkness, figures moved near the far side of the cavern. Lights swung around the space, cutting across each other as the people holding them moved.

"That's gotta be our people—I'm getting a CEC transmitter signal." She pointed to a blue wave form along the bottom of the split view. Her hands flew through the screens, adjusting things here and there. "I'm not getting an audio signal."

"Maybe our people are deeper inside," I suggested. "These could be the ancients. They were closing in from the rear entrance when Juan dragged me out front. They may have been in a better position to follow. Can you get closer without them noticing?"

"I'll try." She poked a couple sections of the visual and swiped to the right. A few more flicks, and a smaller octagonal view coalesced in the bottom of the main screen. This one rose higher above the ground and arrowed across the cavern. The drones flew over the lights and turned to focus downward.

"That's Peter," I said. "And Joss. They don't have comms, except those clunky radios on their belts. Can you talk to them through the drones?"

She smiled and swiped up a control panel. "Peter, this is Aella."

A face looked up at the drone.

"That's Joss," I said.

"Sorry, Joss." Aella chuckled. "I'm one of the journalists covering this mission. We have eyes on the bogies."

"Bogies?" Joss asked.

"That means bad guys," Peter and I said at the same time.

"Is that Siti?" Peter asked.

"Hi guys!" I said. "You're almost out of the cave. There's a big wide space on top here, and the Hellions are hiding about—what would you say Aella? Half a klick?"

"Yes, they're approximately half a klick from the cavern exit." Aella did some more things on her screen and flicked something. "Oh, crap, you don't have visual capabilities. Anyway, they're hiding behind a short drop-off. I think they're planning on attacking when you approach."

"There's no one closer, though?" Joss asked. He stuck his fingers in his mouth and blew a loud whistle. His father and the rest of their team gathered around him, and he explained about the drones.

"Halt!" someone yelled. "Who goes there?" Everyone swung around to face the back of the cavern.

"Explorer Corps," Dad called. "Kassis."

"Dad!" I called.

"Siti? Where are you?" Dad pushed through the ancients to face the drone cloud.

"I'm with Aella. On top of the mesa. The Hellions are between us and you, about a half klick from the cavern exit. Marika and Thor are Gagarian spies." I smiled to myself over my concise and pertinent report.

"Marika is a spy? Don't be ridiculous." His voice softened, as if speaking to ten-year-old me. "She's a decorated veteran. The Gagarian spies are all around us." He gestured to the ancients standing nearby.

Peter opened his mouth, but Zane held up a hand. "Don't bother."

"And frankly, Thor isn't smart enough to be a spy."

"Perfect cover for both of them, don't you think?" I let the sarcasm speak for itself.

"Let me talk to Aella," Dad said.

I rolled my eyes, even though he couldn't see it, and turned away.

"Aella here," she said. "I believe Siti may be correct. Thor has been acting…odd."

"We'll discuss it later," Dad said. "Sit rep."

"Siti gave it to you." She glanced sympathetically at me as she swiped new screens open. "The insurgents appear to be armed. I believe they're planning an ambush. Here's a map with their location pinpointed."

"Roger. Evy!" He turned as the lieutenant materialized at his shoulder. "Get Tam on the horn. Here's what we're going to do."

CHAPTER THIRTY-SEVEN

I glowered at Aella. "I can't believe we're just supposed to sit here."

"I'm an impartial observer." She messed with her holo-interface, sweeping the micro drones into loose circles around the cavern opening and the Hellions. The view fractured into multiple tiny vids, and she pulled a couple of them forward. "Now that you've got backup, I'm going to send this direct to G'lacTechNews as it happens." She stretched six of the drone screens into a grid and pulled up her comm screens. "I'm connecting to the jump server, so this can go out almost live."

"Doesn't all that stuff get cleared through CEC?" I reached over her arm to pull one of the screens larger.

She slapped my fingers away. "This is the outgoing vid. Don't mess with it. Wait 'til I get it set, and you can grab another view." She flicked and swiped some more, then shifted the whole grid off to the side. "And yeah, CEC gets a shot at censoring it, but they aren't going to. This is Earth. Too many people know about the mission and want to see what's happening."

She flipped one of the screens, and a larger drone rose into the air. She pulled a device from her pocket and set it on the ground. With a flick of her wrist, the screens jumped to hover above the device instead of her holo-ring. Then she checked her hair and makeup, using the larger drone and another screen as a mirror.

She turned to me. "You ready to be on cam?"

"On cam?" My hand flew to my hair. "Like this? I've been concussed, tied up, stunned, nearly drowned, and flown across an alien world! Do I look like I'm ready to go on cam?"

"You're perfect." Her eyes sparkled as she turned to the drone. "This is Aella Phoenix with G'lacTechNews, embedded with the Colonial Exploration Corps Earth Return team. With me is Serenity Kassis, daughter of mission commander Nathanier Kassis."

She turned to me. "Siti, can you tell us what's happening here on Earth?"

"I'm not sure anyone knows exactly what's going on," I said slowly. "And I'm not really authorized to speak on behalf of the Corps. I'm a civilian."

"Perfect." Aella winked at the drone and turned back to me. "As a civilian, you can freely tell us what's happening."

I froze, probably looking like a grendadeer in a spotlight. Technically, I was a civilian. But I wanted to become an Explorer Corps officer. I hadn't been sure before, but now I wanted it more than anything else. Even my fifteen minutes of fame.

Anything I might say today could be held against me when my admission packet reactivated. I took a deep breath. "I think you need to talk to the commander."

Aella swiped something, and the tiny holo of her froze. "Work with me girl! You have the opportunity to be part of the biggest news in the 'verse!"

"Not if I want to get into the academy." I crossed my arms. On my shoulder, Liam stirred and made a cheeping sound then went back to sleep.

Something pinged, and Aella swung around to look at the screens on her holo-projector. "They're moving. We can do the interview later. Like you said, it's not really going out live."

She dragged the projecting disk closer and fiddled with the holos. I twisted onto my knees and peered over the camouflaged air bike. The

Hellions had shut down their lights, and the explorers were undoubtedly using low-light visuals. From here, we could see nothing.

"There." Aella pointed at one of the drone vids. She grabbed it and stretched it, pushing it into place on her grid of six. The displaced vid minimized to a thumbnail on the projection.

On screen, a line of crouching explorers exited the cavern and fanned out across the mesa. Another screen flickered, and Aella pulled it into the grid. This one showed Maj. Origani and a team from the base landing.

"Where are they?" I whispered.

"About a klick that way." She pointed away from the cliff edge. "They're going to come in from behind. They'll be here in a few minutes."

We watched in silence as Origani's team flew across the stone mesa. They circled behind the Hellions, who appeared to be oblivious.

"Drop your weapons! You're surrounded!" Origani's voice rumbled through the vids. An echo rolled across the mesa to us.

The Hellions didn't listen, and all hell broke loose. Pun intended.

Tran launched himself at Origani, shoving his weapon away. The two of them went to the ground. Another explorer turned to assist, but one of the Hellions fired at him. The man dropped, screaming in pain.

Across the mesa, the team from inside the cavern raced across the stone, followed by a gaggle of ancients and villagers. The Hellions erupted in all directions, surging to meet the attackers.

Explorers were trained in basic self-defense and weapons use. They hadn't been trained for all-out war. The Hellions waded in, firing and swinging guns as clubs. Ignoring Aella's yelp of frustration, I grabbed the drone screen showing my father and pulled it closer.

He fired off a couple of shots as he ran, then closed with a scruffy-looking Hellion. Dad's weapon was knocked aside, and the men traded blows. Another Hellion came up from behind, a large club hefted in both hands.

"Dad!" I screamed. "Duck!"

Dad swung around at my voice, and the blow took him in the shoulder instead of the head. He went down, and the other men leapt on him.

"Dad!" In a feat of adrenaline-fueled athleticism, I leaped over the air bike and lunged toward the fight. Weapons fire, screams, and yells battered my ears, and the scent of blood caught in the back of my throat.

I put on a burst of speed and plowed into the back of a ragged Hellion, taking her down. My knees slammed into the rock, jarring my teeth and pounding head. I shoved off the woman's back, lurching to my feet again. Disoriented by my fall, I stared into the darkness

A clicking sound brought me around, face to face with an evil-looking, ancient weapon. The muzzle looked huge, pointed right at my face. I dropped to a crouch and swept out a leg, catching my opponent in the knees. Pain ripped through my shin, but the man went down.

I jumped up and stumbled away. I needed to find Dad. I turned and met Flynn's eyes.

"On your right!" he yelled, his blaster coming up.

I swung around in time to see the Hellion crash to the ground, a huge, smoking hole burned in his leg. He screamed. The sound burned into my brain like a brand. I'd never seen the results of a blaster attack before. The smell of charred flesh clawed at my nose.

Flynn clapped me on the shoulder. "Get out of here!"

"I need to find my dad!" I yelled back.

"He was over there, but he doesn't need your help!" Flynn grabbed my wrist and shoved my hand down to my stunner. "Get that thing out of the holster and use it. Then go that way!" He shoved me away from the moaning Hellion.

The stench seemed to thin as I stumbled away. Another Hellion roared at me, racing out of the darkness. I yanked the stunner out of my holster and fired. Blue lightning jetted from the muzzle and hit him in the stomach. The man seized, his eyes, mouth, and nostrils flared in a soundless scream. Then he collapsed. I leaped over him and looked for another target. The sooner this was over, the faster I could find my dad.

The world turned into a single, endless blur. Turn, fire, duck, run. The never-ending screaming and moaning. The timeless stenches of ozone, burned flesh, and blood.

Clinging to my shoulder, Liam screeched, a blood-curdling drill in my eardrums. I whipped around to see Tran lumbering at me. His clothing was soaked in blood, and black burn marks covered his legs and arms.

"YOU!" He yelled, lurching toward me.

I raised my stunner and pulled the trigger. Blue lightning lanced out, hitting him square in the chest.

He kept coming.

I fired again. He didn't even flinch. He just kept barreling forward, hands outstretched, teeth bared.

I squeezed the trigger again. The stunner clicked. Crap! Out of juice. I flung it into Tran's face.

He swiped it away, like an insect, and grabbed my forearm.

A man launched out of the darkness, ripping Tran's hand from my wrist. Tran stumbled and swung around to meet the new threat.

"Dad!" I cried.

The two men grappled. Tran had the advantage of size, but my father had training. Tran swung wildly, his hands sliding off Dad as he twisted and turned. Dad got a grip on the larger man and strained to tumble him to the ground.

I darted forward, pulling the second stunner from my shoulder, grateful Aella had insisted on giving it to me. The jolt from the first hadn't fazed Tran, so I flipped it around in my hand and slammed it into the side of his head. He growled and shook me off. I fell hard on my butt, and the second stunner flew away into the darkness. Crap.

Dad jabbed his elbow into Tran's mid-section. He grunted then yelled. I swung my foot out again, catching Tran behind the ankles just as Dad pushed. The two men went over, my father on top. I scrambled back, crablike, stones digging into my palms.

Tran heaved and bucked, and suddenly, he was on top. I shrieked. I needed a weapon. The loose stones on the ground were too small. My belt pouches were empty.

My father made a gargling sound. I threw myself at Tran, wrapping my arms around his neck. I wish I'd paid more attention when Marika tried to teach me to choke someone out. Who knew that would be a necessary skill? I pawed through my memories, moving my arm into different positions to try to cut off his air.

Tran let go of Dad and grabbed my hair. I screamed and clamped my legs around his waist. His free hand jabbed at my face, one thick finger poking hard into my cheek. I turned my head and bit his finger. Hard.

He howled and threw back his head, slamming it into my forehead. Pain slammed through my skull, ringing it like a gong. I grabbed my face as I fell from his back.

I lay on the ground, cradling my throbbing head. Noises broke through the pain. There was a crunch, like a giant mouth biting down on a huge snack chip. A shout of pain. A holler for help. I curled up into a ball, wishing it would all just go away.

"Siti!" Dad's voice cut through the pounding, breathless and concerned. "Are you hurt?"

"My head," I moaned.

"Can you stand? We need to get you out of here." He took my arm and pulled me upright. The movement sent waves of nausea through my whole body. I clenched my teeth, breathing hard.

"Tran!" Juan's raspy voice cut through the cacophony.

"Dad, watch out!" I tried to yell, but nothing seemed to come out of my throat.

Time seemed to freeze as I dragged my head up and forced my eyes open. My father stood beside me, holding me up. Behind him, Juan stood over his prone brother, his ancient weapon pointed at Dad's back. His face contorted, fury blazing from his eyes.

Behind Juan, Peter moved forward, a club in his hands. He ran in slow motion. Juan's finger tightened on the trigger.

The gun roared. Something slammed into us, forcing us to the ground. A yell. A scream. Pain lanced through my arm.

CHAPTER THIRTY-EIGHT

TIME SNAPPED back to normal speed.

"Siti!" Dad crouched beside me, peering into my eyes. "Are you hurt?"

"Deja vu," I joked, my voice coming out feeble and creaky.

"ZANE!" Peter yelled.

I turned my head. Juan lay across his brother's body in the darkness, a line of blood dripping down his cheek. His eyes were closed, and he moaned. Blood gushed from his skull.

Peter jumped over Tran's legs, stumbling as his foot caught on the prone man. He caught himself and hurtled forward. With a herculean effort, I lifted my head to see what he was doing.

Zane lay on the ground. A dark stain soaked his shirt, growing larger as I watched. Peter pressed one hand against Zane's throat, the other clamped over his chest. "I need help!" he yelled.

"Chasin!" Dad's voice was low. "Med kit to me. Now."

The sounds of the battle diminished. I imagined the explorers must be winning, but I couldn't muster enough energy to care. "Is he going to be okay?" I asked.

Dad glanced over his shoulder at Peter and Zane. "I don't know. We'll see what Chasin can do for him. Where are you hurt?"

"I'm fine," I lied.

"No, you aren't."

Chasin dropped from the sky beside Dad, his medical kit in tow. Li landed beside him.

"My daughter is injured," Dad said.

"Help Zane," I said. "He's been shot."

Chasin looked from me to my dad, clearly torn between following orders and his medical training. Li had no concerns. She pushed off in a smooth arc, landing beside the two men. Her case was open before she hit the ground, and she pulled out supplies while asking questions in a low voice.

Chasin opened his own case and crouched beside me. "I'm going to use the ScanNSeal on you. Depending on your injuries, it might sedate you. Don't fight it."

Dad loomed over Chasin, fidgeting nervously.

"Did we win?" I asked.

A grin twitched across his face. "Yes. Kind of. I need to get the report."

"She'll be fine, sir," Chasin said.

"Go do your job, Dad." I closed my eyes. "I'm busy."

He chuckled. A hand caressed my cheek. "I won't be far away," he said.

I WOKE to an antiseptic smell that said "medical." My head felt light and pain free. I rubbed my crusty eyes and looked around.

I lay on a cot folded down from the wall in the clinic. Rustling and breathing issued from above and below me, as well as across the room. I squinted in that direction. Two stacks of cots—each three high—hung from that wall. All but one was occupied.

I sat up, the movement easy and painless. The top of my head brushed the cot above me, and I ducked instinctively. My fingers prodded my head. My hair felt like a rats' nest, but there were no sore spots.

I peeked over the edge of my cot. The one below me was empty, so I swung my legs out and hopped down. A loose shirt covered me to mid-thigh, and the air was cool against my bare legs.

The two med pods at the far end of the room each held a patient as well. Katy sat near one of the med pods, her head pillowed against the hard plastek. Li sat behind the desk, her eyes closed. I started forward to wake her, then noticed the blood on her wrinkled shirt and the dark circles under her eyes. She needed to sleep.

I went to the door and placed my hand against the access panel. It lit up and displayed a message. "Serenity Kassis. Health nominal. Release at will." The door slid open.

Chasin sat at a desk outside, also asleep. He roused when the door opened and lifted one eyelid. "Oh, it's you." He sat up and pulled something from his pocket. "Here's your holo-ring. It's been cleaned—digitally and physically. Locker room is down the hall." He leaned back in the chair, and his eyes snapped shut.

A uniform dispenser provided me with new clothing, and the shower felt like heaven. The water ran dark with dirt and blood as I scrubbed my hair and body. When I was clean, I dried and dressed. Feeling one hundred percent human again, I pulled on the camp booties that came with the uniform and headed out the door.

The sun streamed down, warming the stone plateau. A group sat around one of the tables on the patio. Maj Origani looked up and waved me over. As I approached, my father stood and hurried to me.

He stopped a half-step away. "How are you feeling?"

"I'm good. You?" I shifted back and forth, not sure if I should hug him in front of all these people.

He reached out and pulled me close. "I was afraid I'd lost you. Twice."

"I'm hard to get rid of." I sniffed. My eyes prickled, and I blinked hard to keep the tears back. Why was I crying? I should be happy. "Is everyone okay?"

He let me go and turned. Putting an arm over my shoulders he pulled me toward the table. "Our team is alive. Some of them are still in the clinic."

I nodded. "I saw them. Chasin and Li need sleep, though."

He squeezed my shoulder. "I know. They won't leave until everyone is stable. Good leadership instinct, Siti. Gotta take care of your team."

Warmth washed through me at the compliment. I slid my arm around his waist and squeezed my thanks.

"Marika and Thor are missing. We've sent a team to look for them, but with their comms off, they can hide forever. I guess we'll find them when the Gagarians land." He nodded when I jerked on the bench beside him. "Aella filled me in." He shook his head. "I can't believe Marika...she'll have a lot to answer for if I get my hands on her."

Although she'd treated me badly, I couldn't help but still think of her as my friend. We'd had so much fun together. And she could have killed me or left me with the Hellions, and she didn't. A part of me hoped she'd get away.

Dad glanced at Seraphina and Mara. "Zane is still in the med pod. Two bullets to the chest. One went completely through, but the second lodged near the heart. Lots of repair to be done."

Maj Origani slid down the bench, making room for me to sit beside my father. Evy, Wronglen, Seraphina, and Mara sat across the table with a large gap between the ship's officer and the New Lake women. Everest stood behind Mara, leaning against the building. Peter, Eric, and Jake sat near him.

"Where are Zina and Joss?" I asked.

"They were in the clinic," Origani said. "Asleep in the bunks last time I looked."

"Oh, I thought those were all casualties," I said.

Dad shook his head. "Flynn and Anivea are still recuperating, but everyone else is back on duty. You were more seriously injured than most of them."

"Except Zane," I said.

He tapped a pink line on my arm. "The bullet that went through his chest grazed you. It's amazing he's still alive."

I nodded. "What about the Hellions?"

"They took some casualties. We patched up their leader, and he's locked up in the cold storage right now. That's part of what we're here to negotiate." He raised an eyebrow at Mara. "Under the ICT and CEC regulations, I can pass judgement and execute punishment in my capacity as mission commander. Once Hydrao returns, it gets a bit more complicated, so we should make the decision now."

"Wait a minute," Wronglen protested. "I officially represent Capt.

Hydrao. I am authorized to make decisions and lodge arguments with her full authority."

Dad swiveled to face Wronglen directly. "Fine. What do you suggest? Is the *Return in Glory* prepared to take custody of the suspects and return them to Grissom for a hearing?"

Wronglen's lips pursed, and her face went red. "No."

Dad nodded and turned back to Mara. "Good, then it's between you and me. I could probably frame this as an act of war if I pushed it. Gagarian terrorists attacking a peaceful CEC mission and taking hostages."

Seraphina raised her hands. "As long as they can't attack us again, you can do anything you want with them."

Dad's face went slack in surprise.

"I can't agree to that," Mara said. "Many of those Hellions need help. We can work with them."

Dad looked from one woman to the other. "Why don't you two figure out how you want to handle this? With my team all alive and safe, I leave their punishment up to you."

Mara and Seraphina eyed each other in silence, then nodded.

"Now what?" Origani asked.

"Now we go back to the table." Dad nodded at Mara. "We implement the ICT."

Mara raised an eyebrow. "The ICT?"

"Inter-Colony Treaty of 2430," Evy said. "It makes Earth a protected, neutral planet. All of the colonies will have embassies here, scientific research stations, etc. But we all share it."

"What about those of us who live here?" Mara asked. "Don't we get a claim to our own planet?"

Dad took a deep breath. I could almost hear him counting to ten. "You've obviously been here for some time, but that doesn't nullify the treaty. There's no way Gagarin landed here before 2430—you didn't have the tech for that."

Mara pinched the bridge of her nose. "What do we need to do to prove to you we're not Gagarians? That we were all born and raised on this planet?"

Dad shrugged. "Maybe you were born here—although that would be a stretch. You're over forty, surly?" He ignored her stony expression. "Or maybe your parents brought you here when you were very young and raised you to believe you were locals."

"I can show you the gravestones of my ancestors," Mara said coldly.

"That can all be faked," Wronglen said flatly, her voice loud.

Dad shot her a glare.

"What about blood tests?" I asked. "We must have records of Gagarian genetics. Couldn't we do some kind of analysis to track these people's ancestry?"

Origani rubbed his chin. "That seems possible. Li would know." He started to his feet.

"Don't wake her!" Dad and I said in unison. He grinned at me.

"We have time." Dad's smile faded as he stared across the table at Mara. "I hate to waste resources on that kind of thing. If you just give up this ridiculous claim, we can move on."

Everest growled. "Do your precious Gagarians have telepathy?"

Dad shrugged. "They have integrated audio implants, just like us. It's almost the same thing."

"No, it isn't." I pointed at Jake. "He can do pictures."

"Pictures?" Origani stared at me like I'd suddenly sprouted a second head. "*We* can't even do visuals yet. No way the Gagarians can. Their tech is all copied from us."

"There's your proof, then." I waved to Peter. "Jake, come show my dad what you can do."

The boys exchanged a look. Peter stood and stepped in front of his brother. "He doesn't want to. I think he's afraid of the commander." Jake's leg swung. "Ow." Peter said.

Everest snorted, trying to keep his face straight.

I got up and walked around the table. Peter gave me a considering look, then stepped aside. I sat beside the younger boy. "May I?" I held out my hand.

Jake's eyes slid to me, and he nodded.

I put my hand on his arm. *We need him to believe you.* I thought the words as clearly as I could. *He represents the Unified Colonies. If your people want to stay here, you need to convince him. You've seen what we can do.* I pictured the shuttles, the grav-belts, the battle atop the mesa. *Do you want that against you?*

A flood of emotions poured through me. Anger, fear, uncertainty.

I leaned closer so I could whisper. "I know you're only a kid, but you can do this. You can save your people." A little over-dramatic, perhaps.

A smile tweaked the corners of Jake's mouth. I got a wash of humor and a clear sense he'd heard my self-commentary. Then acceptance.

Jake stood. I took his hand and led him across the patio, Peter right behind us.

"Dad, turn around."

My father pulled his legs over the bench and turned to face us, arms crossed over his chest.

"You've got to be open," I said. "You won't hear him if you're sure you won't." I didn't know if that was true, but it seemed likely. "Also, you need to touch him. Our shields—or maybe something in our brains—cancels out their abilities."

He looked even more skeptical. "When did you become such an expert?"

"Come on, Dad. Please? Just try to be open-minded." I pulled Jake closer.

Dad sat up straight and uncrossed his arms. "I am nothing if not open minded. What do I need to do?"

"Just let him touch your arm. Or hand. And listen."

"I thought you said he does pictures." Dad held out his hand.

"He does. But 'watch' doesn't really work, does it?" I smirked. Jake's hand twitched in mine, and he pulled back a bit. "He's not sure what to show you."

"Show him when we left the Dome," Peter said. He put his hand on Jake's shoulder. "When we first came outside. That's a strong one."

I raised my eyebrows, but he didn't elaborate.

Jake released my hand and took Dad's outstretched one. His eyes bored into Dad's in an uncharacteristically direct stare.

CHAPTER THIRTY-NINE

NOTHING HAPPENED. Dad watched the boy, his face blank. After a while, he took a breath, as if to call off the whole experiment. Then his eyes went wide. His face paled. His breathing sped up, as if he were experiencing a nightmare while still awake. Sweat sprang up on his forehead and upper lip. He trembled and tried to pull his hand away. Jake's grip tightened visibly, and they stood locked together for almost a minute.

When Jake released his hand, Dad slumped against the table, eyes closed.

"Nate! Are you okay?" Origani shook Dad's arm gently.

Dad shook his head and opened his eyes. He looked at Jake. "Was that real?"

Jake nodded once. Behind him, Peter nodded, too.

Dad glanced at Origani. "I—I don't know how to describe that. If that was Gagarian technology, then... they're lightyears ahead of us. I didn't just see—I felt—all of it. Fear. Amazement. Friendship. Wow." He closed his eyes again for a moment.

We waited in silence. Finally, Dad's eyes opened. "Thank you, Jake."

Jake ducked his head and skipped away. Peter's eyes met mine, and he nodded. I wasn't sure what he was trying to say.

"Is this what happened to Levi?" Dad gestured to Jake. "He lost this?"

Mara nodded. "Whatever you did to his brain—it broke his gift. He only hears with his ears now."

Dad rubbed the back of his neck. "Ouch. No wonder he was upset. After Chasin gets some sleep, I'll have him work on this. What if we could not only repair Levi's gift, but give it to others?"

"What are you talking about?" Wronglen demanded. "Gifts? They must be using some kind of hypnotic effect or hallucinogen! I'm not buying it. And Captain Hydrao won't believe it, either."

Dad's head snapped around to Wronglen. "I suspect Tisha will take my word."

"Not if you've obviously been suborned!" She leaped to her feet, banging her legs against the bench.

"Lieutenant, you may be excused," Dad said.

She crossed her arms. "I will not. My duty is to represent the captain in her absence."

"Then do it silently," Dad said.

Wronglen glared. Dad raised an eyebrow. She plopped down on the bench hard enough to rattle our teeth.

Dad turned back to Mara. "As I was saying—"

A message ping from my holo-ring distracted me. Who would contact me? Everyone must know I was in a meeting with my father. I pulled up the message and gasped.

"Siti, is something wrong?" Dad broke off his conversation with Mara, concern written on his face.

"I—I have a message from Marika." I stared at it in wonder.

"What? Throw it up on the table!" Dad said.

I flicked the icon, and the holo appeared in the projector above the table.

"Siti, I'm really sorry." She glanced around, as if making sure she was alone, and leaned closer. "You've been a really good friend, and I wish I could be as good a friend to you. But this was my mission from the start. Tell your dad it was all my fault—I don't want him blaming you for my work. I was sent here to do this, and now I'm going home. I—I hope we see each other again some time, and I hope you don't hate me too much.

I'm only doing what I was ordered to do—what my nation deemed necessary. Just as you've been doing."

Her right hand reached forward—to flick the ring off? Then she paused. "Please don't tell anyone about this message. They won't believe you anyway, and there won't be any proof. As they used to say on the ancient videos, this message will self-destruct in five seconds. Goodbye, friend."

The screen went blank. I counted to five, but nothing happened. No poof of smoke or sizzle. I guess deleting digital information isn't as dramatic.

"What does that mean?" Wronglen demanded.

I pulled my earlobe. "She expected the Gagarians to arrive in the next few days. I'd guess they're here."

Dad's eyes widened then his head snapped around to glare at Wronglen. "Get Hydrao on the comm. If a Gagarian ship is inbound, they should see it. Siti, send me a copy of that message."

I nodded and flicked the message. "It's gone."

"What do you mean?" Dad asked.

"It's disappeared." I swiped through the interface. "Deleted. No record of it."

"I'll get someone on it." He muttered into his audio implant. Even now, when he wasn't trying to hide it, his voice was so low I couldn't hear what he said.

The door of Alpha mod opened, and a small group came out.

"Zane!" Peter called. "Over here!"

Joss, Zina, Katy and—was that Zane?

"Dude, your hair is back!" Eric cried.

Zane shoved his hand through the inch-thick stubble covering his head. "Isn't it weird? That medical machine is amazing."

"They fixed the bullet hole, and Chasin said they cured his diabetes." Katy's eyes glowed. "He's been living with that since before we met."

Eric laughed. "That's so cool! Is the hair here to stay? I never did get used to the bald look."

"It's been years. Way longer than you knew me with hair." Zane grabbed the younger man in a headlock and rubbed his red head.

"You forget, we watched you way before we met you." Peter hurried to join them, thumping the older man on the back. "We felt like we knew you."

"That was InZane!" Eric crowed. It sounded like a quote.

Dad's head popped up. "What did you say?"

Zane's face flushed, and a sheepish grin twitched at the corner of his lips. "That was my catch phrase. Back when I did VidTube."

"InZane Vidman was a popular VidTube artist during the Exodus." Wronglen's voice took on a lecturing tone. "He stopped broadcasting after he arrived in the colonies."

"I stopped broadcasting because the internet went down when the Exodus ended. No point in making videos if no one is going to watch them." He kissed his wife's cheek, strode the three remaining steps to our table, and sat beside Mara. "And no way to get them to the colonies after that, anyway."

"You're InZane Vidman." Dad stared at Zane in wonder. "*The* InZane Vidman."

Zane peered at him. "Why do you know about that?"

"*Ancient TēVē,*" Dad, Wronglen, and I said together.

I stared at Wronglen in surprise. She flushed and looked away, muttering something about research for the mission.

Zane made a face. "If I'd known they'd be around for centuries, I might have thought twice about doing them."

Katy rested a hand on his shoulder. "I always knew you were timeless."

"Strange as it might seem, this changes things." Dad tapped a finger on the table in front of Wronglen. "Are you willing to agree that this man is the videographer known as InZane Vidman?"

Wronglen looked away, her chin raised. "I am willing to entertain the idea."

"Great." Dad turned back to Zane. "Based on Jake's, eh, let's call it a demonstration—I will attest to the Colonial government that this planet is already occupied by—" He turned to Origani. "I don't want to say 'stragglers.' What should we call them?"

"Remnants?" Origani said the word like it tasted bad. "No. Homesteaders? Indigenous people?"

"There's a tribe up north that might be offended by that term. I'm only one eighth indigenous ancestry." Zane glanced at Katy.

"Don't look at me. My grandparents were born in Africa." Her nose wrinkled "How about 'Survivors'?"

"Survivors of the Exodus." Dad nodded. "We'll still probably need DNA samples to convince the official government drones, but my testimony will count heavily in your favor." He smiled self-consciously. "They like me back home."

"Then what?" Mara asked. "You'll leave us alone?"

"Well, we won't try to deport you." Dad turned to Mara. "Your people present a bit of a problem. We can still label you 'survivors.' Or maybe descendants of survivors. But your special abilities are going to make a lot of scientists froth at the mouth."

"Maybe don't mention that?" Katy suggested.

"Actually, it might be a good thing," I said. "If there's one thing I learned in my history classes back on Grissom, it's that situations like this —where a technologically superior group encounters a less tech-y people—" I gestured to the survivors. "The second group rarely fares well. But if they have capabilities we don't—and that we don't understand—it will give them some leverage to keep the pokers and prodders at bay." I put my fingers to my temples. "A kind of 'try to scan me and I'll blow up your head' thing."

Dad chuckled. "Maybe. For now, I'll leave it out of my report. We'll get some DNA samples—from those ancients who are willing—and match them to known relatives. The Historical Society started keeping full genome maps during the Exodus. It was supposed to keep them from leaving anyone behind. Do any of you have close relatives who, er, went?" He made a swooping motion like a shuttle lifting off.

Peter cleared his throat. "Our dad went to Armstrong on the Lief Erikson."

"Yes, we can use that." Dad flicked his holo-ring and muttered a voice note to himself. "Tam, talk to young Peter here, and see if you can track down his father's data." His eyes slid to me and back to Peter. "That must have been difficult for you."

Peter shrugged and exchanged a look with his brother. "It was a long time ago. We found our own family."

Dad nodded and cleared his throat. "Eventually, under the terms of the ICT, we'd like to establish an embassy here. We've just received information that the real Gagarians are on their way do the same. The Leweians may also want one. Sometimes they let Gagarin represent them, but for something like this?" He raised his hands, palm up. "Who knows?"

"It's a big planet," Mara said. "I'm sure we can allocate a little room for extraterrestrials."

Eric chuckled. "ET phone home."

Wronglen choked, her face turning red.

Dad smirked. "Yes, Elliot. We don't need to make any decisions right now. Except maybe the Hellions situation. We still have several days before the *Glory* returns." He grinned at the word play. "It would be good to have that settled before Hydrao gets here." He challenged Wronglen with a raised eyebrow.

She pretended she didn't see it. "I just received a message from the captain. They have identified a ship near Jupiter's orbit. Likely the Gagarian ship. She backtracked their path—they've been hiding behind the gas giants on their way in."

Dad nodded. "We'll just have to be ready to welcome them. In the meantime," he got to his feet, "we'd like to see more of *your* planet. Will you show us?"

I HOPE you enjoyed *The Earth Concurrence*. If you'd like to find out what kind of trouble Siti gets into next, follow her to the CEC Academy in *The Grissom Contention*.

ACKNOWLEDGMENTS

Author's Note
November 2020

Hi Reader,

If you're still here, I guess you enjoyed my story. Thanks for reading! If you liked *The Earth Concurrence,* please consider leaving a review on your retailer, Bookbub, or Goodreads. Reviews help other readers find stories they'll like. They also tell me what you like, so I can write more stuff you'll enjoy.

If you'd like to be notified when my next book becomes available, download free prequels—including one featuring Zane as a teen—and find out about sales, sign up for my newsletter. I promise not to SPAM you.

It's November in the year that just won't end. So, although the US election has been decided (if not yet confirmed) and a vaccine is in production, the governor of my state just released new lockdown rules. We're at record high infection rates in the US. Luckily, I live in a rural area, so my life is not impacted greatly, at least not on a daily basis.

It's been raining all day here, which is unusual, and a little depressing. I live on the "sunny side" of the Cascade Mountains in Oregon, and while we frequently have snow in the winter, we also have an average of 300 days of sunshine per year. Rain like this is why we don't live on the wet side.

As always, I have a list of people to thank for helping me with this book. Thanks to my alpha readers, AM Scott and Jim Caplan, who make sure I write a good, mostly hole-free story. Thanks to my new editor, Paula Lester, who made time for me between her other projects and her own writing. Thanks to Jenny Wilson at JL Wilson Designs for the fabulous book cover. I've never had one with a 3D character before, and I love her. Thanks to my excellent ARC team for catching all those tiny errors that make it through the process.

My eternal gratitude goes to my sprinting partners: AM Scott, Paula Lester, Tony James Slater, Alison Kervin, Kate Pickford, and especially Hillary "The Tomato" Avis.

Special thanks to my husband who finds other things to do when I sit down at the computer, even though he'd like us to do something together. And thanks to Pippin, the Wonder Westie, who keeps the gremlins away by sleeping under my desk.

In the time it's taken to write this, the rain has turned to snow, and I don't mind the darkness so much anymore. I hope your clouds have silver linings as well.

Thanks so much for reading.

Newsletter signup:

Printed in Great Britain
by Amazon

49126446R00169